AND DARKNESS FELL

David Berardelli

AND DARKNESS FELL

GRAVESTONE PRESS

ISBN: 978 1 78695 710 8

Gravestone Press
is an imprint of
Fiction4All
www.fiction4all.com

This Edition
Published 2021

When the light of life and happiness was destroyed, the darkness came, bringing with it an insatiable lust for death and destruction.

All that will exist from now on will be despair, and a cold nothingness that will forever chill the bones.

When the living can no longer feel the despair or the cold, they will know the end has finally come.

PART I: THE BATTLEFIELD

CHAPTER ONE

Beneath the blood-red sunset, a six-car pileup forming a grotesque sculpture of twisted metal and broken glass blocked the interstate.

I slowed the van and veered right until I reached the shoulder. The short-barreled, .38 Special revolver rested on the console beside me. If someone popped out of the wreckage and lunged, I could easily shoot him.

The bitter irony of it all nipped at my bones. Not long ago, I would have called 911. But now, since there were no more ambulances, I handled all emergencies with a gun.

I could see only three bodies. The others probably lay dead in the back seats or beneath the vehicles. A woman slumped behind the wheel of the smashed silver SUV, her long dark hair a heavy shroud covering her shoulder and arm. Two men in light-colored sweat shirts and baggy sweat pants lay on their backs on the pavement. Splotches of blood covered their faces and shirts. No one moved.

A black handbag lay among the shattered glass, its contents strewn some twenty yards from the crash site. A crushed tan suitcase jutted out beside a flat tire. A shabby brown teddy bear sat in front of the SUV, gazing up at the darkening sky.

Staying clear of the broken glass, I eased onto the shoulder and crept past, until the bodies showed up in my side mirror. Just as I'd moved past the wreckage, a glittering gun barrel directly to my left made me cringe.

A young man sprawled on his left side beneath the rear bumper of an overturned sedan. He lay perfectly still, his left arm outstretched, a revolver pointed in my direction.

Instinctively I reached for the .38 but thought better of it. I wouldn't need it. The boy's glazed eyes were pointed in my direction but did not flicker or blink. His hand was open. The gun barrel rested on the macadam. He was dead.

I accelerated, avoiding the mirrors until I was confident the tiny, glinting nightmare behind me had disappeared from sight.

A couple of miles later, I decided it was safe to start breathing again.

***

Twenty miles north of Jacksonville, small towns and boroughs peppered the wooded areas flanking the interstate. Years ago, many of these places were reduced to shadows of what they once were, as progress stripped them of their dignity. Their anorexic remains had become grim remnants of a time long past, when the world was smaller and quieter and moved along at a much slower pace.

According to my grandparents, life was much more tolerable before the computer age stepped in to change the world. Microwaves hadn't been invented. Cell phones weren't even thought of. Television provided only a handful of working channels. Telephones often had party lines to contend with, and office workers frequently had to rely on their memories, common sense, and other skills to get the work done.

Nevertheless, life trudged on, and people were content and happy with its limitations.

My grandfather believed life began deteriorating when the huge, sprawling monster called Interstate 95 bulled its way into our lives, slicing deeply into the earth, leveling land and trees, destroying homes and farms, and burying this quiet way of life beneath thousands of tons of pavement.

I'd never been a fan of the interstate. In the past, I'd avoid it whenever possible, choosing country roads as a much more restful—and safer—alternative. But when ninety percent of its traffic vanished, travel along the roadway changed drastically, turning into something much more frightening.

I zipped through the Jacksonville area, drove for another ten minutes, and took the first exit. I'd been driving for several hours and needed to stretch my legs as well as take a whiz and hunt for money and weapons. I went straight up the ramp and that dreaded highway quickly disappeared behind a cluster of dirty brick buildings and a row of corroding tenement houses.

I crept down the debris-cluttered street, carefully avoiding bottles and broken glass. A couple of skinny dogs trotted along the sidewalk, searching for food scraps. Cars, vans, and pickups lined both sides of the cracked pavement. Some were fairly new while others appeared much older, abandoned long enough to begin their slow deterioration into misshapen husks of rust and grimy glass.

The two- and three-story houses lining the block had also begun their journey into death and decay. It didn't take long. Their windows were filthy, their paint peeling. Shingles had pulled loose, some still clinging to sections of exposed tar while others had simply given up and dropped to the ground. Trash, toys, rusty lawn furniture, and skeletons of vehicles on blocks littered the overgrown front yards.

Halfway down the street, I found a place to park. I wasn't afraid of blocking anybody—I hadn't encountered another vehicle all evening. Still, I didn't want to bring attention to myself. People usually stop what they're doing and stare if they see something strange or unusual. And if they've never seen you before, they're bound to be suspicious if you show up in their neighborhood. I didn't see anyone wandering about, but I knew better than to lower my guard. I wasn't about to risk my life on the off-chance that someone might be lurking in the shadows.

As I pulled into the vacant space and switched off the engine, I realized at once I'd been correct in my thinking. Two large, beefy guys sat watching me from the now-tall grass in front of the brick house across the street. I hadn't been able to see them through the wild hedges obscuring the view at the corner, but as soon as I'd passed the collapsed picket fence separating the properties, there they were.

They were obviously brothers and close in age, maybe twenty-five. They were fairly dark, their scraggly long hair the same color as their unkempt beards. They wore bib overalls, and each gripped a beer can. They probably went close to three hundred pounds apiece, and I doubted they'd have any trouble pounding me into hamburger. On the other hand, if they'd been doped, I wouldn't have to worry; by the time they decided I was a threat, I'd be long gone.

I thought about trying a different house, but I really didn't want to waste the time—the pressure in my bladder had increased, and I squirmed in my seat.

I watched as they both hoisted their cans to coax some drink into their mouths. The process was excruciating. They took at least ten seconds for each to raise the can, another five to tilt it, nearly ten seconds to swallow the mouthful, and another ten to lower the can. About thirty seconds after all that, they both belched.

Nope. Nothing to worry about—at least from those two. The house could be another story.

I twisted farther around toward Reed, who was sitting in the rear seat amid the canned food, beer, and other stuff I'd stolen before leaving St. Cloud that morning. He sat quietly, his head tilted to the side. He was probably listening to his friend again.

"Reed?"

He turned and focused his small, light-blue eyes on me. Reed always gave me the impression he'd just awoken, even if we'd been talking only seconds earlier. That was okay. Reed wasn't normal by any stretch. But that didn't matter. Abnormal had been the norm for some time.

"Reed, have him check out the house, the one over on the right, where those two big guys are sitting."

He turned and stared out the passenger window then went right back to his listening mode. I should explain at this point that he was listening to someone even though no one else was there. But as far as Reed was concerned, the voice was real—just as real as I was.

"Well?"

No reply. When he listened, he blocked out everything else. Reed wasn't a moron. He was actually very intelligent and well-educated, but his attention focused on things others couldn't fathom. Like Elwood P. Dowd, that lovable dipsomaniac played by Jimmy Stewart in the movie *Harvey*. Dowd claimed he had an invisible friend, too, a six-foot rabbit. I had no idea who or what belonged to the voice Reed heard. I didn't know if he was listening to a leporine six-and-a-half footer, a stacked blonde, or one of those voice-generating computers I saw on an old TV show.

It didn't matter; the voice was real. I'd seen clear evidence of it.

"It's okay to go inside?"

"Don't know," he said in his soft, high-pitched voice.

"What did your friend say?"

"He doesn't hear anything."

"He can't tell if anyone's in the house?"

He shook his head.

12

I tried evaluating the situation. Judging by their actions, the two out on the grass probably had been doped. Families usually ate the same foods and took the same medications, so anyone inside the house probably would be in this same condition.

"I guess I'll go in, then. I need to make a pit stop. How about you?"

Reed shook his head.

That was another thing I couldn't understand about Reed. He seldom had to use the bathroom or stretch his legs. He'd rather sit back there and listen to the voice. Reed didn't eat or drink much, either, but you expected him to use the bathroom once in a while. I'd only seen him slip into the john once since we'd hooked up, but that was only because I'd done something that made him sick to his stomach.

"Want anything special if they've got food?"

"An apple would be nice."

"Anything else?"

"A peach. Or maybe a banana."

"You having a regularity issue?"

He frowned. Reed wasn't the best audience for the casual one-liner.

"It was a joke, Reed."

He didn't reply, and his silence made me wary. I didn't think he'd keep anything from me, but his blank expression made me wonder if I should even bother with this place. I could just piss in the bushes, and I could always look for guns and money somewhere else.

On the other hand, it was getting dark, and I didn't want to be caught in a strange place at night. Some sections still had working street lights; this one didn't. If they'd been working, they would already be on, and those guys sitting in the front yard probably wouldn't mind if I just took a leak at the corner. Still, I needed to do some hunting while I was there. I needed stuff that could substitute for cash.

When most of the ATMs went down, cash became the only form of money acceptable—cash or something of intrinsic value. If I found another gun, for example, that could substitute. Of course, you could never have enough guns. Gas stations had become the most dangerous places in the country. Luckily, I wouldn't have to stop for a while. I'd filled up the tank south of Jacksonville and still had plenty left.

Which brings me back to that house. I thought it would be a safe bet. Two of its occupants were obviously doped and getting drunk out in the front yard. They wouldn't be able to move fast enough to catch me. Also, I wouldn't have to worry about encountering a locked back door. A flickering light showed in the side window. I assumed it was from a kerosene lamp.

Reed suddenly looked worried.

"What's the voice saying now?"

"You might wanna take a gun with you."

I stiffened. "Trouble?"

"He saw something move inside, but says it's small."

Small? That could mean anything from a cockroach to a baby pit bull.

14

My pulse raced as I grabbed the .38, which I'd found in a house I'd raided in St. Cloud. I hadn't fired it yet but was familiar with the caliber.

I shoved it in my back pocket and hoped I wouldn't need it. I hated killing people. I hadn't done it in years and promised myself long ago I'd never do it again. I didn't know certain grisly events beyond my control would soon prevent me from keeping that promise.

My heart thumped as I climbed out of the van.

The jumbo twins watched me as I circled in front of the van, stepped over the collapsed fence, and trudged through the weeds. The one closest to me lowered his hand in the grass.

I froze. My imagination went crazy. He might have been reaching for a gun he'd brought with him. Or, maybe he was bracing his arm so he could get up and rush toward me. He might even have rigged some sort of homemade booby trap for trespassers, and was about to toss it at me.

I hoped I was being ridiculous, but I had good reason to be scared and confused. It had been weeks since I'd encountered anything remotely normal. Judging by the events of the previous six months, I strongly suspected nothing would be normal ever again.

I forced myself to stay calm. If they came at me, I'd sprint back to the van and get the hell out of there. If they were doped, I'd have plenty of time to drive away. Even if they drew guns, their slowness and lack of coordination would prevent them from getting a clear shot.

Still, I'd be in real trouble if I'd mistaken their condition. I'd already stumbled across several people who appeared doped but actually weren't. I'd seen this many times in the work force, under normal conditions. People came to work hung over and strung out all the time. Some managed nicely, getting their job done and leaving at the end of the day without suffering any consequences. Others didn't do so well, stumbling about and spending most of the workday hiding, or in the john.

Nowadays, being doped meant the difference between life and death.

Heads tilted, the jumbo boys continued watching me in confusion.

Reasoning is nearly impossible when you're doped. Getting one's brain to function becomes a horrendously slow, painful process. It's like getting a car to fire up on only one spark plug.

One of them slowly hoisted his arm again, coaxing more beer into his mouth. He belched, lowered his arm, and continued watching me.

I waved. No response.

Keeping my eye on them, I trudged through the weeds. Just as I reached the corner of the house, they both hoisted their arms and waved slowly and awkwardly, as if their arms weighed half a ton.

I veered around the corner, cautiously climbed the loose wooden steps of the deteriorating porch, and stepped through the front door.

Kerosene lamps sent flickering shadows that danced across the walls of the foul-smelling kitchen. An old woman sat in a rocker in the corner beside the stove, crocheting. She wore a stained flowery

16

dress, white socks, and smudged white tennis shoes. Her head was lowered. Her matted, curly white hair obscured her face. She didn't look up when I walked in.

"Hello," I said softly.

No reply.

"You wouldn't mind if I used your bathroom, would you?"

Although I could barely see her arthritic fingers moving, the old woman continued her work. Gaps and holes ruined the center of the afghan in her lap. Yarn hung in loose loops all over the works. She'd obviously been at it a while. She probably had been thinking clearly when she started but began failing as time went on. The bottom section of the afghan, neat and uniform, did not match her recent efforts. I guessed she'd remain in the rocker until she could no longer function and die before anyone noticed.

One of the kerosene lamps lit up the wooden table in the center of the room. A loaf of moldy bread and a few tins of sardines covered a small section of its stained surface. Something had spilled recently. Flies feasted on it.

I saw no fruit on the table or on the kitchen counter. Reed would have to wait a little longer for his fructose fix.

Stepping over hordes of busy roaches, I crossed the filthy linoleum floor and opened the fridge. The pungent smell assaulted my nostrils. The food on the shelves had already reached the beginning stages of putrefaction. The temperature inside matched that of the kitchen. I should have realized by the dead street lamps that this family had lost

17

power. Finding food would become increasingly difficult. The people who could still function would use coolers or freezers, loading up with any ice they could find. Reed and I would have to be content with canned stuff.

I slammed the fridge door, but the old woman didn't flinch. She was either deaf or would react to the sudden noise after I'd gone. Or, maybe she was just so engrossed in her work she didn't care. I took a few deep breaths to rid my lungs of the foulness, but the air in the kitchen was only slightly better. I had to get out of there shortly or I'd be sick.

Then I heard a soft noise and turned to it.

A little girl stared up at me, her large brown eyes glazed.

Small--just like Reed said.

About ten years old, she was dressed only in a stained pink tee shirt and filthy white undershorts. She was also barefoot. Her greasy dark brown hair clung to her forehead and cheeks. Her face was smudged with dirt, her nose glossy with snot. She obviously hadn't been near bathwater in a while. It figured. Their water had also been shut off.

"Mind if I use your toilet?"

She slowly raised a bony arm and extended it toward the archway beyond the cabinets.

Dodging more roaches and a mouse nibbling on something, I took a kerosene lamp down the hall. Dirty clothes and food wrappers littered the carpet. The foul odor followed me from the kitchen.

The bathroom was the first room on the left. I went in, closed the door, and gagged at the stench. The toilet lid and seat were up, the basin brimming with feces. Holding my breath, I depressed the flush handle. Nothing. I tried again. Silence.

Idiot. No power or water. Do the math.

I dashed out of the room.

The little girl hadn't moved. I didn't want to leave her but had no choice. I had nowhere to take her and wasn't able to care for a kid. Reed wouldn't want the added responsibility, either.

"I'll be leaving now." Something tugged at my heart when I said it.

She watched me in eerie silence.

A black cowhide wallet sat on the counter in front of a scratched, red tin can labeled COOKIES. I picked up the wallet and opened it, finding several credit cards and some bills. The plastic wasn't usable anymore, so I ignored them. I found two twenties, three tens, and two ones. I took two tens then glanced at the little girl and the old woman, who continued working on her afghan. This was probably all the money they had.

Stealing from this family would haunt me. I'd always wonder if some of it had been earmarked for milk—or maybe fresh underwear.

I put the money back and returned the wallet to its place on the counter. The little girl still hadn't moved. I waved and went back outside.

I'd originally wanted to search the place for firearms. If the two outside were hunters, they might have guns lying around, possibly in one of the upstairs rooms. But I couldn't spend another moment in that house. The disgusting situation had made me nauseous.

I rushed over to an overgrown hedge in the trash-cluttered back yard, unzipped my jeans, and urinated in the bushes.

The two jumbos still sat in the same place on the front lawn. They watched me as I returned to my van and began waving after I'd slipped behind the wheel.

I hoped they'd remember to buy milk for that little girl.

Maybe if I go back inside and leave a note...

A wasted effort at best. They wouldn't be able to read it.

I saw the little girl watching me through one of the windows. For a moment, I imagined her dying, her big brown eyes glazing over moments before her head dropped. I forced my mind off it.

Sympathy and regret had become wasted emotions in this bleak new world.

***

I got back on the interstate and headed north, keeping the speedometer at about ninety. I wasn't afraid of being pulled over—I saw no traffic. The few people still functioning knew how dangerous the roads had become. The others could no longer operate a moving vehicle.

Depression set in. I forced it away. Depression could be lethal nowadays. I generally had no trouble keeping it a safe distance away, but this time I couldn't help it. That little girl had no future. No one did any more, but it seemed so much worse for kids, who'd never had the chance to experience any joy in life.

I'd seen forty years of it. I'd served in the military, defended this country in many unspeakable ways, and witnessed things that would stay with me the rest of my life. I fell in love several times, married and divorced once, met all sorts of people, made friends and enemies, and operated my own successful business.

I'd seen what the politicians had done to this country. I'd seen people kill one another and steal from one another. I'd seen love turn to hatred, hatred to murder. I'd seen envy. And deceit. I'd seen stupidity in all its forms.

Worst of all, I'd seen the end of life as we all knew it.

Viewed this way, the little girl was fortunate she wouldn't have to endure much more. The young shouldn't be forced to watch hell emerging from the darkness to claim the lives of everyone on this godforsaken planet.

"What happened back there?" Reed asked.

"An old woman and a little girl. Their water and power were cut off."

"I guess they didn't have any fruit, then."

Reed's statement sounded selfish and callous, but the survival instinct had emerged in many forms. Selfishness and callousness were merely two. I considered Reed's reaction a form of denial.

"There were roaches, flies, and rats. It was pretty disgusting in that house."

"How old was the little girl?"

"Nine or ten."

"How bad ... was she?"

"A few more days, maybe."

21

"Bummer." Reed sighed.

"If things were different, we might've taken her with us."

"If things were different."

"But they aren't."

"No. They aren't." Reed settled back in his seat. He probably wanted to talk to his friend about the little girl.

CHAPTER TWO

As I forced the van into the darkness of the night, I found myself once again trying to believe the last six months hadn't actually happened. I wished it had all been a hellacious dream, because all dreams end, so things would eventually revert back to the way they once were, and the world hadn't *really* become a gruesome hell filled with death and slobbering idiots. The powerful, intelligent people running the planet's governments would *never* let such horrors happen.

Would they?

Unfortunately, after spending so many mornings gazing out the bedroom window of my apartment and staring numbly at the growing number of bodies lying on the pavement behind the complex, I came to the frightening realization that I wasn't dreaming at all. And the stench assaulting my nostrils whenever I opened my window served as yet another clue.

A living nightmare had been born, sending reality gasping in the dust. In just a few short years, the System finally broke apart and began its decline into chaos and death, gaining momentum as things deteriorated, and turning society into a dark wasteland.

For ten years, I had been running my own auto detailing business, employing six men who drove to people's homes and thoroughly cleaned, washed, and polished their vehicles. I provided a terrific service, using hard-working, professional-minded young men and offering an unconditional money-back guarantee. The business earned much repeat service and many valuable contacts. But when the phones stopped working just a few months ago, customers could no longer call for appointments. And when my boys and my faithful secretary Leona stopped coming in to work, I knew the business was finished.

I remained in my apartment, scraping by on what cash I had left. I didn't have enough for rent, but that no longer mattered. The association running the apartment complex had suspended all activities and collections weeks earlier.

Orlando Utilities suffered serious changes that damaged their service. As the doping grew to mammoth proportions, their billing department turned chaotic, dying quietly over a period of days.

One afternoon, the meter reader showed up, just as she had on the fifteenth of every month. She got out of her small white pickup and shuffled over to my building. Just as she approached my meter, she stopped moving and stood very still, staring at the equipment in her hand. She remained standing there all evening. By next morning, she'd fallen dead on the pavement.

A week later, Orlando Utilities announced it would operate until the end of the month and then terminate its services. That meant all the stores on its grid would eventually follow suit.

Although most of this chaos took effect fairly quickly, it hadn't exactly happened overnight. I'd noticed several bad omens years earlier, for instance, while watching TV in my apartment. Every so often, the broadcasts would suffer signal glitches followed by white noise. It wasn't earth-shattering, so I didn't give it much thought at the time. I would just get up from the sofa, grab another beer, and wait for the program to resume. I didn't attribute such minuscule fuckups to anything serious or far-reaching. The guy running things from the computer room could have spilled coffee on the keyboard. He might have been shooting up, and when the drug penetrated his system, he fell out of his chair, pulling out power cords during his mind-blowing odyssey to the floor. Or maybe Barbie, the stacked, sunny-faced weather girl, had distracted him by walking by.

Signal hiccups and other interruptions quickly took a back seat to other meltdowns, however. Commercials began interfering with programming. Or, the image would become grainy and soft, almost muted followed by a blast of sharp and deafening audio, forcing me to lunge for the mute button. Eventually, normal programming appeared only fitfully, a few seconds here and there, only to revert back into inappropriately timed commercials and signal distortions.

One afternoon, as I watched a documentary, a grainy print of a home movie appeared in the middle of a break, showing two naked teenagers humping away in front of a swimming pool.

Then, a few months ago, the misspellings started, first in the commercials, soon thereafter on the local news, and finally on the national news.

I saw an ad for a local law firm that went something like this:

CALL MARTIN LANG IF YOU WENT TO BE COMPONSATED

FOR YUR INJYRIES

And:

DON'T LET THE IRS BETE YOU UPP—

CALL NORMIN BLAINE, ATTORNIE-AT-LAW—

HELL FIX YOU

The weather report in the screen crawl would read:

LOCL SHOWERS

HIGHTS IN THE EIGHTYS LOWS IN THE SIXTYS

TOPICAL DISTURBENCES ON THE TOPRICS...

DETALES LATR ON, WITH THE EVNING NEWCAST

Inquiries proved pointless. Each time I tried reporting a problem, I received a busy signal or recording saying the number was not valid, or no longer in service. I eventually stopped calling altogether and turned off the set.

Things worsened. My Wi-Fi connection, which normally ran flawlessly, broke down. Telephone service tanked. Internet service grew sporadic and frequently stopped for days on end. Electricity went off for hours. Cell phones lost their signals. ATMs stopped dispensing cash. Credit cards could no longer be scanned and were frequently chewed up by the machine.

As the doping epidemic increased, the chaos intensified. Because of the numbers of people winding down, the cities proved much more

26

dangerous than the rural areas. And as more people became affected, violence increased, and some of it was unimaginable in a normal world.

As for me, for reasons I couldn't explain—because I still didn't know what was going on—I remained unaffected. I wasn't alone. Many others who seemed still able to function wandered about. Like me, they'd witnessed the growing plague and its consequences, determined what they needed to do to survive, and did what was necessary. Their sense of self-preservation, heightened to the nth degree by the horrors they'd seen, forced them to do terrible things.

I'd been doing some terrible things myself. I'd walked into someone's house less than an hour ago to use their facilities and take whatever I wanted. If it hadn't been for the little girl and the old woman, I would have taken their money and anything else I could find. But I couldn't possibly steal from the unfortunate.

Even in this nightmare world, I clung to the principles I'd been following since I was a kid.

I realized that having principles at this stage was a weakness, and if I didn't soon toughen up, it would mean my demise. I understood this but still couldn't bring myself to do certain things. On the other hand, I couldn't bring myself to give up or come to grips with the world dying this way. I was a survivor and always had been. This was certainly a devastating blow to civilization, but I refused to believe it was the final one—though for me it had come awfully close just a few days earlier.

Orlando Utilities, operating with a skeleton crew of functioning employees, was providing service on a very limited basis: one hour in the morning and two hours in the evening. I would use this opportunity to cool off the sweltering apartment by turning the thermostat to 60 and keeping it there until the power switched off.

The severely crippled Internet followed the same pattern as the power company, providing service between 6 and 8 p.m. each day.

I switched on my screen one night during the two-hour window to see if anything was going on. It displayed the usual dated news reports and one new email message.

The email was from my mother, who still lived on the 88-acre property my great-grandparents had bought nearly a century earlier in Western Pennsylvania. Mom was in her mid-sixties and had lived on the farm her entire life. When Dad died five years earlier, Mom moved back into the main house with her older brother, Joe, and rented out the small frame house next door, where Mom and Dad had raised me.

Mom's message made my pulse pound.

HI SON WISH YOU WERE HERE THINGS HAVE BEEN GETTING BAD UP HERE LATLY AND I HOPE I GET TO SEE YU SOONE
MOM

The message was ominous enough in its content, but the misspellings told me the worst. My mother had graduated with honors from Carnegie-

Mellon University in Pittsburgh and taught College English for twenty years.

I had to face reality: Mom was affected.

**

It was the email that convinced me to return home. I had no idea how affected she was, but I'd never seen her misspell a word before. I hadn't seen her since Dad's funeral and felt badly about it. I'd considered moving back to Pennsylvania, but since my business had been doing so well, I didn't want to tempt fate. Now that fate had dealt us all the worst hand imaginable, I had no more excuses. If I didn't go back now, I'd probably never see my mother again.

**

Like many apartment complexes in Florida, mine adjoined the rear parking lot of a major Safeway. Normally, living within walking distance of a supermarket can be a terrific convenience. But the rules had changed dramatically. Even if I hadn't planned to leave the state, I would have moved out of my apartment. I refused to spend my final days next door to a building filled with massive amounts of putrefying foods.

The store normally operated twenty-four/seven, but because of the power loss, even with backup generators, the staff had given up on the facility weeks ago. Now, the evening air hung heavy with decay, assaulting my sinuses. Still, I had an errand to do before leaving town.

The parking lot was practically empty. I saw half a dozen vehicles parked farther down, in front of the local bar. That's where the few unaffected people in the neighborhood had chosen to gather—obviously to get sloshed. If I wasn't heading out of town, I would have joined them. Downing free drinks would have been a sensible way of facing a bleak future.

The Safeway's big sliding-glass doors were partially open. They'd probably stopped in that position during the last power blip and hadn't been reset. Most of the store was dark, while some parts flickered beneath erratic fluorescents. A large, heavyset black woman leaned against one of the registers, watching me with unseeing eyes. If I hadn't seen her blink, I would've thought she was dead.

To my left, Jim, a slender guy around thirty, watched me through the window of the manager's office. I waved, but he didn't move. I'd shopped in this store hundreds of times during the last ten years and had seen and spoken to him often. But now his face showed no recognition. His eyes displayed a fixed gaze. I'd learned to recognize the signs. When the light leaves the eyes and is replaced with a heavy glossiness, death settles in quickly. Jim probably had become affected a few days ago.

I grabbed a cart and pushed it down the aisle, passing a few other shoppers who were moving so slowly they'd probably be dead before they finished shopping. A tall black man around seventy faced the glass refrigerator door, staring blankly at the racks of assorted beers. I edged toward his left, pulled it open, picked up a six-pack of German pilsner, closed the door, and hurried down the aisle. Just before I turned the corner, I glanced back. He still hadn't moved.

I grabbed cans of tuna, chicken, baked beans, and several packets of beef jerky. I dumped them in the cart and headed back toward the front of the store. So far, so good. I seemed to be the only one moving about normally. The store remained quiet. If the cashier still hadn't moved as I was ready to leave, I wouldn't have to pay for my purchases.

Then I stopped cold.

Three large punks in filthy jeans, leather vests, and do-rags blocked my path. They all had long, greasy beards and stunk of B.O., cigarettes, and beer. Two of them wore nose rings. The third had several studs piercing the flesh at the ends of his eyebrows. All three wore ear studs. Two of them had switchblades tucked into their belts. The third gripped a pair of brass knuckles in his right fist.

They were standing still.

My guts churned, and my feet turned numb. I had no idea what to do, because I wasn't sure they were doped. Their glossy eyes suggested they might be doped. Or, they might be hyped up on something. I hadn't noticed them when I walked in the store.

They were spaced a few feet apart, giving me just enough room to slip by. If they were playing possum, they could easily kill me if I moved closer.

Backtrack!

It seemed my only possible escape.

I turned the cart around and hurried back down the aisle.

Just then, one of them zipped past me, stopped, slammed his scuffed boot onto the bottom shelf of my cart, and waved his switchblade at my face.

"Money," he said flatly.

Terrific. The world's been destroyed and I'm about to be mugged.

My pulse pounding, I glanced behind me. The others had crept up to us, stopping about five feet away. The punk with the switchblade held it out. Its razor-sharp blade glittered in the sputtering fluorescents. The other continued gripping the brass knuckles.

I was trapped.

"Your money, motherfucker. Everything you got. Give it up." His large, filthy left palm moved toward me. A heavy whiff of B.O. raked up and down my face.

The other two didn't move, but their eyes stayed on me.

My military training, long forgotten, quickly snapped on. The punk facing me was obviously still functioning. My cart separated us, but he could easily kick it aside and lunge at me with his knife. The other two stood within easy access of my back, with nothing separating us. This made them even deadlier than the first guy. If I wanted to get out of this alive, I'd have to confuse them.

"You really want money?" I asked.

"Give it up."

"Why?"

"Huh?"

"Don't *you* have money?"

"Give it up, motherfucker."

"Did you try the office?"

"Huh?"

"Back there." I pointed. "The office. They have money there. Lots of it."

He turned in that direction and squinted. "Off-office?"

"A small room with filing cabinets, a copier, computer, phone, safe, and money. Lots and lots of money. Piles of it."

"P-piles? M-money?" muttered one of them behind me.

"It's Monday," I said. "They keep it in the safe until Tuesday, when they take it to the bank. But right now there's no one to take it. Even if there was, the banks aren't open anymore. All that money's gonna stay right there, in the safe."

"Safe?" The one with the brass knuckles scowled.

"Bank?" muttered the other one behind me.

"Ain't no fucking banks open no more," corrected the thug in front of me.

"There's probably ten thousand bucks in that room," I said, "right behind the glass. And no one to take it out of the safe."

"Ten ... *thousand*?"

"At least."

"How d'ya ... know?"

The one facing me fought to keep his eyes open. He shook himself. His tattooed arm had lowered. Now I could see it. He was doped, but not yet severely enough to prevent him from functioning. He blinked, and when his eyes focused on me again, they'd turned glossier. The process was accelerating.

The last of his adrenaline might have flushed through his system when he'd raced past me.

"The m-money, m-motherfucker. I'll ... c-cut ... you ... up."

"Why don't you try the office?"

He was squinting again. He'd obviously forgotten our earlier conversation.

"Wh-what'd ... he s-say?" mumbled the one behind me holding the switchblade.

"Said ... s-said ... off ... office."

Someone behind me began snoring.

A switchblade clattered on the tile behind me. The brass knuckles clunked to the floor a few seconds later.

The thug facing me opened his mouth. A soft groan escaped his throat. He lowered his arm. His blade fell from his grasp, smacking the floor. His head lowered.

The two behind me had become living statues. The other just stared at me with glossy eyes.

The cashier didn't move as I pushed my cart through the glass doors and disappeared in the muggy, sour-smelling darkness.

CHAPTER THREE

Fog had covered that following morning with a heavy gray veil.

I had crammed my clothes into the back seat of my classic black Mustang, filled the trunk with beer and the canned foods I'd taken from the Safeway the night before, and left my apartment without looking back.

My first stop—and the most painful part of the trip—was to find a replacement vehicle. The Mustang had been my pride and joy. I'd purchased it nine years earlier from one of my customers and kept it in mint condition. I hated to leave it but I couldn't take it with me. I had no idea what I would encounter along the way, so I needed something that would give me good gas mileage, more personal security, and allow me enough room to sleep.

Rather than drive north and take Highway 50 all the way to the coast, I decided to head south and hunt for a vehicle in St. Cloud. I knew that area well. I'd lived there before moving to Orlando and knew where the best van dealerships were located. I figured that as soon as I found a suitable vehicle, I'd get on 192 and drive east straight to the coast then pick up I-95 and head north.

I drove down South Orange Blossom Trail to Kissimmee and turned left on 192. The fog had lifted, and I saw very little traffic. Sidewalk activity consisted of street punks emptying the pockets of someone lying on the ground, and a couple of skinny stray dogs sniffing the ankles of a man standing motionless at the corner.

I stopped at St. Cloud Motor Works, a large dealership located on the western side of town. The lights in the showroom still shined brightly. I didn't know if they were hooked up to a functioning grid or being powered by a generator.

A long row of SUVs, pickups, and luxury vans in the front lot faced the main drag. A good prospect sat at the far end, near the telephone pole. It was a tan three-seater, with plenty of storage in the back. It had double rear doors and a sliding side passenger door, and the engine was small enough to conserve gas. The third seat was removable—another plus. It would be perfect for my needs.

I turned toward the building and nearly bumped into a salesman who'd snuck up on me. He was tall and well-dressed, about forty, and hadn't shaved in several days—a clear sign that something was wrong. His grin was lopsided and sloppy—another sign.

"I'd like this one," I said.

He nodded slowly. "Wanna ... wanna test-drive it?"

"Got the keys?"

He reached into his jacket pocket. His hand stayed buried.

This was going to take a while.

"Nice day," I said.

He nodded. "Yeah. Nice. Hot, but nice."

"It's always hot."

"Yeah. Hot. Florida, right?"

"Been working here long?"

"Yeah. A long time. Real long."

I decided not to say anything else. Each time he spoke, his hand stopped moving. He obviously could no longer multitask.

His hand finally reappeared. A ring holding at least a dozen keys dangled from his index finger. He brought it closer to his face and began the painfully arduous task of selecting the right one.

This would take a while as well. That was okay. If he switched off, I'd take them from him and find the right one myself.

Nearly five minutes later, he pulled a key from its metal clasp and handed it to me. "I'll need ... I've gotta get your ... your ... your ..."

"Driver's license?"

He grinned awkwardly. "Yeah."

"Don't you need to put a temporary plate on this first?" I didn't want to take the van with him standing here. "Just in case I get into an accident?"

He squinted at the deserted highway. "Hardly any traffic anymore."

I shrugged. "One never knows."

"Sure. Yeah. Better safe..."

"You got it."

He turned, took a step then turned back around and blinked. "What ... am I ... s'posed to get?"

"We need a temporary tag."

"Oh, yeah, a ... tag."

"No problem."

He turned around again, awkwardly. "Be ... right back."

I watched him for about ten seconds. I figured it would take him at least five minutes to reach the building. Using my penknife, I transferred my tag from the Mustang to the van. I didn't think I'd encounter any cops along the way, but I wanted to be prepared.

I loaded my supplies into the back. Forcing myself to ignore my prized Mustang sitting in the grass, I backed out of the space and pulled out onto 192.

The salesman still hadn't reached the front steps of the showroom.

***

I needed cash. I had no idea what would happen during my long trip. I'd brought along a few supplies, but not what I'd need if I faced a real emergency.

The local Walmart would be my last stop before I reached the coast. I could probably spend the night in one of the RV parks in the Cocoa Beach area. After a good sleep, I'd be ready for my thousand-mile journey.

I turned off 192 and cruised down one of the residential streets running perpendicular to the main drag.

Rows of one-story stucco homes, each with its own tiny front yard, extended as far as the eye could see. I stopped in front of a small yellow ranch. A dark-brown SUV sat in front of the garage door. I listened for a few moments but heard only a distant barking dog and some birds chattering away from the pines across the street. A careful scan of the neighborhood revealed no sign of life.

The front door was locked. I went around to the rear of the house. The back door was locked as well, but the bathroom window was partially open. I pulled out the screen, pushed the sash open all the way, and climbed through.

No sign of life in the living room, kitchen, dining room, or hall. In the master bedroom, a thin young guy around thirty sat on the edge of the bed, watching me. He wore only his stained undershorts. A pair of black socks lay on the carpet at his feet. A slender, naked woman about the same age stood in the shower, gazing at the tile.

Two wallets sat on top of the dresser. One contained a hundred bucks, the other nearly two hundred. I took half from each.

They're gone now, a voice inside me said. *They won't need anything.*

I reluctantly pocketed the rest of the cash and felt a stab of guilt. I was no thief.

These are extreme times, my interior voice added. *Those still functioning need to survive—this means you.*

It didn't matter. I couldn't overcome my feelings. I pulled out the wad back out of my pocket and left them two hundred bucks.

I checked the dresser drawers next. Three handguns lay hidden among two stacks of tee shirts. I selected two of them, found them loaded, and pocketed them. I checked the third, verified it was loaded as well, put it back among the shirts, and closed the drawer.

I went back out to the kitchen and found another two hundred bucks in a cookie jar on the counter. I took half and dashed outside before I could change my mind.

The Walmart was practically empty. The few people in the aisles slumped over their carts, gazing dumbly at their purchases. They weren't any more animated than the mannequins decorating the women's clothing section. Other than a few lifeless clerks and about two dozen others lying on the floor in Produce, I had the place to myself.

I left the store pushing two carts filled with supplies—a first-aid kit, sleeping bag, gasoline can, flashlights, batteries, lantern, cooler, butane grill, canteen, bug spray, binoculars, a box of MRE, a can opener, and a hunting knife.

I'd managed to acquire more than a thousand dollars of supplies without having to pay. My cashier had forgotten how to ring me up, and the store manager was too busy trying to remember where'd he'd put the key to the office. I felt sorry for them but was greatly relieved. I could never have paid for everything with the few hundred in cash I carried in my pocket.

I stashed the stuff in the back of the van and slipped behind the wheel. Then I coasted down the center of the parking lot to the entrance that would take me back to 192. Just then, about fifty yards to my left, at the east end of the parking lot, a slender figure paced frantically. Not an unusual sight in normal times but in these circumstances an unforgettable image.

I didn't want to stop, but my soft side had already taken over, and my foot mashed down on the brake pedal. Reluctantly I turned the wheel and moved the van closer to the grove of scrubs, where the agitated figure stomped about, talking to himself—or, at least, that's what I thought he was doing.

He appeared to be around my own age, fairly tall and wiry, with thick, light-brown hair. He wore a loose-fitting, short-sleeve tan shirt, plus jeans and sneakers. I didn't see his face until he spun around and gawked at me. Then I saw the blood covering his forehead.

For some reason, I didn't fear for my safety. I didn't even think of grabbing a gun as I got out of the van. He'd stopped pacing and watched me as I approached. He was obviously not doped. His small blue eyes were glossy, but I attributed this to rage, which I was familiar with. The ugly gash on his forehead hadn't been there very long.

"What happened?" I asked.

"I was attacked!" His voice was high-pitched and throaty. "Right outside the fucking store!"

"Who did it?"

"Kids. Punks."

"How many?"

"Could've been eight or nine, for all I know. Jerks were all over me. They got me from behind and…" He stopped talking and tilted his head. "What? Three? Are you sure?" He sighed. "There were only three of them, apparently."

"But you said…"

"I know. But he said three," he said, jerking a thumb to his right.

"Someone there?" I saw no one hiding in the bushes or behind the scrubs.

"You ... can't see him."

I should have figured something was wrong. This man had suffered a concussion.

"I can't see him, either," he said.

"Then how do you know he's...?"

"I can *hear* him. How *else* would I know he's there?"

This man genuinely believed someone was standing beside him. I didn't know if I should humor him or just politely wave and get back in the van.

"Any idea who he is?"

"He just ... started talking to me after ... after those punks jumped me—when I woke up."

"He wasn't there before?"

His eyes narrowed. "You think I'm some sort of nut!"

The idea *had* occurred to me. Unfortunately, I didn't have time to take him to a doctor. I didn't even know if any doctors were still functioning—or where their offices were. I didn't want to get involved in anything that could delay my trip. But he clearly needed medical attention.

"You really should get checked out. I don't know if I can find a doctor around here, but..."

"You can't."

"You live around here?"

"All my life."

"You have a family?"

"A wife ... two kids." A shadow crossed his features.

"Where ... are they?"

A deep sigh. "At home."

"Where's home?"

He pointed across 192 to a residential area. It wasn't far from the house I'd visited an hour earlier. Iciness slid down my arms. I was genuinely relieved it wasn't his place I had robbed.

"Down that street. They're ... still there."

"Are they ... I mean…"

"They all collapsed three days ago. I spent the last two looking for a damned doctor. When I found one, I had to force him to remember what he did for a living. Just when I thought I was getting through, he closed his eyes and died. On the spot. I've been wandering around all morning, trying to decide what I should do. I've been waiting to wind down as well, but it hasn't happened. I don't understand." He looked me over. "You seem okay, too."

"I'm pretty sure I am."

"Know why?"

"I've got a few theories."

"I've got a ton of them, too, but what the hell good are they? They won't change anything, and they sure as hell won't bring anyone back."

This wasn't exactly the time for a discussion of world events.

"Tell me about the assholes that jumped you."

"Tattoos and jewelry and studs and funny clothes. They were carrying guns and giggling like girls. I was going to the store for a few odds and ends when they pulled me out of my car, slammed me to the pavement, and then took my money and my car."

"You have any money back at your home?"

"I have cash ... in a jar ... on my wife's side of the bed."

43

"Want to go back and…"

"No."

"I can go in and…"

"Please." His eyes glistened. "I can't … see them like that … or know. If they died. If … they haven't."

I nodded.

"You've got no family?"

"I'm divorced."

"Kids?"

"My wife miscarried three times. That last time almost killed her. She went back to Miami to live with her family, last I heard."

"You're lucky."

He was right. Watching my wife die would make all this a hundred times worse. Thank God for small favors.

"Where are you going?" he asked.

"I'm leaving Florida. I'm driving up to Cocoa, then…"

"You have room in that van?"

"You want to go to Cocoa?"

His features tightened. "I don't care where I go. I have to get the hell out of here."

"Listen, fella, I need to…"

"Reed. My name's Reed McCallum."

"Listen. Reed. I'd like to help, but…"

"What's your name?"

"Moss. I'd like to…"

"What's your first name?"

"Alan, but everyone calls me Moss. I'm heading north."

"Like I said, I don't care." Then he tilted his head.

"I really don't have room for…"

"You need to get gas."

"Pardon?"

"You're low. You don't want to run out—especially on that long stretch east."

I glanced at the van, then at him.

He nodded. "Check the gauge."

I opened the door and peered inside. Sure enough, the needle hovered just above empty. I straightened, nearly bumping my head. "How the hell did you know?"

"I didn't."

"Then how…?"

"He did." He jabbed a thumb to his right, again. This was getting weird.

"You *really* don't know who he is?"

"He just started talking to me a little while ago. He ... woke me up."

"You woke up and heard his voice?"

"He *told* me to wake up—yelled at me. Those punks who jumped me, after they beat me up and got in my car, they tried to run me over."

"And he ... yelled at you to get out of the way?"

"Weird, right?"

"Slightly." I was still wondering about that gas gauge deal.

"So ... can we tag along?"

I'd been planning this for myself. Besides, I'd always been a loner and didn't want to be responsible for someone else's safety. A lot of things could happen on a thousand-mile trip.

45

"I don't know..."

"He knew about your gas tank."

"What else can he do?"

Reed glared. "He said he'll pay his way."

"He's ... got money?"

"He'll pay in other ways."

"How will *you* pay?"

"*He'll* pay by telling us things we need to know. *I'll* pay by being his translator. Otherwise, you won't know what he's saying. You can't hear him, can you?"

"No."

"If you need him, you'll need me as well."

I didn't like being pressured, but the gas tank issue had slapped my face with a chilling reality. I had no idea who Reed was talking to, or how this imaginary friend knew about the tank. But he'd been right.

I'd always been cautious in the past. I always checked the door and windows and made sure the contents of my wallet were in order before leaving the apartment. I've always checked gauges, tires, oil, and gas as well before driving off.

On that day, however, I hadn't been thinking clearly. Plus, I'd stolen a vehicle in broad daylight. I'd never stolen anything before, and the experience had shaken me up. As I'd driven away, I worried more about being nabbed by the cops than anything else.

When I'd left Walmart, I was thinking about the items I'd stolen. I probably would have spent the rest of the day checking the rearview mirror and not thinking rationally again until I was halfway to the ocean.

By then, I would have already run out of gas. There were only a few stations on that stretch, and they were all probably closed. If I'd gone empty, I would've been forced to search for another vehicle. I would've been out in the open and totally vulnerable—an easy target for psychos driving around hunting for fresh prey.

"Get in," I said.

Reed nearly smiled. "Would you mind letting me use your first-aid kit? I need to clean up and fix this disgusting gash."

The back of my neck tingled. The first-aid kid sat on the floor behind my seat, beneath the sleeping bag. "How'd you know I bought a first-aid kit?"

Reed grinned. "He saw it when he was checking your gas gauge."

CHAPTER FOUR

After spending nearly two hours finding a working gas station in St. Cloud, we gassed up, got back onto 192, and reached Cocoa around suppertime. Then, for the next half-hour, I searched for a place to rest for the night.

The same eerie stillness I'd seen everywhere else had engulfed the town. The palm trees and palmettos, oblivious to human suffering, surrendered to the cool ocean breeze. The few people on the sidewalks stood completely still or lay dead on the pavement or on park benches. Others sat on front porches, staring straight ahead. It was difficult to tell who was still alive and who was dead. Deserted stores lined the streets, their darkened windows reflecting the emptiness within. Traffic lights blinked sporadically. Neon signs flickered, darkened then flickered again. Vehicles sat in the middle of the street, their drivers slouched behind the wheel. A stray cat rubbed its nose against a shoe of one of the corpses on the sidewalk.

A mile north, across the street from an abandoned gas station, a vandalized 7-Eleven, and a deserted strip mall, an RV park sat silently in a grove of pines. A small stucco building marked *OFFICE* awaited us at the far end, next to a smaller building marked *BATHROOMS.* An ice chest and cold-drink machine shared a concrete slab off to the side.

Half the spaces were taken, but the RVs appeared dark and empty. No candles or kerosene lamps lit up any of the windows. I heard no moaning of generators interrupting the silence. Total darkness had swallowed up the office as well.

Creepy.

I peered at the bushes, half-expecting some undead creature from an old zombie flick to crawl out and stumble our way.

"Where we gonna park?" Reed's voice snapped me out of my delusion.

"I thought I'd ease on over to the empty space near that single-wide in front of the bushes."

"Someone's in there."

I stiffened. "You sure?"

The black windows revealed nothing.

"We're being watched."

"Could be someone just being cautious."

"My friend doesn't think so."

"What makes him so suspicious?"

"He spotted a rifle—and a handgun."

Rifle. Handgun. Two words I didn't want to hear just then. I didn't want to spend the night waiting for someone to rob us at gunpoint, and I certainly didn't want to shoot it out with a paranoid nutcase. Even if I won the battle, he might hit the van and disable it. Then I'd have to waste precious time searching for another ride.

I backed out, turned around, and hurried down the street.

We heard no gunshots.

I drove another two miles until we reached an attractive residential area of large brick homes. Halfway down the block, I stopped in front of an old two-story house sitting proudly behind trimmed

49

bushes and palmettos. A long gravel drive ran up to the two-car garage in the back yard.

An elderly man sat in a rocker on the front porch, his bald head slumped forward. He wasn't rocking and didn't move at all.

I pulled in and coaxed the van down the driveway, stopping about five feet from the garage doors. "This place is as good as any. We can leave the van right here."

"I don't think the old man will mind," Reed said.

"He's probably been dead a while."

"If anyone's still moving around inside, they would've already brought him back in."

"Poor guy. He probably just fell asleep then died."

"Not a bad way to go."

When I was in the military, I'd seen people die in many ghastly ways. Reed was right—falling asleep was the most peaceful way to go. Even so, as I flicked off the ignition, a heavy tug of guilt pulled at my heart. We were going into this man's house to use his facilities while he sat out here, dead.

"I feel badly about this," I said.

"We need a place to spend the night."

"I know."

"He won't mind."

"Won't you feel guilty?"

"I'll get over it."

Reed had a point. I fully realized I should get over it as well, but my soft side had stepped in again.

"I keep thinking someone'll come along, pile them all in an ambulance, and haul them away to a mass grave."

"There's no one to drive the ambulance. No one working the hospitals."

"That's what's eating me up inside. I'm surprised it's not eating you up as well."

"Being beaten up and left for dead changed my outlook," Reed said edgily.

I grabbed a flashlight and one of the handguns. I told myself to ignore the dead figure in the rocker and focus on the house.

The front door, made of carved mahogany, had a large oval pane of glass built into its center. I aimed my flashlight at the glass but saw only the glare from its reflection.

The door was unlocked. I eased it open and aimed my light at the gaping square of darkness facing me. A large tile foyer. Carpeted stairs straight ahead and doorways to my right and left. A light-switch panel on the wall directly to my left.

I tried the switches. The foyer flickered at first, went dark again, then came right back, spraying the area with bright yellow light. The living room blazed, then the dining room, front porch, and kitchen. Apparently the grid handling the area still provided temporary power.

"Nice," Reed said behind me.

I felt as if we'd just won the lottery. To be safe, I flicked off the porch light as well as the kitchen light.

The house radiated comfort and warmth. Framed family photos covered a stretch along the living room wall and extended up the stairs.

The living room boasted a high beamed ceiling, lots of furniture, and polished hutches and shelves. Knickknacks and mementoes filled every niche. A large leather couch sat in front of a big bay window. A smaller couch faced it. An oval coffee table piled with magazines rested between the two pieces. A wicker-back rocker occupied the far corner. A thick, well-worn armchair sitting against the far wall faced the entryway.

Despite its aged attractiveness, the room's silent emptiness and lingering smell brought me back. This home would no longer hear laughter, joy, or any other sounds of life. It would never again exude delicious aromas from the kitchen. It had become yet another mausoleum in a world filled with death.

"I'd better do a search upstairs," I said.

"Be careful. He doesn't hear anything, but you know what that might mean."

"Someone could be up there, waiting."

"Looters have no conscience."

Reed's statement made the hair bristle on the back of my neck.

"What the hell do you think *we* are?"

He blinked. "We … haven't hurt anyone. We're just using the facilities. These people have already died. I honestly don't think they'd mind, Moss."

His reasoning didn't make me feel any better. We'd just walked into someone's house while a dead man slumped in a rocker on the front porch. I was going to see what was salvageable and what we could take with us. That meant searching the rooms and going through people's dressers and closets—just as I'd done in St. Cloud.

These people were dead, but it didn't change the fact that I'd become a looter.

My disgust and self-loathing rose to new levels.

I forced myself up the stairs and stopped at the doorway of the first bedroom. A girl in her late teens lay on the floor, just a few feet from her vanity. Apparently her reflection was the last thing she saw before falling out of her chair and dying on the carpet. She was dressed in a white slip. One of her fuzzy pink bunny slippers had dislodged beneath her vanity. A cell phone lay just a few inches from her outstretched arm.

A middle-aged couple lay in bed in the master bedroom, staring up at the ceiling. They both wore pajamas and held hands. They'd obviously chosen to die together.

In another bedroom, a woman around seventy lay on the bed on her back. She wore a red, flowery housecoat that had opened, revealing her white slip. She was probably the wife of the old man on the porch. Perhaps her husband had slipped outside for some fresh air before going to bed. Maybe he hadn't asked her to accompany him because she'd already fallen. Or maybe he knew he was going to die and wanted to watch the stars one last time.

Holding in my nausea and depression, I went into the bathroom. To my relief, the toilet was usable. I indulged myself then washed my hands and face in the sink. I tried not to stare at my gaunt reflection in the smudged mirror, but I was tired, and my self-control lost out over my curiosity. I ignored the despair, fear, and self-loathing oozing from my reflection by washing my face again.

They're all dead, the little voice inside me said. *You may be a looter, but it doesn't matter anymore. Not to them. Not to anyone.*

Why doesn't it matter? I asked myself.

No one else is around to make things right, came the reply.

I washed my face one more time. Then, leaving my irritating philosophical self at the sink, I went back downstairs.

Reed was lounging on the couch in front of the big bay window.

"How many?" he asked softly.

"Four." I turned off the light upstairs and the one in the dining room. Then I turned on the small lamp beside the living room hutch and turned off the main overhead light. I didn't want to advertise activity to anyone wandering about outside.

"Kids?"

"One, probably in her late teens."

Reed sighed. "I don't want to be around when all this ends. I mean, I don't want to be the last one left. Do you?"

"What choice do we have?"

Reed pointed to the gun in my hand.

I didn't look at it. "Only if the time comes."

"*When* it comes?"

"Let's not talk about this, okay? Things are depressing enough."

"I'll take this couch, if you don't mind. I'm already beginning to feel the last few hours. It's been a long, stressful day."

"We should check the kitchen. Their food might still be fairly fresh."

"In the morning. I'm too exhausted to eat."

I hadn't noticed my own fatigue until Reed mentioned it. I wanted to lie down and sleep for hours. I knew that was impossible, but we could at least grab a few winks and be ready to go in the morning.

"I'll take this armchair. It faces the front doorway."

"You think we'll have company?"

"If we do, I'll need a clear shot."

"Isn't there a deadbolt on the front door?"

"I didn't lock the door."

"Why not?"

"We don't want to arouse suspicion. Anyone will know that with the dead man outside, the door shouldn't be dead-bolted. Even if I did lock it, what good's a dead-bolt with a huge pane of glass in the center of the door?"

Reed said nothing, but he didn't look pleased.

I turned off the lamp and carefully found my way back to the chair. I sat, put my gun in my lap, and grabbed the afghan from the back of the chair.

***

A couple of hours later, the front door flew open, slamming into the wall behind it. I forced myself to remain still. My first instinct was to pull off the afghan and empty my gun at the entrance, but my head quickly cleared away the grogginess of sleep and ordered me not to move.

A flashlight beam hopped across the entryway before turning abruptly and hitting me full in the face.

Play dead.

Without flinching, I closed my eyes. A few tense moments later, the beam left me, sliding over the couch, then moving toward Reed and settling on his sleeping form.

Three figures crept into the room.

The flashlight beam returned to my face. I wondered why Reed hadn't awakened during all this. Was he playing dead, as well? Probably not. Reed had no military training, and wouldn't know what to do in this situation. He'd obviously been more exhausted than he'd let on and remained in heavy slumber. His earlier trauma, no doubt, had done him in.

I was greatly relieved he hadn't stirred. If he opened his eyes, he'd get us both killed.

"Fucker's dead." The one with the flashlight sounded young, probably in his late teens. He lowered the beam to the afghan in my lap. "Both of 'em."

"I'll check upstairs." The second one sounded about the same age. He dashed up the stairs, his flashlight beam guiding the way.

The third looter went into the dining room.

The one near me said, "Where d'ya think *you're* goin'?"

"Gotta find the kitchen."

"You hungry *again*?"

56

"This is hard work, Frankie."

"Well, hurry up. We gotta frisk these two and see what goodies we can find. This is one big fuckin' house. We'll prob'ly be here a while. That old stiff out on the porch didn't have a fuckin' thing in his pockets."

"Won't be long," his friend said and disappeared.

"All right, slick." He aimed his flashlight at my afghan. "Let's see what you got for ol' Frankie." A strong stench of whiskey rubbed my face as he moved closer. He grabbed a corner of the afghan and pulled.

With my left hand, I seized the hand holding the flashlight and slammed his forehead with the butt of my handgun. He went down with a soft grunt, whacking his chin on my knee.

I grabbed him by the ankles and dragged him over to the far corner of the room. I pulled out the rocker, pushed him into the corner, and wedged the rocker in front of him. He stirred, moaning softly. I smacked him again on the back of the head, cracking his skull.

I hurried back to my chair. Before covering myself with the afghan, I pulled back the hammer of my gun, cocking it, and rested my index finger behind the trigger as a precaution.

The second looter came out of the dining room, smacking his lips. "They got chicken wings in here, Frankie. Would ya believe it? Chicken wings." He forced out a belch. "They even got beer!"

He stopped in the archway. I could feel him looking around.

57

"Frankie?" He stopped munching. A click. The flashlight beam settled on my face. "Frankie?" The beam moved away, drifting over to Reed. Without moving my head, I glanced at Reed's face at the end of the beam. He still hadn't moved. Good thing. A panic would quickly turn this into a ghastly nightmare.

The beam floated back to me.

"Frankie? Where the fuck are ya?"

The beam shot back to Reed.

"Ya doin' a number on us?"

I knew he'd find Frankie in just a few seconds, so I made sure my gun was aimed and my index finger in its proper position. I just hoped he wouldn't put two and two together and try the light switch. I wasn't sure I could toss the afghan, aim, and shoot him before he could get me.

Just moments later, the third punk rushed down the stairs. The room blazed.

"Motherfuck! Their lights work!"

"Frankie's missing," the second one whispered.

"Missing?"

"Yeah. Missing. Gone. Disappeared."

"Maybe he went outside."

"Why the fuck would he go outside? All the good shit's in here."

My heart sputtered as they scanned the room.

"What the fuck's that?" They dashed past me, stopping abruptly. I could tell they were gawking at the motionless form in the corner behind the rocker.

"Fr ... Frankie?"

"Motherfuck!"

The two spun around. The one closest to me dropped what was left of his chicken leg and groped for the pistol in his waistband. I yanked off the afghan and shot him in the chest. He grunted and fell, whacking the back of his head on the oval table. Several magazines slipped over the side and dropped to the floor.

The third punk drew his gun and brought it up. "Fucker," he growled, and pulled back the hammer of the revolver.

"What's all the commotion?" Reed sat bolt upright, knocking his pillow to the floor. "Can't a guy get any sleep around here?"

Gasping, the third punk spun around.

I shot him in the back of the head.

Doubling up, Reed turned away from the blood spatter and coughed wetly. He straightened, swaying a little, and took several deep breaths.

"You okay?" I asked.

He didn't reply. His eyes were enormous as he gazed at me. Then he noticed the blood spatter and bits of gray matter on his left forearm. Covering his mouth, he held his left arm straight out and carefully stepped over the two young corpses. As soon as he crossed the room, he rushed through the archway and ran upstairs. A door slammed shut. Muffled coughing followed. A minute later, the toilet flushed.

Ten minutes later, he came back into the living room, wiping his face with a damp washrag. His cheeks were bone-white, his eyes red and wet. His gaping expression told me he'd never witnessed anything like that.

"They were going to kill us," I said.

A nod.

"Then ... why are you looking at me like that?"

"Like what?"

"You're not ... afraid of me, are you?"

"It ... isn't that."

"What is it?"

The corners of his mouth turned down. "You ... handled this so ... well."

"Whaddya mean?"

He swallowed audibly. "As if ... as if you'd had ... practice."

If only he knew.

My reflexes had kicked in, causing me to act instinctively. It was like grabbing an egg before it rolls off the counter, or catching a bottle of beer I'd just tapped with my elbow. I hadn't thought much about it when it happened. My survival instinct had come to my aid just as it had nearly twenty years ago, when I was in the Army.

I hadn't even realized my training had stayed with me. In this case, I was greatly relieved. It had saved our lives.

While Reed continued to apply the washrag to his face, I searched the dead looters. I wasn't surprised to discover they'd all been armed. I found a short-barreled Beretta .22 and a Llama 9-millimeter in Frankie's pockets and an American Arms .22 long-barrel, cowboy-type revolver and snub-nosed American Arms .38 in the pockets of the second punk. The third carried a short-barreled Smith & Wesson .45 in a pancake holster in the small of his back. All the guns were loaded. I found only three empty casings among the revolvers.

I also collected more than five hundred dollars in cash from their pockets. I dropped everything on the coffee table, went into the kitchen, and turned on the rear outside light.

The back door opened up to a small wooden porch with five steps descending to a large concrete slab. A large wooden picnic table, stainless-steel barbecue grill, and several lounge chairs covered the slab. The well-used grill told me the family enjoyed their get-togethers.

A five-foot, chain-link fence enclosed the back yard. The grass had been mowed recently. Three galvanized garbage cans formed a neat row at the opposite end of the property inside the gate.

Reed reluctantly helped me drag the three bodies down the hall, through the kitchen, down the stairs, and across the back yard. I opened the gate and we dragged them out onto the sidewalk and left them next to the curb. The faint orange haze of the porch light ended a foot or so beyond the fence. They lay at my feet, everything from the waist up shrouded in darkness. Only minutes ago I'd murdered all three of them, yet I felt no remorse.

Reed stood beside me, panting from his excursions. Even in the semi-darkness I could make out his pale features. After catching his breath, he said, "Why'd we bring them out here?"

"I don't want their corpses contaminating this family's house or back yard."

Reed nodded but said nothing.

"By the way, thanks for waking up when you did. I'm glad you didn't do it earlier. It would have been … well, really bad."

"I was up long before they broke in."

"How long?"

"My friend woke me as soon as he heard them coming down the walk."

"Why didn't you say anything?"

"He told me to play possum until the right time."

"Did he tell you when the right time was?"

"I sort of used my own judgment."

"You cut it a little close, but it turned out well."

He stared at the corpses for a moment then turned away. "I guess it did—for us, anyway."

"We're still alive, aren't we?"

"Yes. Alive." Then he hurried back to the house.

Inside, I turned off all the lights. I also applied the dead-bolt to the front and back doors. I found towels in the kitchen that I used to cover the blood spatter and brain fragments on the living room floor. For Reed's benefit, I wiped down the spatter on the couch.

This time, I chose the small couch. I was much too tired to spend the rest of the night in a chair.

I'd just killed three people, but I'd sleep peacefully.

CHAPTER FIVE

The next morning, as remnants of the early fog rubbed against the kitchen windows, Reed and I ate breakfast.

Still troubled from the previous night's trauma, Reed had little appetite. He settled for coffee, two strips of bacon, and a dry piece of whole-wheat toast.

I, on the other hand, had no trouble devouring three scrambled eggs, six strips of bacon, coffee, and three slices of toast.

Afterward, we cleaned up the kitchen and put what unspoiled food that remained into my cooler, along with all the ice cubes we could take from the freezer. The power had dwindled during the night, rendering a lot of the food suspect. I briefly considered taking it out to the garbage but realized how futile that effort would be.

Reed followed me upstairs to help search for items we could use on our trip. Luck was on our side. One of the family members had been a hunter. We found an old Winchester .30-30 lever-action rifle; a Mossberg 12-gauge, single-barrel, pump-action shotgun; a Ruger Target model .22 pistol, and several boxes of ammunition for 12-gauge, .22, .38, .380, 9-millimeter, .30-30, and .45.

"What should we take?" Reed asked.

"Get a pillowcase. Fill it up."

"Isn't that a little ... excessive?"

"No reason to leave anything for future looters, is there?"

While Reed gathered up the ammo, I grabbed the rifles and handgun and went back downstairs. I picked up the handguns from the coffee table then pocketed the cash we'd collected from the looters and from the wallets we'd found in the bedrooms.

Outside, we put everything in the back of the van, hiding the long guns as best as we could and putting the ammo boxes beneath the passenger seat. I loaded the Ruger with fresh ammo, adding it as well as the looters' guns to our growing collection beneath my seat and in the console and glove box.

Before leaving, Reed and I lifted the old man from the rocker and set him down on a rug we'd brought from the dining room. Grabbing the rug by its corners, we carried him inside, laying him gently on the large couch in front of the bay window and covering him with the afghan I'd used the night before.

I wanted to say a few words but had no idea what would be appropriate. I didn't know if I believed in God anymore. After what had happened to the world, I didn't know if I believed in anything.

"He wants to know if you're going to say something," Reed said.

"Does he have any suggestions?"

"He says this was a good family, and we should thank them for their hospitality."

I turned to the lifeless form on the couch. His home had sheltered us for the night. We'd been able to have breakfast and use the facilities, and we'd even collected food and other items that would help us on our journey. I felt badly for what had happened to them and for what we'd taken, but I thought they would have approved under the circumstances.

"Thank you," I told the old man's body, "and many thanks to your family. If we could give you a proper burial, we would. But we can't, and for that I apologize. Hopefully, you're all in a much better place and you're together again, this time for eternity."

***

I drove all morning and much of the afternoon, stopping only when we reached the Jacksonville area that evening. After leaving the little girl and the old woman, I drove two more hours before getting off the Interstate. It was nearly 10 o'clock, and after so much driving I needed rest. Reed hadn't offered to spell me, and I didn't force the issue. He'd been silent since we'd left Jacksonville. He was obviously still trying to come to grips with what happened in Cocoa.

I had no idea why the incident hadn't traumatized me. After all, I'd murdered three people. I had done it in self-defense, but it was still murder. My past, that colossal steed of death and vengeance, had galloped out of the darkness to rescue me.

Reed had said I handled things so *well*. To the casual observer, my actions could easily be interpreted as skillful. Reflexes happen automatically and rarely have the luxury of even a moment's rational thought or decision.

As a soldier, I was trained to kill. And kill efficiently. And react quickly without thinking about it.

Viewed this way, Reed's statement had been thoroughly accurate. It *had* been easy for me—much easier than it would have been for someone without military training. I'd spent three years in the Army. The fact that I hadn't killed in nearly twenty years meant nothing. When the situation presented itself, the killer lurking in the darkness of my soul responded with deadly force. He'd done it quickly and efficiently—as if he'd never left my side.

That thought made me shiver.

***

The darkness of the night pressed its mass against the windshield while flicking its angry tentacles at my headlight beams. As we passed the Savannah area, I continued flooring the gas pedal. The jagged line of tall pines whizzed by in a dark blur as I kept the van at ninety, leaving the metropolitan area safely in our wake.

Based on our recent experience with looters, I didn't want to get too close to a city, so I went several more miles before getting off the Interstate. After passing several secondary turns and two minor intersections, I kept going straight.

About a mile later, the two-lane road turned into a series of sharp bends. Half a dozen deserted vehicles sat off the road, but we saw no traffic and passed no one walking.

"We're not looking for another house, are we?" Reed asked.

"Just a quiet, secluded place to crash. Maybe even a gas station, if we can find one that's still working."

Reed sighed. "I think we should stay away from houses for a while."

Damn. He's still gun-shy.

I sent him a glare in the rearview. "I don't plan on shooting anyone if I don't have to."

"I told you I understood, Moss."

"Then what are you talking about?"

He didn't reply.

"Is it Cocoa? Or Jacksonville?"

"It's ... all this death. It's ... this killing you've just done. Nearly everyone's dead and there's still a need ... to kill."

"The few still left are either in hiding or have become savages. We don't have too many options, you know."

Reed sighed. "I just hope ... that is, I don't want you to ... please don't become ... one of them."

The fear in Reed's voice ripped through me. But I couldn't let myself succumb to it. It could mean our death.

"You just told me you understood."

"I ... understood why you did it. I just didn't understand how ... easily you did it."

I didn't respond.

"You were in the military, weren't you?"

"How the hell did you know...?"

"I didn't."

I could barely see Reed's reflection in the darkness of the van's interior. But it wasn't Reed's expression I was worried about.

"Did he get in my head? If he did, tell him to get out. I don't want anyone in there. Hell, I don't even go in there unless I have to."

67

"It's really not much of a stretch, you know. I knew something was up when I saw you handle those guns."

"You can tell I was in the military just because I know how to handle a gun?"

"And by how you ... how easily you killed those three looters."

"It wasn't a question of being easy. My survival instinct came into play. It was them or us."

"He just said an untrained person couldn't have killed those three so efficiently."

"I *was* trained for stuff like that. A long time ago."

"I'd like to know about it. I mean, since I'm here with you and since we kind of depend on one another."

"It's a long story. I'm tired."

He obviously sensed my edginess. Growing silent, he settled back in the seat.

The road deteriorated, becoming narrower. The pavement disappeared, turning into sand. A couple of flickering streetlamps shed a slender sheen of yellow light on the pines straight ahead.

A large, hand-scribbled sign advertising a trailer court appeared around the next bend. I turned onto a narrow grassy path, swerving around pine trees, junked cars, and single-wide trailers. At the end, huddled between an RV and a travel trailer, a small, dimly-lit building awaited us. A heavyset, gray-haired woman in a flowery blue dress stood in front of it. In the flickering haze of the single floodlight above the door, she appeared to be about fifty, with a round face and puffy cheeks. Her tiny blue eyes twinkled. She said we should call her Rozzie.

"Where you two nice-lookin' gents from?"

"Orlando," I said.

Her face wrinkled up. "Orlando? That's ... lemme see ... that's in ... don't tell me, now ... um ... Florida?"

"You got it."

She chuckled then brought her pudgy hands together and clapped. I glanced at Reed, who frowned. When she'd first come outside to greet us, she'd moved fairly quickly for someone her size. I assumed she hadn't been affected. Now I realized I'd been wrong.

"I used to know someone from down that way ... what was his name?" She rubbed her chins, trying to remember. "Ya wouldn't know 'im, would ya?"

I shook my head and just let her ramble.

"I think he told me he lived there. At least, at one time he did. But you know how things change, folks movin' around all the time. He did mention Miami. That's in Florida, too. Think you might know 'im?"

"I don't think so." It was easier than asking questions and confusing her.

She nodded. "You gents wanna spend the night? Don't think I ever saw ya here before. Live around here?"

Her brain was obviously shutting down. So was her body. A strong urine smell emanated from her broad form.

"You have a place where we can park the van?"

"Sure thing. My son's twenty-seven—ain't that somethin'?"

"Sure is."

"He lives with me, ya know."

"I didn't know."

"Luke?" She grinned broadly, displaying several missing teeth. "He's been livin' with me a while, now, since his daddy had his accident. Ya like tater salad?"

"Most of the time."

She rubbed her hands together. "Just whipped up a big batch. Be glad to bring ya some. Ya look hungry. Yer friend, too." She raised her brows at Reed. "Hungry?"

"A little."

"I can always tell when a man's hungry." She chuckled. Luke? Now, that boy can eat all day long. You'd think I starve 'im, to look at 'im. Boy's skinny as a rail, eats like a horse and never gains an ounce. Makes ya wonder, ya know?"

"Where can we park?" She was making me nervous.

She extended a large, beefy arm and pointed. A heavy fist of BO mixed in with the urine slapped my face and made my eyes water. "Down that path past that last trailer. It's vacant, but the folks might come back to pick it up. Didn't say where they was goin', but I can't letcha use it, not knowin' when they'll be back. One of 'em fishes. Wife makes some tasty brownies. Like brownies?"

"It's all right," I said. "We can sleep in the van."

"Just pull in between those scrubs and you'll have yourself some privacy. I'll bring over some tater salad later on, when you're settled in."

"Get much traffic out here, this time of night?" I didn't want any surprises after our trouble in Cocoa.

"Used to, but lately?" She shook her head. "Don't know what's been happenin', folks not comin' 'round like they used to. This country's goin' to the dogs. Can't even get a decent signal on my TV no more. Just bought myself a brand-new set a month back, too. Got it from Walmart, but ya know, ya just can't trust any of 'em no more. Not since those Indians and the Chinese started comin' over and buyin' up everything. I know this fella, lives in Savannah, has this Chinese wife. Maybe you know 'im. Cecil's his name. Wife's okay for a ferner. Don't say much, but they don't talk too much over there. Anyway, Cecil drives a station wagon, does handy work, really knows how to use his hands. Redid my cabinets in the kitchen, where Luke and I live behind the office. Maybe you can come in and see what he done. They're real pretty now."

***

Using the bright light from my battery-powered lantern, Reed made sandwiches with some of the bread, turkey meat, cheese, mayonnaise, and dill relish we'd taken from the house in Cocoa. I grabbed a beer from the cooler and asked if Reed wanted one. He said he wasn't a beer drinker, so I handed him one of the cans of pop we'd found.

71

After supper, it was time to bed down. Rozzie never brought over her potato salad, but we were both glad she hadn't. I didn't want to insult her by tossing it in the bushes. She might have been great in the kitchen at one time, but judging how fast her mind and body were deteriorating, I couldn't trust her.

I let Reed use my sleeping bag while I delegated myself for sentry duty. I chose the passenger seat so I wouldn't have to worry about getting hung up on the wheel if I had to move quickly. I inclined the seat as far down as it would go, adding a small pillow to support my lower back. It made a fairly comfortable bed. I'd have no trouble falling asleep.

I didn't want to leave the windows open, but the mugginess of the night left me no choice. I couldn't leave the engine running all night with the AC on. We had to conserve gas at all costs.

I sprayed my face, neck, and hands with the mosquito repellent I'd picked up at Walmart. Before settling down, I grabbed one of the handguns from beneath the seat and placed it on top of the console. In an emergency, I could snatch it up quickly.

I settled into a comfortable position. I knew better than let myself relax totally. Rozzie's kid was out there somewhere, and I had to be wary. He could be in the same shape as his mother. My gut told me to expect the worst.

In the military I'd learned that it is a fatal mistake to underestimate one's adversary. I didn't know if Luke could be classified as an adversary, but it was definitely something to consider. That was another thing I'd learned: always expect the unexpected.

I scanned the heavy veil of darkness surrounding us and listened carefully as the warm breeze whispered through the branches of the pines. In the distance, an owl hooted, and a whippoorwill made its nocturnal territorial declaration. A dog barked twice. Nature appeared totally unaffected by Mankind's demise. Since Nature had always displayed a seething contempt for Mankind, ignoring our ultimate end came as no surprise.

Just as I closed my eyes, Reed asked, "Where were you stationed?"

Damn. I'd hoped he'd forgotten about this. I wanted to relax, not rehash that terrible period in my life. The present situation was bleak enough.

"I'm tired."

"He tells me you were wounded."

What the hell?

I sat bolt upright and twisted around. "How the hell did he…?"

"He says he can feel it."

"If he can feel it, he must also know how I got it."

"How would he know that?"

"He seems to know everything else."

Reed went silent for a moment. "He says he can feel the hurt in your voice. He also says you were wounded more than once."

My uneasiness grew. "Why so interested?"

"We're in this together. Don't you think we should know a little about one another?"

73

"Maybe later, after we've both had some sleep."

"I was a high school teacher ... for a while."

"A while?"

"Until I finally realized what a useless, unrewarding profession teaching actually was. I denied it for years, but it finally kicked in. It wasn't my idea, though. It was decided for me."

"What happened?"

"I'll tell you about it … later."

Judging by Reed's tone, I suspected the story was not pleasant.

"So ... where were you stationed?"

I lay back in my seat and rubbed my eyes. "Brighton Beach was my first tour of duty."

"My God." Reed gasped. "It must've been horrible."

"I spent three months handling riot control at Little Odessa then three months at Pakistani Brighton."

"I read those places averaged a major riot every three days."

"When I was there, we saw at least three skirmishes every week."

"How'd you get picked? I mean, the National Police Force was recruiting heavily around twenty years ago. Was that about the time you went in?"

"The NPF was going strong a couple of years before. When I went in, the military was having major problems with Russians, Albanians, and Muslims in the New York City area, so they sent most of us there. Since I'd already been deployed to Pakistan for two months following Advanced

Infantry Training, I had more practical experience than most of the other guys, so they picked me and a few others from my old unit to work with a special group of undercover cops in Little Odessa.

"They stuck us right in the middle of that shithole to nab a white-slavery ring responsible for sending underage girls to other countries for profit. With our help, the Metro cops were able to rescue a large group of eight- and nine-year-olds during the course of the sting. We were about to nail a couple of the top traders when our operation was blown. Half a dozen cops were killed and it turned into a really messy firefight. We were pinned down by Russians and some traffickers brought over here from Albania. I was stabbed in the thigh, arm, and back."

"How long were you hospitalized?"

"About a month. It was the only vacation I ever got. Riot control sucks even in the best of conditions. Undercover work is much worse—especially when you're dealing with Russians. Like the Muslims, Russians are savages and have no regard for human life. You can't scare them and you can't intimidate them. They won't cooperate and they won't listen. We didn't even bother trying to bring them in. We just cuffed them and tossed them in the back of the wagon."

"Were they deported? Or just put in prison?"

"They never made it that far."

"What happened?"

"I really don't think I should…"

"Moss, we'd like to know."

"They were transported to the docks, shot twice in the head then dumped."

Reed fell silent.

"You have to understand cops. They're overworked, underpaid, overstressed, and backlogged. And with the court system so messed up, the criminals beat the cops back out onto the streets. It was beyond frustrating."

"I know about frustration," Reed said softly. "Teaching is frustration at its most extreme."

"From what I've heard, police work and teaching, especially in the big city school systems, are probably more similar than most people think."

"What you heard was absolutely..."

He suddenly stopped talking.

"Reed?" I started to turn around.

"Hi ya!"

A tall, skinny guy in his late twenties stood just a few feet from my door, grinning stupidly. The long-barreled revolver gripped in his right hand pointed directly at my face.

I froze. Judging by the dead silence behind me, Reed wasn't moving, either.

My heart thundered in my ears. It had been a long time since someone had pointed a gun at my face, and I quickly realized that twenty years had done little to change the icy terror raking through my body.

But instead of surrendering to the panic, I felt my military experience kicking in again.

Breathe normally. Keep your head. Avoid any sudden movements.

I forced my gaze off the big revolver and studied the boy, taking in everything from the hand holding the weapon to the position of the boy's feet. It was crucial to find signs of weakness.

The enemy's body language will tell you all you need to know. Study his position, his posture. His attitude. Anything that will betray him. A twitch. Excessive blinking. Rapid eye movement. Sweating. Shaking. Labored or irregular breathing. Continuous swallowing. Nervous shifting of the legs. Sudden movement in the lip or jaw area.

Only the blankness in the boy's eyes registered. They were somewhat dull, exuding the same confusion and disorientation I'd seen in Rozzie's eyes. This boy had those same tiny blue eyes, the same broad nose and loose features.

"You must be Luke."

His face lit up. "Yeppers. That's me. Luke."

Despite my inner turmoil, it was time to bond. To share experiences. It was the only way to talk him out of using the gun.

"Your momma said something about tater salad."

"Yeppers," he repeated, perking up. "Good stuff! Momma makes it up *real* good!"

Even though the gun did not waver, relief washed through me. This boy was just as far gone as his mother. With any luck, he'd find it difficult to operate the revolver properly. Even so, I had to proceed carefully. It was always extremely dangerous to talk someone out of using his gun. As with the punks I'd encountered in the Orlando supermarket, I had to confuse this boy.

77

"That sure is a scary-looking gun."

"Got it from Daddy. He hunted, Daddy did. Squirrels and rabbits. Deer, too."

"Good hunting out here?"

He nodded eagerly. "All year round. Feller said just the other day, tweren't no good huntin' out here in the boonies. I showed 'im, though—showed 'im *real* good."

I knew better than ask for details. "Is that the gun your daddy used for hunting?"

"For deer. He used bird shot for squirrels and rabbits."

"Would you mind if I looked at it? Just for a minute?"

"No. No-no-no!" He shook his head. "Daddy told me, said *never* give nobody your gun. Nopers."

"Just a quick look? I promise I'll give it right back."

"Nopers. Nope-nope-*nope*."

The gun twitched and I knew I had to get it out of his hand quickly. I had no illusions of grabbing my gun from the console. It would take too long. Besides, I didn't want to kill the boy. He wasn't all there and had no idea what he was doing.

"I just thought..."

"Nope-nope-nope! Daddy told me, said 'Luke, never give...'"

"Did your dad have it inscribed? With your name?"

He tilted his head and squinted. "S ... Scribed?"

"With your name, no one can take it from you. I'll bet your name's there, on the side of the barrel.

78

Take a quick look. I'll bet it says, 'To Luke, From Daddy.'"

He brought the gun up to his face.

With a flick of my wrist, I reached out and swatted his hand. He smacked himself in the nose. The gun flew and he fell backward, landing with a loud grunt on a pile of dead leaves.

I jumped out of the van, snatched the gun from a mound of pine needles, and held it behind my back.

He sat up sharply, looking around, trying to get his bearings. Even in the darkness I could tell he was dazed. He reached up and touched the blood covering his mouth, squinted at it, and squealed. He wiped his hands on his trousers, wiped his nose, and stared at his hands again. When he noticed me, he cringed.

"You okay? You just tripped on one of those dead branches and went down hard. You must've hit your nose on the ground. Does it hurt much?"

He sniffed again. "Hurts ... really hurts!"

"You need to go back home and clean yourself up. Ask your momma to help you."

"Momma?" He frantically rubbed his buzz cut. "Momma!" He jumped up and spun around. "She'll skin me alive, she sees me out here, gettin' my duds all dirty and messed up."

"You'd better hurry on back. Blood stains are hard to get out, you know."

He spun around again. Stooping over, he gawked at the ground. "Daddy's gun. Where's Daddy's gun?"

"You lost your father's gun?"

79

"I thought I ... just had it ... brung it on over..."

"You didn't have it with you. You probably left it in your room."

"I coulda swore I..."

"I didn't see it. Maybe your mother hid it so you wouldn't get..."

"Momma. I gotta get back now." Gasping loudly, he dashed into the trees, tripped on a deadfall, jumped back up, and stumbled into the darkness.

I climbed back in the van, slammed the door, and collapsed. My pulse raced and my limbs trembled. The gun in my hand had gone cold. It was no wonder. My palms were covered in cold sweat. I put Luke's gun on the dash and wiped my palms on my jeans.

"That was impressive, Moss," Reed said. "He even said so."

At the moment I didn't care what anyone thought. I hadn't been ready for that and found it disheartening to discover how badly it had affected me. But I was in no mood to argue.

"Didn't have much choice." I picked up the gun again, clicked open the cylinder, and checked the ammo.

"What kind is it?"

"A Smith & Wesson .357 Magnum revolver. As deadly as they come."

"Loaded?"

"All six cylinders. This one's a Model 686. In my opinion, one of the most powerful guns made."

Since I couldn't examine the ammo in the dark, I rubbed the tip of one of the bullets with my finger.

"Lovely. Hollow points." I slipped it back into the cylinder, snapped it shut, shoved the gun under the seat, and lay back. "If he'd shot me, you'd be finding skull fragments and chunks of brain matter in the upholstery for weeks."

Reed swallowed audibly. "Think he'll ... come back?"

"One never knows."

"What if ... what if he does?"

"Ask your friend to give us a little more warning next time."

"We were talking when the boy snuck up to us, Moss. My friend said he was distracted."

"Is he distracted now?"

Reed sighed. "He said he'll give us plenty of notice next time."

It took about ten minutes for my nerves to finally settle down. Then my breathing returned to normal. Despite Reed's assurance, I picked up the gun from the console and placed it in my lap. Then I closed my eyes and focused on sleep.

CHAPTER SIX

The next morning, a heavy blanket of fog settled amongst the pines, turning the woods into a canvas of wavy gray shadows.

To avoid another encounter with Rozzie or Luke, I awoke early and, using only my parking lights, forced the van through the thick fog and back out onto the main road.

Reed didn't say much as I hurried along the Interstate. He was probably still troubled by the incident the night before. I welcomed the silence. The confrontation with Luke had rattled me.

The passage of years takes a toll on the human soul. Stress, trauma, and frustration wear one down. When I was young, I tolerated punishment easily and healed quickly. I was invincible and had no qualms about engaging in dangerous activities. I didn't even entertain the notion of death at such a young age. That came much later, when I'd personally seen some of the horrors life can deliver.

After recovering from the knife wounds I'd sustained in the firefight with the Russians and Albanians, I was sent to Pakistani Brighton, where a bloody revolution was taking place. Fundamentalist Muslims frequently battled the extremists, prompting daily suicide bombings as well as massive destruction to mosques and stores. My unit was given an intensive bomb-deactivation training course then immediately deployed. I spent my first two weeks locating and disarming bombs and tracking down the terrorist cell responsible for planting them.

Chasing a vest killer—we called them veekays—is terrifying. He is not reasonable or balanced, is interested only in blowing up as many people as possible in the name of religion, and seldom leaves clues.

I was forced to read body language and evaluate clothing at a glance then react instinctively before a bomb could be activated. Capturing a veekay alive, without endangering my own life and the life of anyone else in the kill zone, was impossible. That's why they gave us strict orders to kill all vest killers before they could detonate their bomb.

I found more than twenty pipe bombs in nearly a dozen locations during my stint. I'd killed four veekays and successfully evacuated three groceries and one business center minutes before the entire block exploded into rubble.

I'd served with forty other men. We guarded twenty square blocks of Muslims, all of whom claimed to be a peaceful people and tolerant of everyone. But late at night, their rogue gangs routinely prowled the neighborhoods, shooting and stabbing innocent people, setting fires and planting car bombs.

One night, an argument broke out and assault weapons came into play. The crowd scattered, but many were cut down in the crossfire. People lay dead or dying in the street. A Hispanic boy about ten years old crawled beneath a parked car for safety.

As I sprinted across the street to save the boy, someone lobbed a grenade that exploded dangerously close to my former position. I hit the ground and crawled over to the vehicle to grab the kid and pull him out of the line of fire.

Cold fear rolled heavily down my back when I saw the gun in his hand that was aimed at my face. Before I could duck out of the way, another grenade went off, this one closer. The kid's gun fired, slamming me in the left shoulder. I rolled out into the street. Just then, one of our armored vehicles crept by. The crew spotted me and stopped, enabling me to crawl underneath for cover. Another grenade whizzed by. Seconds later, the parked car exploded, turning the kid into a husk of screaming flame.

***

After about an hour on the road, Reed broke his silence. "You never said where we're going."

"I'm driving back home to be with my mother."

"Where's home?"

"Gibsonia, Pennsylvania. It's about half an hour north of Pittsburgh."

"You think she's all right?"

I didn't want to voice my suspicions. I figured that if I kept my fears silent, Mom might be all right. I knew the reasoning was silly, but I couldn't help it. "I don't know. I've got to find out. This could be my last opportunity."

"My parents are both dead," Reed said. "I know it sounds harsh, but I'm glad they're gone. They don't need to see any of this."

"No one does."

He sat back in his seat and stared at the roof of the cab. I could tell he'd gone somewhere else.

"Bad memories?" I asked.

No reply.

"It couldn't be worse than what's happening now. Nothing could be worse than that."

"Sometimes I feel that way."

"Just sometimes?"

He didn't reply.

"Does this have anything to do with your teaching days?"

"That's what scarred me up," he said. "Even now, after all this ... this horror ... I can still feel them."

"I've got the time."

"It's complicated."

"Most things are."

"I wanted to get in my car and just drive," he said softly, as though speaking to himself. "I wanted to go somewhere I'd never been. A secluded place, with trees and land and no people. I didn't want to hear traffic ... or planes ... or any sounds of modern civilization. I wanted to hear birds singing. I'd been living in St. Cloud much too long. I felt like ... like I needed fresh air. I ... had to get away."

"You never got the chance?"

"Family activities and business pressures got in the way. I soon forgot all about it. But I never forgot my needs. My urge occupied me constantly. I'd been so wrapped up in business and family issues I lost my sense of direction."

"When were you planning to take this trip?"

"Three or four years ago, I guess. I'd left teaching and started in software. I did well financially, but it was a culture shock. A whole different class of people. It didn't take me long to immerse myself in it. Once I did, I trudged on. But in doing so, I'd forgotten who I was. What I was. How I felt. I'd found another profession but lost myself. So I decided to take a leave of absence and just drive."

"You and the family?"

"I needed a clean break. I know how callous this must sound, but I thought my family would influence me somehow. I wanted to discover things by myself, without interference. But by the same token, I was afraid of leaving them. Of coming back and feeling differently toward them. It had been so long since I'd been by myself I didn't know how I'd feel once I returned."

"What triggered all this?"

"My teaching nightmare ... it came back one day to haunt me." Reed's voice changed, growing softer, weaker. "My kids ... they were having problems at school, and when my wife and I went to talk to the principal, and I found myself in the midst of all the chaos I'd left not long before, I suffered a severe panic attack. They had to take me out of there immediately. I thought I was going to die."

"What happened to cause all this?"

He didn't reply.

"Reed, it's all over. It can't hurt you now. Everything's gone."

"In my mind, it'll never go away. The scars ... like I said, they'll always be there."

I knew what he meant. My military horrors would be with me until the day I died.

"I know what you went through last night," he said suddenly. "I didn't have a gun thrust in my face, but I know what it's like to fear for your life."

"My mother taught English Lit and Composition at Carnegie-Mellon until she retired. She had a few stories to tell but never said anything about…"

"She obviously hadn't seen the same horror I did. College kids usually go there to learn. High school's much lower on the food chain."

His expression had become dark, as if someone had slipped a veil over his face.

"I was a damn good teacher. I was conscientious. I actually *wanted* to help my students find the right path."

"Teaching used to be an honorable profession," I said.

"It stopped being that long ago."

"Why'd you even go into it?"

He groaned softly. "Like most everyone pursuing the profession, I wanted to help another generation get a fair chance. In those days, I thought education was everything."

"What made you quit?"

"The Internet—what else? The ridiculous practice of texting, in my opinion, lowered the level of the last few generations to that of pond scum. Texting and cyber-bullying. The Web was originally a marvelous invention. But in the hands of idiots it quickly became as dangerous as a handgun."

87

"It's been dehumanizing people for the last fifty years. We should be used to it."

Reed squirmed in his seat. "Forget this damned plague. Those idiots have been walking around like zombies for years—texting in the halls, the classrooms, on the roads, in their homes. I've seen them text at urinals, and what they're texting is worthless drivel. 'Guess who's fucking who?' 'Guess who wants to fuck who?' 'Guess who's not fucking who?' 'I have a hard-on.'" He frowned. "It's disgusting."

"How did all this get you to quit?"

"One day during lunch I noticed a large crowd of students standing outside the men's room, some staring at their cell phones while others texted. I suspected right off that something bad was going on. All kids made me suspicious in those days—especially when they were congregated in a large group. I knew I had to see what was going on. I wanted to stay away, but I still possessed a modicum of principles in those days, so I braved the crowd and went in."

Reed fell silent again. He stared down at his lap. When he raised his head, his face had turned bone-white. "It was a scene right out of hell. There must've been thirty students of both sexes grouped in a semicircle, watching the local jocks taking turns raping a thirteen-year-old girl. They were standing in line, for God's sake. Those not participating were recording it on their cell phones. The ones waiting in line were texting. Would you believe it?"

I didn't reply. There was no need.

"I tried to break it up, but several of them rushed me and tossed me out. Literally picked me up, carried me back out into the hall, and dumped me—as if I were garbage!"

"Did you report it?"

"That's what got me in trouble. The parents of at least twenty of those vicious savages brought in their attorneys and threatened to sue me for assault if I pursued it."

"Assault?"

"When I tried breaking it up, they said I pushed a couple of them too hard. I hadn't noticed at the time because I was running on pure adrenaline and concerned about the poor victim. One of the idiots I'd pushed tripped, while another slammed into a urinal. The first one complained of a wrenched back and sprained wrist. The second showed up with photographs of bruises on his arm. He also claimed I'd knocked his shoulder out of its socket."

"What about the rape victim?"

Reed shuddered. "She was dead before the police arrived. I have no idea how or what caused it. They'd beaten her during the rape. Her face was a mess. A bloody nose, swollen lips, and numerous lacerations. But the actual cause? I can't say. They could've choked her, accidentally or otherwise."

"And that was that?"

"The jocks didn't have to worry. Their daddies all had political clout, as well as an arrangement with the football coach. Two of them had already landed full athletic scholarships at big schools. Apparently, their daddies had been greasing the right pockets for years, so they were untouchable."

"Big money killed the whole thing."

"They told me the dead girl was a slut who'd been coming on to the jocks for weeks. They also said she'd arranged the whole thing. Everyone said her death was an accident, so that was the end of it."

"What about her bruises?"

"They said she liked it rough."

"And since everyone filmed it, it could probably be argued that she actually consented to it."

"It never got anywhere near the courtroom, but the whole world saw it online. I'm surprised you never heard of it."

"I was never big on using the 'Net and never liked watching the news."

"They put it on the 'Net and it received more than three million hits in one day. One of them even charged twenty-five cents a hit. He made a fortune."

"So you had to drop it."

"The death threats convinced me."

"Death threats?"

"It started with the clowns in the men's room, then their friends, relatives, and so on. Hundreds of threatening emails arrived in my inbox every day. I got them at school and at home. I received regular mail threats, too, and anonymous phone calls at all hours. When I found a dead pigeon in the front seat of my car, I knew it was time to move on."

"Can't blame you."

"I was stupid and naïve to think I could actually do something about it. I blame society for letting it happen. We're all guilty when we let an atrocity happen without doing anything about it."

"None of the other teachers backed you up?"

"Many were threatened for talking to me. It was a horrible, impossible situation."

"Maybe."

"Just maybe?"

"Look what we're facing now."

***

We crossed into North Carolina and reached Fayetteville just before noon.

A glance at the gas gauge prompted me to take the exit ramp. The needle had settled just above a third of a tank. I didn't want it to get lower. I also needed to stretch my legs. Reed still appeared somewhat despondent after telling me his story and had said little since. He obviously needed a break as well.

Just beyond the exit ramp, the road went straight. About a hundred yards from a stop sign, an abandoned service station sat quietly on its concrete slab, its yellow flags flopping intermittently in the breeze like the wings of a dying bird.

I pulled up to the pumps closest to the gray-block building that said *BUD'S ONE-STOP* in large letters with something printed in Chinese characters directly beneath it. The Chinese restaurant and souvenir shop next door displayed dark, dirty windows. Six abandoned vehicles sat beside the building, but none in front. The car wash at the other end of the lot showed no activity, and the six pump islands were abandoned as well.

"Anyone in the office?" I asked Reed.

"He said he doesn't think so."

I saw no movement behind the large, dusty window. To be safe, I decided to check it out. If someone was inside, I didn't want to pump gas without paying. For all I knew, this area could still be using an active power grid. If the office was empty, I'd probably have to turn on the pumps myself.

"I'll be right back."

Reed made a move to climb out as well.

"Since that last can of pop, I…"

"Wait until I get back. Someone could pull in while we're both inside and steal the van."

The small office showed no signs of recent activity. A couple of half-empty coffee cups sat on the counter and desk. The smell of burnt coffee languishing in the pot clung to the stale air. The coffeemaker was switched off, and the pot was cold to the touch. There was no sign of food in the room.

I opened the door marked *RESTROOM*. It was empty, but the strong smell of urine and feces tainted the small area. I cracked open the window.

When I had emptied my bladder, I flushed the toilet and did the same to the one in the next stall. Both flushed slowly, barely emptying their contents. The tile below the stained urinal had darkened with the contents from the bottoms of hundreds of shoes.

I found the controls for the gas pumps and switched ours on. Luckily, they still had power. I went back outside just as Reed was getting out of the van.

"I left the window open. It might help."

"I appreciate the heads-up."

I circled the van and went over to the pump. Just as I unscrewed the cap and slipped the nozzle into the opening of the tank, I heard the soft whining hum of an engine easing up to our pump island on the other side.

My scalp tingled. I reluctantly forced the anger away. After all, I wouldn't be the only one needing gas. But I couldn't shake the darkness of suspicion building inside me. With five other sets of pumps available, they'd chosen mine.

To be safe, I locked the catch on the gas nozzle then pulled open the driver's door. I reached under the seat, grabbed a revolver, slipped it in my pocket, closed the door, and returned to the pump.

A tall, skinny guy with his head shaved to the bone peered between the pumps just as I pulled the nozzle out. Tattoos of stars ran down his left cheek. A row of studs covered his left ear. A nose ring dangled above his upper lip.

"Hey," he grunted.

I nodded but said nothing.

"Quiet around here, huh?"

He looked early twenties, wearing a black tee shirt embellished with white stars, faded jeans, and scuffed white tennis shoes. A gold necklace with a peace sign hung around his neck. A large gold bracelet encircled his skinny left wrist.

I remained cautious. He was obviously capable of operating a vehicle and safely pulling up to the pumps—a small feat for a normal person but an impossible task for someone doped. My deadly encounter with Luke had convinced me to treat everyone as a potential enemy.

"Yeah," I said. "Pretty quiet."

He nodded, over and over. His eyes were a little bloodshot but not the least bit filmy. My scalp continued to tingle.

He grabbed the nozzle and shoved it into the tank with a resounding *clunk*. "Guess the fuckin' pumps are on if you're fillin' up too," he said, snickering.

My distrust grew. He gave me the impression he was hiding his left side behind the pump.

"Things are really fucked up ... know what I mean?"

I made no comment.

He shook his head. "Everybody's so fucked up now. Me, too. Even when I don't take any shit. Forget my own name, sometimes. You forget your name, too?"

"No."

"You're lucky, ya know? One lucky motherfucker."

I kept my eyes on him and hoped Reed would come back out so we could leave.

"Forgot where I live, even went to the bathroom the other day ... ya know, to take a leak? Forgot to pull down the fuckin' zipper. Ol' lady thought that was funny, so I belted her. Know what I mean?"

"No."

He squinted. "Y'ain't very friendly, mister."

"I get that a lot."

"I got an aunt. She ain't friendly, neither."

"Small world."

"She's got these horses on her place. Know horses?"

"Not personally."

He took another step closer but kept his left side out of sight. "One of 'em's got this funny thing. She bucks when ya try gettin' on 'er."

"Maybe she doesn't want anyone on her."

He leaned against the pump. He appeared to be thinking it over. "Ya just might just have somethin' there, ya know?" He turned back to his ride. "Yep, ya just might have somethin' there."

While his back was turned, I stepped to my left and peered around the corner of the pump. His car was one of those cheap rice-burners they'd brought over a few years ago, when China began its mass export program to help the thirty percent of the population who couldn't afford new vehicles.

The passenger's door was open.

My military training kicked in once again. Before I realized it, I'd taken out the gun and pointed it at the figure circling the pumps at the far end.

This boy was about the same age but shorter and slightly broader, with a nose ring, earrings, and lip ring. Like his buddy, his head was shaved. When he saw my gun, he froze. "Hey, man! What's with the fucking gun?"

The first guy nearly stumbled off the concrete island. "You got a fuckin' gun?"

I immediately sensed my dilemma. Since they were at least ten feet apart, I couldn't hold the gun on both of them. I stood too close to the pumps and

95

fumes. Any spark from a ricochet would vaporize the three of us. But this was no time to show fear.

"Yeah, I guess you could say this is a fucking gun."

"What's he's got a fuckin' gun for, Eugene?"

"You gonna ... shoot us, mister?"

"Not unless you want me to."

"Hey, man," said the second punk. "You shoot us, you're gonna blow us all up--ya know?"

That statement alone told me they still had all their faculties.

"Thanks for the advice."

"He's gonna shoot us, Eugene."

"He ain't gonna shoot us. You ... ain't, are you, mister?"

"I already said..."

"I'm gonna puke! I'm gonna fucking puke!"

I glared at the second punk. "You turn right around and maybe I won't use this gun."

"I'm gonna be fuckin' sick!"

A slight metallic sound to my left made me turn sharply. The first punk was gripping a crowbar and had pulled it overhead to strike.

Just then the loudspeaker came on, crackling all around us.

"Number Nine, you need to come to the office so I can turn on your pump and complete your transaction! Thank you, and please have a nice day!"

The first punk twisted around toward the building.

I grabbed the hooked end of the crowbar and yanked it toward me. It pulled him off-balance and he fell back against the pump, hitting the back of his head. Then I slammed him on top of the head with my revolver.

The second punk rushed toward me, a ball peen hammer held high above his head. I kneecapped him with the crowbar then pounded him on the back of his skull as he went down.

I gripped the crowbar with both hands, ready to use it again as Reed emerged from the building. Neither moved, not even when I dropped the crowbar loudly onto the slab, inches from where the second punk lay, looking up at me with glazed eyes.

CHAPTER SEVEN

My heart thrashed wildly as Reed and I climbed back into the van. Nausea had caused a heavy throbbing in my gut, and my fists went numb as I gripped the wheel. I was surprised I hadn't lost control.

By the time we had gotten back on the Interstate, my pulse rate slowed and the gut throbbing eased up. Feeling returned to my hands, and a warm tingling raced up my arms.

"That was quick thinking, Reed," I said, my voice sounding weak and unsteady.

"I can't ... take the credit for that," he said, sitting forward, his face in his hands. Something was obviously troubling him.

"It was your voice I heard on the speaker."

He didn't reply.

"What happened in there?"

"I was at the urinal when ... when he told me to hurry up and look out front. As soon as I did, I saw the one with crowbar moving toward you."

"Then you switched on the PA system."

"It wasn't that simple."

"However you did it, you saved our bacon."

"I ... I didn't know *what* to do. I was in a panic. I wanted to rush outside and startle them, but he told me that would be very stupid, and might get us both killed. He suggested I stay inside and switch on the speaker system instead. Even so, I almost screwed up. I'm a klutz—I admit it. I can't remember the number of times I wanted to call a plumber, electrician, or handyman, when my wife Alice stepped in to fix the emergency with the simple twist of a screwdriver. No, that announcement thing was a fluke. I ran over to the cash register and fumbled around blindly. For one horrible moment, I couldn't even remember what I was looking for. When I finally remembered, I couldn't find the right button. He ... told me which one to press."

I didn't want to argue with him. I'd probably be dead if his friend hadn't intervened.

"He always comes through, doesn't he?" Reed said.

"He always seems to know what's about to happen."

"Then what's the problem?"

"Problem?"

"He says you have a problem with him."

"He knows too much."

"Look how it helps us in the end. How it saves our lives."

"It's not normal."

"If things were normal, the jerk with the crowbar would've killed you."

"If things were normal, none of this would've happened in the first place."

We both grew silent.

I began thinking how things once were. Not long ago, I could stop for gas without worrying about being killed at the pumps. I couldn't possibly walk into someone's home and take what I wanted. I couldn't even walk onto someone else's property without some consequences.

In those days, people were everywhere. They clogged the roads and the streets, the shopping malls and the flea markets. The cities. The suburbs. The country. They made a mess wherever they went, leaving garbage and trouble in their wake.

To be alone, you had to find a large parcel of ground the developers hadn't yet grabbed and leveled. But even then, you knew you wouldn't really be alone. Planes would fly overhead. Dogs would bark. Gunshots from hunters would echo for miles, warning you of violence and death. Distant traffic sounds would provide constant reminders how close civilization actually was.

People had turned peace and quiet into a thing of the past.

So why did I long for those days?

Reed said, "We've turned society into a wasteland. With our innovations, our high-tech toys, firearms, and weapons of mass destruction, we've made ourselves extinct."

"We always knew we could do it. We even invented the necessary technology to speed up the process."

"Each generation has given us highly intelligent people in all fields. Why has it always been so difficult to listen to them?"

"We've been living in a mentally defective society all our lives. The average teenager couldn't tell you the name of our vice president, but they could easily give you their favorite music diva's cup size."

A maroon van with dark-tinted windows registered in my side mirror. It was coming up fast.

I tensed in my seat. My hands clutched the wheel more tightly.

"Something wrong?" Reed asked.

I pried my right hand from the wheel, reached beneath my seat, found Luke's long-barreled .357, and laid it on the console. "Someone wants to make nice with our rear bumper."

Reed gazed out the rear window. "My God." He spun back around. His face had turned pale. "He's coming up really fast. What are we going to do?"

"I don't think we can outrun him. Even if we could, I don't want to waste the gas."

I pulled my foot off the gas pedal. The vehicle behind us slammed on its brakes to avoid ramming us.

My gaze stayed on the large object in my side mirror as I let the speedometer drop to sixty ... then fifty ... then forty.

"What ... are you doing?"

"Pulling over."

"Why?"

"To see what they want." My pulse hammered loudly as I eased onto the shoulder.

The maroon van pulled over behind us. I coasted to a stop and put the gearshift in park. Then I found a small revolver and handed it to Reed.

He gawked at it, shivering. "I can't ... I've never..."

"It's a revolver." I thought it would be easier for him to operate. It was also much smaller and less cumbersome than the .357. And the lighter kick wouldn't scare him as much. "Just aim and squeeze the trigger."

He blinked. "The trigger?"

"Hold it like this, with both hands. If I'm dead, this'll be your only chance. Got it?"

"I ... think so." He took it and nearly dropped it.

The other van crawled up to us, stopping about twenty feet from our rear bumper. My flesh grew cold and wet.

"Now what?" Reed held the gun out and away from him—as if it were a poisonous snake.

"We wait."

"For what?"

"For him to make the first move." I kept my gaze on the side mirror. Lucky for us, our visitor had parked far enough away to give me a good view of both sides of his van. I could spot any movement on the far side by checking the other side mirror. Sneaking up on us would be impossible.

My blood rushed hotly through my veins. I squirmed in my seat and wiped my wet palms on my jeans. It had been a long time since I'd been forced to wait for something potentially bad to happen. As a former sniper for the Border Patrol, my job was to lie in a sandy ditch for an eight-hour stretch. My rifle, knife, and canteen were my only companions, as I waited for the enemy to show among the cacti and wild brush peppering the desert.

Now, after nearly two decades out of the military, I once again found myself waiting for the enemy. This time, the enemy didn't come from another country but from my homeland—the place where I was born and raised, where my parents and

102

their parents were born and raised. Someone just like me could be sitting in that van, just as frightened of me as I was of him.

I had no idea what I now faced. I couldn't see the driver. Both windshield visors were lowered. The sunbeams bouncing off the glass hurt my eyes. The driver could be waiting for me to get out of the van. He might have crept up to me because he wanted to talk to someone else whose brain still functioned.

He could also be cradling a gun, just as I was, and was waiting to kill whoever stepped out of this van. Maybe he was a potential serial killer taking advantage of the chaos by quenching his blood-lust without fear of prosecution.

"No one's getting out," Reed whispered.

"I noticed." Once again I wiped my palms and suddenly caught my reflection in the rearview. My face was sweating as well, but I hadn't noticed. I wiped my glistening forehead while keeping a close watch on the mirrors.

Finally the driver's door swayed open.

My body trembled, but my fingers automatically closed around the large plastic grips of the .357. I expected to see the huge gaping hole of a shotgun barrel resting on the door hinge. Or the long, thick barrel of a sniper's rifle. Or an automatic.

Instead, an open-toed white sandal lowered to the pavement. A long, shapely leg followed as a tall female with long blonde hair appeared from behind the driver's door.

"Damn," Reed said, fidgeting in his seat. "Do you ... do you see that?"

"I'd have to be blind not to."

A babe. Son of a bitch. That's all we need.

A couple of guys with machineguns would have been much easier to deal with. At least we'd know for sure what sort of trouble we faced.

She wore a tight red tank top, light-blue shorts, and those open-toed white sandals. The top showed off her bare midriff as well as the glistening silver stud piercing her navel. Her breasts were perfect. A silver necklace hung around her tanned neck. She wore silver bracelets and several rings and silver studs on her left earlobe. Large-framed black sunglasses covered her eyes and cheekbones, hiding much of her face.

In different times, I wouldn't be able to resist this woman. But now, instead of wondering how she looked naked, I wondered where she was hiding her gun.

"What are we gonna do?" Reed whispered.

"Any suggestions?"

Reed shook his head. "Moss, I never ... I've never been able to ... women who look like that. I've never had any luck ... dealing with them."

"Neither have I." I'd always found gorgeous, statuesque females cold, arrogant, demanding, and selfish. This wouldn't play out any differently. I didn't want to confront her, but I had no choice. She'd gotten out of her van and obviously wanted to talk. I was going to have to do likewise.

Before stepping out, I swapped the heavy .357 with the tiny .22 Beretta I'd taken from the looters in Cocoa. I took it off safety and shoved it in my front pants pocket. Before opening the door, I glanced at Reed. He was staring at me, the revolver gripped in his trembling hands, its barrel pointed in my direction. I gently pushed it down so it pointed to the floor.

"If she kills me and comes at you, point that and empty it. It holds six. Use 'em all. Keep firing until the gun's empty, all right?"

Reed swallowed. "There are t-two others w-with her. Both females."

My spine grew cold. "You sure?"

He nodded.

Lovely. I felt as if my gut had been jabbed with a hot poker. I pulled the Beretta out of my pocket, switched it back on safety, and shoved it under the seat. I selected the larger .9 millimeter with a twelve-clip. I took it off safety, cocked the hammer, and slid it very carefully down my back, over my shirt, so I'd have no trouble getting it out. Before climbing out of the van, I laid the .357 on the driver's seat, butt facing me.

My nerves twitched as the bottoms of my feet connected with the macadam, but I forced myself to stay in control. I took two steps and stopped, making sure I was close to the open door. If I needed cover, I could duck behind it and circle the front of the van. It wouldn't stop a bullet, but it would minimize the impact before it hit me.

My training told me to expect the worst. I glanced to my left and made a quick mental note of my escape route. I planned on the other two females to use the blonde as a distraction. Like me, she was standing about a foot from the edge of her opened door. One of her companions could be lying across the driver's seat, holding out a gun for her.

I sincerely hoped this wouldn't play out badly. I didn't want to kill anyone else—especially a woman.

"What's the problem?" I asked.

She smiled. "No foreplay?"

"Foreplay?"

"How about hi, neighbor? What's going on? How's every little thing?"

"Hi, neighbor. Now ... what's your problem?"

She laughed. "Do I look like I have a problem?"

"*I* sure do."

"Tell me about it, baby."

"You scared the shit out of me then tried to run me down. That would be a problem, wouldn't you say?"

A gust of wind pushed thick golden strands across her face. She reached up and flicked them over her shoulder. A strong whiff of something sweet drifted over. She'd probably slathered on the perfume just before getting out of the van.

"I didn't mean to scare you, baby. It's been a while since I've met up with someone who isn't wandering around like a fucking zombie."

I kept watching the driver's door.

"I'm Carla."

She looked more like a Bambi. Or Ursula.

"You got a name?"

"Moss."

"Is that your first name?"

"I go by Moss."

She nodded, and more hair rubbed her cheek. "Okay, Moss, how's about we get better acquainted?"

"Why?"

"Not too many of us walking around these days. We've gotta stick together."

"I prefer sticking to myself. It's less complicated."

She brought up both hands and pushed more stray hair away from her face. Another cloud of sweetness wafted my way. In different circumstances, I'd have been a goner.

"You're tough, Moss."

"I have to be."

"Even with someone who wants to be friendly?"

"Especially with one of them."

"I'm a hot lady, Moss. I like my fun. Not much of it these days, so I've gotta take it where I can find it. I can make you feel really good."

You're really playing hardball, baby.

"I'll bet you can."

"I've got half a case of some pretty good Scotch in my back seat. C'mon over and we'll have a little party."

"Thanks, but I've got to be going. How about a rain check?"

"What's wrong? You don't like women?"

"Love 'em. Dream about 'em. I've been obsessed with them since I was a kid."

"What don't you like about me?"

"For one thing, you tried to run me down."

"I do crazy things when I'm lonely and frustrated."

"I don't know many women who don't."

"You know what they say, don'tcha?"

"What *who* says?"

"People."

"What do they say?"

"The crazier the chick, the wilder the ride."

"I've heard that one a few times."

"You'd better believe it, too."

"You're one delicious-looking babe. I just don't have the time now."

"Why not *make* time? A little Scotch and some of that sweet coke I picked up a few days ago? We could be making sudsy memories in my back seat."

Her right arm raised a couple of inches, and brought her hand closer to her door. I placed my right hand on my hip, which brought it within six inches of the automatic.

"C'mon, Moss. I don't know about you, but I'm really horny. Haven't had any in weeks. You're hot looking and probably just as horny as me, so let's get it on and…"

"No, thanks."

I could see her scowling behind her sunglasses.

"What the hell's wrong? Got something against a little nookie? When was the last time *you* had any?"

"Can't remember. Weeks. Months. Doesn't matter anymore."

"C'mon over, then. We'll climb in back and see how much Scotch we can kill. And how much coke we can snort. I just picked up this van. It's new and the shocks are a little stiff. Let's see what we can do about breakin' 'em in."

She raised her arm a couple of more inches. Her palm slowly turned upward.

My instinct kicked in. She was about to grab something. Her thigh muscles tensed and she turned her face slightly to her right.

Christ, I don't wanna do this. I snatched the automatic and put three quick holes in a horizontal pattern across the center of the door. A loud shriek issued, and a machine pistol clattered to the pavement near Carla's white sandals, which quickly pitted with blood. Carla dove for the pistol, her head disappearing behind the door. As soon as it reappeared, I put a hole in her forehead. Her sunglasses split in two and flew in opposite directions, as her head jerked back.

I put three more quick rounds in the gap between the door and the frame, just above the rifle barrel that had appeared. A scream blasted from the inside of the van. The barrel jumped in the air, whacking the roof. The rifle came back down, slapping the driver's door, then the running board, before landing on Carla's still form.

Long red hair appeared beneath the doorframe, stopping when it touched the pavement. Two hands slid down. I waited. A female body slid out head-first, thumping the macadam then landing across Carla.

My gun pointed out, I approached the bloody scene. I suspected my shots had all been kill shots, but I'd seen countless training films and heard horror stories of the enemy successfully operating a weapon after sustaining mortal wounds.

The body lying on the console was another young blonde. One of my shots had hit her in the side of the head. I kept my gun trained on each body while tapping the two on the bloody pavement with my foot. I tapped the third on the shoulder with my gun.

No reaction from any of the bodies. I drew nearer, squatted, and felt for pulses. There were none.

I finally put my auto on safety and returned it to my waistband. I bent over, picked up the redhead, draped her over my shoulder, opened the side door, and dropped her onto the seat. She was solidly-built, and it took considerable effort. It was also messy. I'd clipped her high in the chest, and the massive blood loss quickly stained my shirt. I left the other blonde lying across the front seats.

Just as I got into position to pick up Carla, Reed walked over. When he saw the blood on my shirt he backed up, spun around, and doubled over, coughing and hacking away. Once he got it under control, he cleared his throat. Then he straightened and turned back around. His features had gone pale again. "I d-don't see how ... how you d-did that."

"I just aimed and…"

"I didn't mean that!" He wiped his mouth with his sleeve. "I meant, how could you…?"

"They were going to kill us. Just like those looters in Cocoa."

"I know. It's just ... well…"

"These girls all had guns—like the looters. Make no mistake—females are much more dangerous. You know that."

Reed made no comment.

"I'll bet they already whacked a slew of other guys before stopping us. Probably used the same shtick, too."

Reed stared at Carla, a pitiful expression on his face.

"Is that all you'd like to know?"

He just nodded.

I grabbed Carla beneath her armpits, pulled her up, and draped her over my shoulder. She was solid, too. I opened the side door and flipped her gently onto the seat, next to the redhead. I stood there a moment, looking at the three females now dead by my hand. I no longer felt remorse. I was tired of being judged. This damned plague had reduced life to a savage existence. I saw no reason to waste my time explaining my actions.

I circled around to the van's rear door and opened it. Crates of booze, food, and ammunition filled the back.

"My God." Reed had followed me. "They had more stuff than we do."

"They've definitely been busy. Let's take along a couple of these crates."

"Just the food, right?"

Knowing how he felt about beer, I figured he wouldn't want to load up on the booze.

"You're talking about the alcohol, right?"

"Actually, I'm quite fond of Scotch."

"Really? I figured since you don't like beer…"

"Beer makes me pee too much. What would *you* like?"

"I usually drink rum or bourbon."

While Reed moved the booze, I set about looking for ammo. I found six green canisters shoved against the seat. There were also boxes of shells for .38, .357, .44, .45, 9 millimeter, .22, 30-30, and buckshot for various shotgun gauges.

Wedged between the canisters and the driver's seat was a small cooler. I opened the lid. It took me a few moments to realize what I was looking at. Then it hit me. It was a pile of human penises. Carla and her brood had been preying on the men they'd met on the highway. Most of them probably hadn't had any sex for a while, were hungry and not thinking clearly. Carla and her gang enticed them, murdered them, and looted what supplies they could find. Once they acquired their booty, they separated the manhood from each of their victims for a trophy and tossed it in the cooler. I had no idea how many lay on top of the bag of ice, nor did I want to count them—but the pile was impressive.

Disgusted and nauseous, I slammed the lid shut, picked up two heavy canisters and lugged them to our van. I now felt less guilty for killing them.

Reed was shoving a crate of bottles into an empty space in back. He'd also brought over a crate of canned goods. I pushed the canisters in his direction then went back to pick up the machine pistol. I tossed the assault rifle into the tall grass off the shoulder. I hated assault weapons. They reminded me too much of Brighton Beach.

Before getting back behind the wheel, I pulled off my shirt, wiped myself down, and swapped it for a clean one from my suitcase.

"We're just going to ... leave them here?" Reed asked.

I stuffed the bloody shirt into one of the Walmart bags we used for garbage. I saw no reason to tell him about Carla's disgusting penis collection. "You want to toss them in this van, drive them to the nearest cemetery, bury them, and say a few words about what fine people they were and how much they meant to us?"

The hopelessness and sorrow showed prominently on Reed's pale features. He obviously needed to be reminded of the situation.

"You have to remember something. It's extremely unpleasant, but it's the truth. It's what you told me in Cocoa, when I suffered that brain blip."

"There's no one to drive the ambulance," he said softly, gazing at the bloody pavement. "No one working the hospitals."

"There's nothing left. Never forget that." Despair and sorrow filled my being as well, as soon as the words left my throat.

CHAPTER EIGHT

Engulfed in an eerie stillness, Washington sprawled before us on the other side of the Potomac River, its remaining survivors as shocked and bewildered by the plague of death as those we encountered in Florida and all the way up I-95.

The sun had already dropped low in the sky, turning pink and lifeless among the shredded clouds brushing silently around it.

I'd passed dozens of vehicles pulled over or stopped on the interstate and back at the Beltway. Only three were moving, inching about at a snail's pace, their affected occupants struggling to control the last precious moments of their lives.

I pulled onto the side of the road just before the 14th Street Bridge to survey the situation. The gas gauge had drifted steadily toward empty. Once again I faced the risky task of finding a place to fill the tank.

As we had approached the D.C. metro area, I also worried about being stopped by a cop. My driver's license was current, but if the cop checked the tag, he'd discover that it didn't belong to the van. Any working databanks would know I was driving a stolen vehicle. A search would follow. The cop would find the guns, the ammo, and the booze, as well as my illegal Walmart acquisitions. The garbage bag containing my bloodied shirt would not help my situation.

I had to face facts. If I was stopped, I'd have to shoot the cop.

The realization terrified me. I'd always been a law-biding citizen and had risked my life for my country many times in my brief military career. Aside from a couple of speeding tickets picked up during my hectic teen years, my record was clean.

But in the last few days, I'd stolen food, guns, sporting goods, money, and a van. I'd also killed eight people.

I'd done what was necessary to survive. Very few people still functioned and were probably doing the same unforgivable things I was doing. But that didn't make me feel less guilty, and it sure didn't make me feel any better. I was brought up to respect others, the law, and my country. And no matter what happened to society or the rest of the world, stealing and killing just wasn't right.

"I've been wondering about those women," Reed said.

"Why?"

"I think about people, Moss. It's the teacher in me, I guess. I'm always trying to get a fix on things. Even as a kid I'd always wanted to find out why something happened. Everything's important in the great scheme of things. Background influences everything. Maybe Carla had a rotten childhood and…"

"Background means nothing in a catastrophe. Everyone's lost everything, and the primeval urge takes over. Fight or flight becomes the order of the day. Most people don't even realize what that is until it's too late. Getting a fix on mass chaos is impossible. And it doesn't solve anything."

115

"I can't help wondering what she was before all this happened. Where she came from. If she had family, friends. She might've been a teacher, for all we know. Or a software CEO. Or maybe even a lawyer."

"Now she's dead."

"It bothers you, doesn't it?"

"I shot the woman. Killed her and her friends. They were all young and pretty. Now they're rotting in their van. Yeah, it bothers me."

"But ... you were ... *taught* to kill." Reed said, sounding confused.

"They taught us how, when, and who to kill. They even instructed us to seek professional help if we found we couldn't cope properly in society. They neglected to teach us how to kill without feeling badly about it."

"Even though you were forced into it?"

"We were ordered to eliminate the opposition and proceed with our mission. Do it quickly and efficiently, and then forget about it. They didn't feel the need to guide us through an acceptable period of mourning for those we killed. That wasn't in their budget."

Reed fell silent.

I decided to avoid going into the city, where the streets might be impassable by now. I didn't want to risk getting trapped by a marauding gang. I also didn't want to chance running into a military roadblock. So I backed up the interstate a few hundred feet and took the exit onto the George Washington Memorial Parkway. I remembered that it ran along the river and headed northwest toward the affluent Virginia suburb of McLean.

After about five miles I took the first exit, which spilled me onto Dolley Madison Boulevard. The first service station we passed, right off the parkway, had been ransacked. Office furniture lay on its side in front of the building. Broken bottles and crushed beer cans trashed the area near the service islands. Someone had shattered the glass facing of both pumps. The plate glass window of the office had been shot out as well.

I passed by the entrance to the Central Intelligence Agency. I saw no activity—something that frightened me quite a bit. If the U.S. Government was no longer functioning, we truly were on our own.

I drove a couple more miles and turned into downtown McLean. I found another gas station. It had been similarly pillaged. Chairs, tables, and office supplies covered much of the front lot. Trash had been taken from the cans and scattered.

The third station appeared just as unpromising. There were only two pumps. Three vehicles sat in line on one side, an old pickup on the other, its driver slumped over the wheel. The body of a man lay on the pavement in front of the office doorway.

Three larger stations at the crossroads appeared in even worse condition, as though there had been a full-scale riot by people trying to buy gas and get out of town.

I meandered through the shopping center and past rows of once-grand three-story townhomes. Wide-open front doors revealed the dark emptiness

117

beyond their marble foyers. Toys and discarded furniture lay on the overgrown front lawns and in front of garages. I spotted a few souls just sitting in their driveways, staring out at the dying world with glazed, unseeing eyes. No one moved.

I realized I probably hadn't needed to worry about being pulled over.

I headed back onto Dolley Madison and toward the glistening towers of Tysons Corner, with its twin shopping malls and opulent office buildings. Again, there were no signs of normalcy.

Finally I saw a station that looked open. The only activity was a scrawny black Lab that had stopped to sniff a wrapper on the cracked pavement. As soon as we pulled in, it trotted across the road and disappeared behind an overgrown bush.

I stopped next to one of the vacant pumps. A sloppily handwritten sign on yellow paper taped to the front of the pump said: *CASH ONLY--PAY INSIDE*

I dug into my pockets, peeled off five twenties, and stuffed the rest of the wad in the console between the seats. I pocketed the hundred and grabbed the .22 Beretta beneath the seat. I checked the clip, took it off safety, and slipped it in my front trouser pocket. It was the smallest gun I had and the easiest to conceal. I didn't like relying on such a tiny gun, which was good only for close work and rarely accurate beyond twenty feet. But I didn't want to walk inside with anything larger. It would show under my clothes, and if whoever had scribbled the note on the pump was still functioning, he'd consider me a looter and shoot me.

I glanced at Reed in the rearview. "Anyone in there?"

"Yes."

"How many?"

"He sees only one man. He thinks it's the owner."

"Any guns?"

After a pause, Reed nodded once.

My scalp tingled.

Pull yourself together. You have to get gas. There's no other way.

"If I don't come back out in a couple of minutes, get the hell out of here, get on the Beltway north, back at the bottom of the hill, and keep driving."

Reed said nothing.

"You can drive, can't you?"

"Of course I can drive."

"Then be ready."

"You think it'll come to that?"

"At *this* stage of the game? Yeah. It just might."

"How will I know if ... if I should ... if you're..."

"Tell your friend to follow me inside. If something happens, you'll only have a few seconds to get away. If it gets nasty in there, he might come out blasting. Understand?"

Reed's nod was slight. I could tell he was scared.

I took a couple of deep breaths then got out and stood beside the van, waiting for my nerves to settle down. I took another deep breath, told myself things would be just fine, and forced my feet to start moving.

As I trudged across to the office, I heard and saw nothing. No traffic buzzed by. No other sounds drifted over with the cool evening breeze. A few pungent odors wafted over from a dumpster, but didn't frighten or alarm me. A sour-smelling dumpster won't kill you. I focused my gaze on the darkness of the open doorway just ten yards ahead.

I paused a few feet from the threshold. In my present state, I remembered old westerns I'd seen as a child. I envisioned myself as the wandering gunman stopping in for whiskey and a few supplies before getting back on his horse and riding off.

It wasn't a farfetched thought. Modern times had somehow reverted back to how things were two centuries ago. I'd stepped into a situation that could easily turn volatile. Although it had been over a hundred years since barroom gunfights had been the norm, the tide had shifted, bringing back its ghosts. To survive, I had to expect any conceivable scenario. My only solace lay in my resourcefulness, instincts, and the tiny automatic in my pocket.

The large room was arrayed with merchandise shelves that were now mostly empty. Likewise the upright freezers that used to be filled with food and beer, a couple of junk-food machines and a cold drink cooler, which stood against the far wall, next to the green door marked *RESTROOM*.

A Middle Eastern man in his late fifties—from my Brighton Beach experience I guessed he was Pakistani—bent over the counter, smoking a cigarette and working what looked like an Arabic version of a crossword puzzle. He was beefy, broad-shouldered, and balding, and he wore a white tee shirt. A double-barrel shotgun sat on the counter, inches from his elbow. It was pointed at the doorway.

"I need some gas," I said.

He took his time sizing me up. I couldn't tell if he was affected or trying to decide whether I was trouble or a potential customer. He slowly straightened to his full height, which was around six-two or -three. He pushed a thick plume of gray cigarette smoke in my direction.

"Got cash?" he asked in a low, raspy voice.

"Sure do." I slowly reached for my pocket.

His left hand jumped for the shotgun.

My pulse raced, and I froze. "I'm only going for my money."

He nodded, but his hand stayed where it was. I pulled out the hundred and held it up. He raised a bushy black brow. "How much you need?"

"I figure about ten, maybe twelve gallons."

"Hundred bucks. Just put it on the counter and I turn on the pump. If you need more, it all right. But I switch it off when you finish, and I turn it back on when you pay more."

I did as he said, then backed up.

He picked up my hundred with his right hand then took his left away from the shotgun. My nerves immediately stopped jumping around. He counted the money then moved to the register. He opened the cash drawer, put the cash inside, slammed it shut, and pressed some buttons. "It is on."

"Thank you." I didn't want to turn my back. I began backing up again.

"No, you are all right," he said, raising his hands.

"I take it you've been robbed once or twice."

He snorted. "Wish it *was* only once or twice."

"That bad?"

He jerked his head to his left. "I nail a stupid fuck couple days ago with shotgun then toss his ass into dumpster. Then I figure how stupid that was. Has not been garbage pickup in weeks. So, had to close station, dump him in back of pickup, haul him somewhere else then haul ass back here so I don't get robbed again."

I turned toward the door.

"Mister?"

I turned back around.

You just give me money?"

"You just put it in your register."

He frowned.

"Problem?"

He tapped his scalp, signifying that he couldn't remember.

Suddenly I pitied the poor guy. "I'm sorry to hear that."

He pointed to the shotgun. "Time come when I can't remember my own name? That when I use this."

"Get roaring drunk first. It might help."

He nodded then lit another cigarette and went back to his puzzle.

***

A couple of hours later, we reached Breezewood—at the junction of Interstate 70 and the Pennsylvania Turnpike, which for decades had been a popular comfort thruway of motels, fast-food places, tourist attractions, and buffet restaurants—and more gas stations.

The main stretch was deserted, and the stench of death clung heavily to the air. Restaurants and motels displayed black windows. Vehicles of all makes sat in the parking lots and take-out lanes, and next to the pump-service islands. Passengers slumped over steering wheels. Bodies sprawled on the pavement near car doors.

"This is horrible," Reed whispered.

I made no comment as I pulled up to one of the pumps. I figured I couldn't keep my tank full enough. Many of the street lamps still flickered. Forcing myself to ignore the sourness drifting over, I got out of the van and tried the pump. It seemed to be working, then...

Something's wrong.

I turned around and listened. I heard only the cool breeze slapping flags and banners, but my gut told me something else was going on. I scanned the darkened windows, my eyes and ears alert for glints of light, sudden changes in the darkness, and odd sounds in the breeze. I saw nothing, heard nothing—yet I couldn't shake the feeling that Reed and I weren't alone.

The urge growing in my bladder and bowels wrenched me from my observations, reminding me of more pressing matters. I opened the driver's door and stuck my head inside. "I need to use the john."

Reed tilted his head. "Can't you just ... go right there, behind the pump?"

"I've ... got more intense business to tend to."

Reed frowned.

"Something on your mind?"

"My friend says someone could be in there."

My gut had obviously been right. I considered getting back in the van, but my sphincter was growing more active. There were other places that would suffice, but this one was only twenty feet away, and I wanted to tend to business and get out of here. The stranger in the building could be dead, dying, or still functioning. If he was the manager of this place, he'd want money for the gas. He might even be a looter or a psychopath. Reed's friend hadn't given me any details, so I had to assume the worst.

But just in case Reed's friend had underestimated the situation, I grabbed the .22 Beretta and slid it down the front pocket of my jeans again. Then I got some cash from the console and stuffed it in my pocket, just like I had done back at Tysons.

"Same procedure as the other place?" Reed asked.

"I'll be a little longer this time. Send him in if you're worried."

I crossed the lot and went inside.

In the dim light of the dying fluorescent, the cluttered office reeked of burnt coffee, motor oil, and stale air. Dog-eared hot rod magazines covered the table in front of the well-worn couch. The tin ashtray in the center of the table overflowed with cigarette butts.

A slender young woman with thick chestnut hair sat on a metal stool behind the counter. In her mid-thirties, she had fine features and high cheekbones. The back of her head rested against the block wall. Her eyes were partially closed. She was dead or very close to it.

I moved closer.

Her lower lip, bloody and bluish, ruined the overall picture. A jagged trickle of blood had reached the bottom of her chin, forming dark drops on her light-blue tee shirt.

Someone had obviously backhanded her.

I decided to check her pulse; corpses don't bleed very much. If I found a pulse, I'd carry her over to the couch and lay her down gently. I didn't know how much longer she had left, but I didn't want her to stay perched on that stool. She'd eventually fall and slam her face on the corner of the counter. I didn't want her to fall if she was still alive and I didn't want her to die on a filthy floor with a couch less than ten feet away. She deserved to spend her last moments in comfort.

I took a few more steps. She still didn't move, but when I leaned against the counter, I saw her hands. A large-caliber revolver grew from them like a giant black finger. The barrel was aimed at my face.

My insides twisted hotly.

I raised my hands. I wanted to disappear, go back in time. I wanted to close my eyes and tell myself I was imagining this, but I didn't want to do anything to startle her. I forced myself to stand calmly and hope my military training would kick in again. But my mind refused to cooperate. I could only stare at that huge barrel and imagine what would happen once the trigger was pulled.

Fight it. Force away the panic. Let logic take over.

Despite my shattered nerves, my brain began working. As with Luke, my eyes wandered from the gun to her eyes.

The eyes will reflect whatever lies within a person's soul. And unless one is facing a cold-blooded psychopath, the eyes will predict this person's next move.

The girl's eyes were large and a deep shade of green. They were dead-steady and focused directly on me. I could feel the heat of anger emanating from them. The sensation was terrifying.

Her hands shook. She wanted to use the gun, but her index finger kept pulling away from the trigger. She was obviously torn between shooting me and lowering the gun. I envisioned her lowering it and putting it on the counter top.

The barrel refused to move away from my face.

I swallowed the cold, gooey lump in the back of my throat and struggled to keep my voice calm. "I thought you were ... there's no need for…"

"Shut up."

"I … I was gonna ... I came in to…"

My bowels were the least of my concerns right now.

"I told you to shut up."

126

Keeping the gun steady, she slowly raised herself off the stool and stood her full height. The top of her head reached the level of my eyes, putting her at about five-six or -seven. Her slender frame gave her a distinctive vulnerable quality. If she hadn't been pointing the damned gun at my face, I would have felt sorry for her.

Two live brass rounds glinted from the open end of the cylinder. They looked like full metal jackets. Due to the structure of the frame, I couldn't see what lay in the top or bottom chamber. My experience told me to assume there could be four live rounds in the cylinder.

"Don't move."

I did exactly as she ordered.

She circled the counter and came back around, stopping about five feet away from me. She wore a pair of tight jeans and tennis shoes. The shoes were scuffed, the jeans smeared with dirt. Dark stains smudged her tee shirt, and scratches and cuts covered her forearms.

"Who ... hit you?"

"I told you to shut *up!*"

I went back to studying the gun. The hammer wasn't pulled, which told me she might not be familiar with double-action revolvers. Judging by the barrel opening, it was a .44 or .45, and would deliver a deadly kick. She held it with both hands, but unless she cocked the trigger first, she wouldn't have a prayer of nailing me on the first shot. If she closed her eyes while squeezing the trigger, I'd be able to duck out of the way. She probably tipped the scales at one-twenty on a good day. Her arms were very slender, her hands small. She might wing me, but could lose her grip and drop the gun after that first shot.

But I had no desire to test her. She'd obviously been traumatized and considered me a threat. Judging by her actions and speech, she hadn't been affected and was totally aware of her surroundings. I didn't want to make things worse for either of us.

I wondered if Reed was getting worried. Probably not yet. Staring down the wrong end of a gun barrel feels like an eternity. The gas pumps were almost directly in a straight line from the doorway. Reed would have a clear view of my back and raised arms. His friend might have even drifted over, glimpsed what was going on then returned to the van to warn him.

With luck, Reed wouldn't try to help. If he showed up at the wrong moment, he could easily get us both killed. Reed wasn't the most collected person I'd ever met. He'd already demonstrated his aversion to violence. If he did make a clumsy attempt at bravado, he knew nothing about guns. It was one thing to know how to handle a gun but another matter entirely to talk a gun out of the hands of a desperate female.

"Why'd you come in here?" she asked softly.

I didn't reply.

Her hands trembled. The gun twitched. She took a deep breath. "I ... asked you a question."

"You also told me to shut up—three different times, as I recall."

She took another breath. "You can ... you can talk now."

I lowered my arms.

She stiffened, but the gun didn't waver. "I ... didn't say you could do that."

I raised them again.

"Answer the question."

"I ... wanted to use the restroom. And pay for gas, if I found someone working here."

"Why don't you have the money in your hand?"

"I had to find out if someone was in here, first."

"You really expect me to believe such a stupid story?"

"It's the only one I've got right now."

"It's piss-poor. I don't believe you."

"That should tell you something."

She blinked. "Huh?"

"If I was gonna make up a good one, it would be a damned sight better than that."

The gun barrel dropped an inch. She was staring at my forehead.

"Now what's wrong?" I asked.

"Your hair."

"What about it?"

"It's covering your forehead."

"I came here for gas, not a TV interview. Besides, I don't think we could find a studio that's still working."

"That's not ... what I'm talking about."

"So ... what's the problem?"

"I can't see ... your forehead."

"I've been trying out the boyish look. Is it working?"

"Push it back."

129

"What?"

"You heard me."

I reached for my back pocket.

She stiffened again. "Watch it."

"Don't get tense. I'm only going for my comb."

"Use your fingers."

What the hell? I had no idea what was going on, but since she was the one holding the gun to my face, I did as she ordered, while she continued to stare at my forehead. "Is there something I should know?"

She abruptly stopped staring. Her eyes shifted, darting to her left.

"You okay?" Reed's voice drifted in through the open doorway.

The girl's arm jerked to her left, in Reed's direction. I immediately twisted to my right, grabbed the gun with my left hand and rotated my wrist, forcing the barrel straight up. I squeezed her wrist with my right hand, pulled her hand down, wrenched the gun free, and elbowed her away. Then I broke open the gun, upended the cylinder, and emptied it. Four live rounds of full metal jackets spilled into my opened palm.

I snapped it shut and handed it back. She took it, watching me in stunned silence. I dropped the brass on the counter. "You can have these back when we leave."

"What did you ... why did...?" She gawked at me, at Reed, at the gun in her hand, at the counter, and at me again.

"Like I said, I came in to use the john and pay for my gas." I reached into my pocket, peeled off three twenties from the wad, and held them out. "I know how things are now, but I still don't want to stiff anyone."

She stared at the bills. "I don't ... work here."

"Why *are* you here?"

She pushed some hair back over her shoulder. Only then did I realize how thick and shiny it was. "I'm sorry," she said softly and moved to the counter. She laid down the gun and sighed. She looked like she was ready to collapse. I took a step closer, but she immediately tensed and backed up.

"You looked like you were about to faint."

She pushed more hair out of her face. "I'm ... all right."

I pointed to the couch. "Sit down. I promise we won't try anything."

She stared at me then at Reed. "We really won't," he said.

She plodded over to the couch and collapsed onto it. I sat down beside her.

"Now, what happened? Who hit you?"

She rubbed her eyes and sighed deeply. "A couple of guys ... no, three. They were weird and scary. They ... they were walking around, looking ... looking for things."

"What sort of things?" Reed asked.

"I don't know. Bodies."

"Were they looters?" I asked.

"They didn't act like looters. I mean, they weren't carrying anything."

"How did they act?"

"Weird, like I said. And scary. Dazed, but not like ... like everyone else."

131

"Drugged?"

"At first I thought they were, but I changed my mind when I saw how they moved. They'd walk over to a body, kneel down beside it, and check for a pulse. Then they got back up and walked away."

This made no sense. She was obviously leaving something out.

"You're still alive. What exactly happened? And why'd they hit you?"

She shivered. "My car died, and I was checking around to see where I could pick up another one. They came around the corner and bumped right into me. I tried running, but they caught me and pulled me right off my feet. One of them picked me up with one arm and swatted my face. He didn't do it very hard, but it really hurt. I almost blacked out. Then I fell and they stood over me, looking down at me. I had the weird feeling they were studying me. I thought ... I really thought they were going to kill me."

A tickling began at the crown of my head. "Did they ... say anything?"

Her eyes grew before she spoke again. "They didn't say a word. Not one of them. I thought of those stupid zombie movies I'd seen when I was little. That's what they reminded me of. They had no expressions on their faces. They looked almost like department store dummies. I thought I was a goner, but a car went down the road right then and they spun around and ran after it like a pack of wild dogs."

The tickling vanished and was replaced by a heavy throbbing low in my gut.

"Did they ... catch it?"

"That was the *really* scary thing. The car was moving at around twenty or thirty, I guess, and much faster than you and I could ever run." She took a deep breath and shuddered. "They actually caught it. I know it sounds incredible, but they actually ran down a moving car! They forced open the doors while it was still moving, pulled out the driver and the female passenger as if they weighed nothing at all, and started beating them. I got up while the poor lady was screaming and took off. I don't know what kept me going, but I made it here. I figured if I could stay in here a while, I could sneak away and find another car. That's why I didn't move when you came in. I was playing dead."

"Where'd you get the gun?"

"It was in the drawer under the cash register. The drawer wasn't locked. No one was here, so..." She shrugged.

Judging by what she'd already told us, the gun had supplanted my digestive tract as the least of our worries. Despite my growing fears, I had to find out more about this.

"What did they look like, the three who assaulted you?"

"Young, maybe mid-twenties. Fairly tall, and really strong and fit. I mean, if they could pick me up with one arm..."

"Go on."

"They were about an inch taller than you. And they all wore black caps. Their clothes were dark, too. And they wore black boots."

The more she spoke, the more terrifyingly familiar it sounded. The throbbing in my gut had become a hot coal raking at my insides.

"Were they armed?"

"They all wore those belts I've seen soldiers wear. Yes, they had guns, but they didn't use them. They were covered with those leather flap things and were snapped shut. The flaps and holsters were black leather, and matched their outfits. I didn't even notice their guns until I saw them at a distance."

"What else?"

"Their eyes ... they were ... Asian-looking."

My heart skipped a beat. "So these guys ... were tall Asians?"

"They didn't look Asian. Just their eyes. And they all looked ... alike."

"You mean...?"

"Like twins. Or triplets."

My God. This can't be happening.

My head felt hot. "Anything else?"

"They all had these weird little black dots in the center of their foreheads. That's why I wanted to see your forehead. To make sure you weren't ... you know. You don't look like them, but I was scared and had to make sure."

Dots. Asian eyes. Looked alike.

Memories from my military days, shoved away in the darkness for so long, rushed back into the light. Chills ran down my arms. I wanted to leap into the van and floor it, and keep it floored until we were a thousand miles from here. But I had to keep

134

this inside me—at least, until we were a safe distance away.

Gas.

In the excitement, I'd almost forgotten. The pumps were working. I'd fill up here and do it as calmly as I could. I didn't want to panic Reed or the girl. I could relieve myself at one of the motels down the road—I thought I could make it that far. Filling up the tank would only take a minute or so. I'd be just a few feet from the driver's seat and could jump in and make tracks in seconds if I had to.

"I've got to fill up the tank," I said, standing up. "Would you like to come with us?"

"Moss?" Reed gawked at me. "What's wrong?" His friend had obviously picked up on my anxiety. This was not the time to tell them my suspicions.

"Nothing's wrong. I just don't want to meet up with ... well, whoever this lady's talking about."

"But don't you ... I mean, you said you have to use the…"

"I'll wait. This place is creeping me out."

CHAPTER NINE

Cold numbness consumed me as I filled the tank. My entire being focused on the deserted highway as well as the strange sounds of the night. The pump, amplified by my fears, clickety-clacked loudly behind me. The shrill breeze sounded like the desperate wailing of lost souls. A Styrofoam cup hopped frantically across the lot, making me jump.

It seemed like forever to fill the tank. I knew it was only minutes, but every pulsating second slammed into me with the force of a sledgehammer. My hands shook so much that it took me three tries to replace the hose nozzle and another three to screw the gas cap back on. I managed to climb into the van without tripping or whacking my knee. Using only the parking lights, I pulled back onto the highway and raced through the main intersection. We passed no one, and I spotted nothing in my side or rearview mirrors.

About three miles later, heading west on U.S. Route 30, I pulled into a deserted motel. Before stepping out of the van, I grabbed a flashlight and Luke's .357. I also left the engine running. If necessary, the girl could climb over the console, get behind the wheel, and drive away in a hurry. I wasn't afraid she'd leave me there. Reed wouldn't let her do it unless it was an emergency.

"I'll be five minutes," I told them. "If you see anyone, do what you have to do. Reed, you know where the guns are. I won't hold it against you if you decide to split."

"We won't leave you," Reed replied, a glint of anger flashing in his small blue eyes. "No matter what."

His sincerity touched me, but there was no time to waste. I sprinted across the pavement, where a motel room behind the abandoned office awaited me.

A quick scan of the room with my flashlight revealed a large shape lying on the bed. I slid the hazy orange beam over his features, stopping at his broad, heavily jowled face. He appeared to be around fifty, and his bloated belly was partially covered with a towel. Judging by the faint smell in the room, he hadn't been dead very long. Forgetting myself, I tried the light switch. The lamp and overhead light flickered then brightened.

Idiot! This light can be seen for miles!

I flicked it right off with a swipe of my hand and hurried into the bathroom.

Five minutes later, I jumped back into the van. Staying on Route 30 until Bedford, I rushed up the ramp to the Turnpike, accelerating to seventy and keeping it there. With only the parking lights on, my visibility was limited, and I had to be extremely careful. My skin had grown cold, and my gut churned heavily. I kept glancing at my rearview and side mirrors, alert for any flashes or sign of movement behind us.

The girl watched her side mirror as well. Once we were safely on our way, she placed her gun on the floor between her feet.

"Have you ever fired that thing?" I asked.

"No."

"Have you ever fired a gun, period?"

"A few times. My uncle taught me when I was young. He was a hunter."

"Do you know anything about that gun?"

"It's a revolver, and it's really heavy."

"It's a .45. With a four-inch barrel. The kick alone would probably sprain your wrist. If you're not used to it…"

"Is this a male thing? I told you, I've…"

"This has nothing to do with that. Going by your size and frame, I'd say you need a smaller gun. You've really got to be familiar and comfortable with large-caliber guns before you try and use one for protection."

"What do you suggest?"

Keeping my gaze on the darkness ahead, I reached beneath my seat and found one of the smaller autos Reed and I had picked up.

"This is an automatic. Just take it off safety like this." I flicked the catch with my thumb then flicked it back on and handed it to her, butt-first. "The kick isn't bad at all, and the gun's pretty accurate up to about twenty-five yards. Just remember to pull the hammer before you start shooting. Once you shoot the first round, you don't have to cock it again. Just keep pulling the trigger until the clip's empty. You don't have to pull it very hard, either. There should be eight rounds in that clip. You can empty it a lot faster than a revolver."

"Thank you." She handed me the .45, which I put beneath my seat.

"How many of those do you have down there?"

"Several."

"That's what your friend said. Where'd you get them?"

"He didn't tell you?"

"He didn't want to talk about it. He was ... kind of distant."

"I'll tell you about it later."

She went back to watching her mirror.

Although the blackness pressing against our windows reassured me, I knew better than to let down my guard. If my suspicions rang true, what this girl had stumbled upon was something none of us would be able to deal with. They could be out there right now, and they wouldn't have to see our headlights or tail lights to know where we were. They could function extremely well in total darkness. The mere thought of what might happen urged me to gain as much distance as possible. If they found us, we'd have no chance at all.

But something about her story made no sense. It also made me somewhat suspicious, and I had to find out about it quickly. After all, I'd just given her a loaded gun.

"Let me get this straight. They didn't care that you got away from them? They just ... let you leave?"

"They seemed more concerned about that car driving by. It was really weird—a kind of predator/prey thing. Like how an animal reacts when you try running away."

"What did they do when they'd finished assaulting the passengers?"

"I didn't wait to find out. I got away as fast as I could."

139

"I can't say I blame you," Reed said.

"I was so terrified I didn't know what else to do. I really wanted to help those poor people. If only I'd found that gun earlier..."

"They would've just taken it from you before you could use it."

She stared at me. Even in the darkness of the cab I felt the intensity behind those green orbs. "You ... know about them, don't you?"

"I'm ... not sure."

"Back at the station ... when I told you about them, you seemed ... tense."

"Like I said, I'm not sure."

"But you've got some idea."

"Moss?" Reed shifted forward and rested his forearms on the console. "I could tell something was wrong. Is she right? Do you ... know anything about this?"

"Like I said, I'm not sure. I'm only guessing. I could be wrong."

"What if you're right?"

I didn't want to tell them my suspicions.

When I was in the service, a program the military and a government research agency were working on at the time hadn't progressed beyond its initial stages. I never thought I'd ever see it in my lifetime. At least, I hoped I never would. I'd seen how slowly the military and the government operated, and I assumed it would be at least fifty years before something of that magnitude would ever come to fruition.

But now? And at a time like this?

140

"Let's hope I'm not," I said. "Let's just make some distance so we don't have to worry about them anymore."

Neither spoke, but I knew the subject would come up again.

"Where are you guys coming from?" the girl asked a few minutes later.

"Florida. How about you?"

"Walter Reed."

"You're a doctor?"

"Nurse."

"I suppose that place is in shambles," Reed said.

"Right out of a horror flick. Bodies were everywhere, and the stench was horrifying. We ran out of beds two months ago. People would come in by the dozens and stagger around, looking for treatment. An hour later, half of them would be lying dead in the corridors. Two hours later, the rest would be dead. We didn't have enough people to handle them all because our own people were dropping like flies. I just couldn't stand it anymore. I had to get out."

"That's understandable," Reed said.

"Both of you are from Florida?"

"The three of us," Reed said.

She turned sharply in her seat. "Three of you?"

"You can't see my friend. He's invisible."

She twisted around to the front and felt for the door handle. "You can just leave me off right here, if you don't mind."

"I can't drop you off in the middle of nowhere."

"It's all right. I'll just…"

"Listen. I know how crazy this sounds, but it's true. Reed's friend is invisible, but if it weren't for him, I'd be dead. So would Reed."

She turned and stared at Reed then at me. She was probably trying to decide what was going on with us. "You're okay? I mean, you're not…"

Reed sighed. "Crazy? On meds? In spite of the circumstances, I'm perfectly okay."

She didn't reply.

"Want some proof?"

"Proof?"

"My friend says you can use that antiseptic packet you've got in your back pocket to tend to your swollen lip. Or, if you'd like, we have a first-aid kit."

The girl blinked. Her mouth fell open. Once she accepted the reality of the situation, she closed her mouth, swallowed, and cleared her throat. "H-how did he…? H-how did…?"

I grinned. "You needed proof, right?"

She kept staring--first at me, then at Reed. Then she pushed her hair out of her eyes and reached into her back pocket.

As she applied the antiseptic to her lip with help from the visor light, Reed handed her a small baggie of ice from the cooler. She gently applied it to the swelling.

"I'm Moss and he's Reed," I said, figuring an introduction might break the ice.

"What about ... his friend?"

"What about your friend, Reed?"

"He hasn't told me his name."

"Why not?" I asked.

"It never came up."

"You're not curious?" she asked.

"Not really."

"Strange. Anyway, what's the story with you guys?"

"I met Reed in Florida. He'd just been beaten up by a gang of punks. He said he started hearing a strange voice when he came to."

She nodded.

"It's not what you think," Reed said.

"What do I think?"

"Head trauma. Hearing voices. Imagining things. Going bonkers."

"Since he said you came to, I assume you were unconscious. A head trauma would cause all that—especially if you suffered a concussion. But since I'm not a doctor, I have no idea what's going on up there."

"He's real," Reed said.

"I'm sure he is."

"Why do I think you're humoring me?"

"I wouldn't know. Anyway, I just told you I'm not a doctor. Just a nurse."

"A nurse with no name," I said.

She sighed. "My name is Brooke Fields."

"What do we call you? Fields? Brooke? Nurse Fields? Nursie?"

"Whatever you like. Except Nursie."

I kept driving and watching out for movement in front of us as well as any lights in my mirror. The thick, impenetrable darkness reassured me somewhat, but I remained uneasy.

"So now that we're acquainted," she said, "maybe you can tell us why you acted so weird back there. Just before we left Breezewood, when I told you about those ... those guys."

I didn't reply. I was reluctant to say anything. Telling them my suspicions would certainly frighten them.

"Why are you stalling?"

"I'm ... not quite sure who they were. Or even if you could call them guys."

She lowered her ice pack again. "What would you call them?"

"I didn't see them."

"Moss?" Reed was fidgeting. "Is there something you're not telling us?"

"I'm ... not sure."

"What *are* you sure about?"

"They're dangerous."

"I got that, too. I was there. I saw what they can do."

I said nothing.

"I'm not in the mood for games," she said flatly. "I was almost killed back there. If you have any idea what's going on, the least you can do is..."

"They're guys," I finally said. "Sort of."

"*Sort* of?"

"It's a long story."

"Start telling it."

"It involves the military."

"Moss," Reed said, "are you saying the three men who attacked her are military personnel?"

The facts more or less confirmed it. They were strong enough to pick up an adult woman with one arm and run down a moving car. However, the small black dot in the center of their foreheads told me the most important—and scariest—part of the story.

"Possibly," I said.

"Now that I'm thinking about this," she said, "something about those three struck me as very odd."

"Go on."

"They didn't talk to one another."

"You mentioned that before. How is that odd?"

"It just didn't make any sense. They didn't speak or even laugh. Guys always, you know, joke around with one another, even when they're out to hurt or rob people. But these three didn't even talk when they surrounded me. Or even when they ran down that passing car. It was like a sci-fi flick, where the alien touches down and has its first look at our civilization but doesn't talk because it doesn't communicate as we do. Know what I mean?"

I'd seen enough training films to know where this was going. During my tour, several of us were given special treatment in exchange for giving them written permission to put us through a series of stress tests. At the time, we'd welcomed a few weekends of R&R and light duty. We weren't concerned what the military was doing, or that some secret program would result. At twenty, one doesn't think too much of the future.

But now that future had finally arrived, and it was vitally important to learn all the facts.

"You mentioned getting away from them while they were distracted," I said.

"I didn't want them to see me running, so I found a good hiding place at the end of the block. I crawled underneath an SUV. I was afraid they'd guess which direction I'd come and would hunt me down when they were finished with the other two people."

"What happened?"

"They didn't seem to care about me or where I'd gone."

"Not at all?"

"I watched them turn around and march down the street, and when they were out of sight, I got out of there."

Walking around. Not talking. Hunting down the enemy. Attacking then marching away. This sounded like a program the military had initiated while I was stationed at Brighton Beach. The government commissioned the military to devise a sophisticated method of monitoring the movements of undercover cops and informants. The program involved microchipping, but only voluntary subjects were to be considered. Top-level military people headed the program, and little was heard about its progress. What Fields had seen could be evidence that the program had succeeded or was later abandoned in favor of something more effective.

"Any idea why they all looked alike?" Fields asked. "Why Asian eyes?"

Asian scientists were handling the program at the time. They were concerned about mass production and uniformity, but I wasn't totally sure of their motives.

"No idea."

"What else don't you know?" Reed asked.

"I'm not hiding anything. I do suspect a few things, though."

"If it's something we need to know," Fields said, "don't you think you should tell us?"

"During my three-year hitch, I learned that the Army had gotten together with two other branches of the government for a special project adapted from a top-secret experiment Black Ops had been working on."

"Black Ops?" Reed asked.

"This is getting more and more frightening," Fields said.

"You're sure about this?" Reed asked.

"I only know what I heard."

"What did you hear?"

"Our government was working with the military to improve survivability under combat conditions."

Fields swallowed audibly. "Are you saying those guys I stumbled across are Black Ops?"

"No."

"Then what are you saying?"

"The government has been experimenting with all phases of combat conditions and warfare for the last hundred and fifty years. Their studies and tests have varied, of course, but it's always been to the same end. They're obsessed with creating the newest and most efficient methods of winning wars. They want to create the best soldiers, the best weapons, the best technology money can buy. During a national crisis, they take over and pull out all the stops. Take September 11, 2001, for example.

After it happened, we put ourselves on red alert and kept it there for years. When Homeland Security started up, the government went crazy with every conceivable method of high-tech intel regarding terrorism surveillance and warfare. But this wasn't exactly a new pattern of behavior. Nearly a hundred years ago, when we considered communism our biggest threat, the military experimented with chemical and biological weapons, including the Ebola virus."

"What does that have to do with any of this?" Reed asked.

"They knew Ebola was somehow related to HIV, the AIDS virus, because both originated somewhere in Central Africa. Except Ebola acts with lightning speed. Its victims die within hours or days instead of years."

"Many people still believe AIDS was created in a lab by the CIA," he said. "I read it on the leftwing blogs for years."

"Yeah, well, the real stuff was going on with Ebola, anthrax, bubonic plague—strains like that. Part of the research was to develop vaccines to defend against biological attacks. But another part was experimenting with even more virulent strains. They wanted to see if they could make a virus that would sweep through a population so swiftly that it would overwhelm their ability to combat it." I took a breath. "That was their plan. Look what's happening now."

"We were never told any of this," Fields said. "The general consensus was that what's happening is the bad-seed effect of the massive antibiotics campaign the government pushed through over the past decade."

"What do you know about that campaign?"

"Anyone with any sort of medical training could tell those antibiotics weren't right. A chemist friend of mine told me the batches she studied contained a cocktail of nearly a dozen chemicals she couldn't isolate."

"But you weren't allowed to say anything, were you?"

"We were ordered to keep it to ourselves."

"They always play it this way," I said. "Always with the best intentions, and always with unintended—and tragic—results. It was the same when they launched their campaign to fight the narco gangs sneaking across the border during Mexico's war with the cartels. They'd been mixing in with the illegals for years, but it got much worse when we started letting assault weapons flow south under that ridiculous Fast and Furious program. Then, when the cartels took over the Mexican government, our most learned superiors decided we'd better get serious about protecting our sovereignty.

"I spent six months on the Arizona border as a sniper. They posted two dozen of us at various checkpoints and ordered us to shoot everyone we saw sneaking across the border."

"Everyone?" Fields asked.

"Everyone." Nausea immediately filled my gut.

CHAPTER TEN

The miles rolled on uneventfully. We passed through the Allegheny Mountain tunnel, which unnerved me a bit, because its lights were off. But on the other side, headed toward Somerset, the night grew even darker and more ominous than inside the tunnel, and sourness infiltrated the chilled air. More corpses, obviously. I wondered if a field of death awaited us straight ahead.

I felt the urge to turn around but didn't want to alarm Fields and Reed. Besides, where could we go? I wasn't familiar with this area, and didn't want to flick on my headlights and risk being seen. Luckily, no one else had mentioned the smell. I could be imagining it.

I decided to keep driving. If something prevented me from going further, I'd handle it when it happened. But until then, it was best to stick with my plan and stay calm.

Then, about a quarter of a mile down the road, I saw something that told me I'd been right in my suspicions.

Half a dozen vehicles sat off the shoulder. A battered pickup, its bed stacked with furniture, sat in the rear. A slender arm dangled from the driver's window. A large figure lay on the pavement beneath the doorway, forming a dark blur on the pavement. I wondered if the poor souls had packed hastily to rush off to some safe place, unaware that death had gone along with them.

As we passed the other vehicles, I veered out of the way of the bodies sprawled in the slow lane. There were eight of them; five adults, the rest small children. Fields and Reed gazed out the window in stunned silence.

When it was clear, I sped up to get away from the horror. No one said anything for the next few miles.

Fields, regaining her composure, rubbed her face. "Death. It's everywhere. Where does it end?"

"It doesn't," Reed muttered. "It's become our reality."

"Does any of this bother you?" she asked, staring at me.

"Why shouldn't it?"

"You were in the military."

She might've said "you're a cold-blooded killer."

Reed had also mentioned this to me. Many who'd never served assumed military people were cold, calculating killing machines unaffected by death and destruction.

"You never get over it," I said.

Fields stared straight ahead at the darkness smothering the windshield. "It must have been sheer torture," she said, her voice a whisper.

"That more or less sums it up."

"I'll never understand how people can do such horrible things to one another."

"Border Patrol was a nasty gig." Even after all these years, going back to those days brought a bitter taste to my mouth. "At twelve o'clock each night, a dozen of us were driven out to the desert in

151

jeeps and placed in various strategic spots. I spent the next eight hours lying in a shallow foxhole surrounded by sandbags. It was just me, my knife, canteen, and my Falcon 12.7 sniper rifle and bipod. My assigned kill area went straight out for about twelve hundred yards and covered four hundred yards in either direction."

The Falcon, an effective, formidable weapon, had saved my life many times. The round, equivalent to a .50-caliber Browning, was designed to penetrate armor at a hundred meters. Wounding someone was nearly impossible. It was like shooting a sparrow with a .357. I chose not to mention this.

"How many ... did you kill?" she asked, still staring straight ahead.

"I never counted." I'd forced myself to rid my mind of the actual number. For years, the images haunted me. It took a great deal of sheer will power and sleepless nights to get me through it.

Fields still didn't look at me. "Did you ... shoot women and children?"

It had been very dark during my shifts. At twelve hundred yards, it was impossible to tell the age or sex of those I'd killed.

"Most of the time, it was too dark to see. Luckily, nearly all my hits turned out to be scouts for the cartels. All were armed with machineguns and grenades. They also wore vests—which is why the Falcon was necessary."

"How long did you do this?"

"Six months."

"What happened after?"

"They took away my rifle and gave me a pair of binoculars with laser sights and built-in camera. I was told to keep track of the illegals and photograph them as they came over."

"What was that all about?" Reed asked.

"They didn't share the details with us, just told us to take pictures. Then, after just a few weeks, they changed our orders again and sent us all over the place. For six weeks I sat in a Quonset hut in the middle of the desert in New Mexico, collecting spent ammo the other snipers had brought in. I had to count it, categorize it, file the information, put all the ammo in canisters, and load them on a truck."

"Sounds like busy work to me," Fields said.

"It was the most boring six weeks of my life. During that time, the public was growing tired of the daily death tolls and urged the politicians to do what was necessary to reduce the size of the border-defense program. The military then launched an early out program for anyone who didn't want to re-up when their tour was over. I jumped at the chance. I was completely bummed out by military bullshit."

"I just don't understand what happened with that border stuff," Reed said. "The illegals kept coming over."

"I'd heard things about some sort of deal with Mexico and the drug cartel, but nothing definite. Too much was going on at the time. The United States started dealing almost exclusively with China, and for the next few years, everything sort of went crazy."

"That was around the time the food-poisoning epidemic started," Fields said. "When I started at

Walter Reed ten years ago, the hospital had already endured five solid years of poisoning cases."

"Those days were ghastly," Reed said. "At least one food recall per month, thanks to China. I was afraid to buy anything. Every time I turned around, one of the kids was sick. My wife developed every conceivable sort of food allergy and stayed in bed most of the time. She and the kids practically lived on antibiotics back then." He sighed. "I honestly believe that's what killed them so quickly."

Another group of vehicles showed in the dim yellow rays of my parking lights. This time, more than a dozen formed a jagged line just off the shoulder. Several bodies lay nearby, three of them directly in the slow lane. Their heads were cocked at an odd angle.

"My God." Reed hunched over, his elbows on the console. "What happened here?"

It looked like the handiwork of the same trio that attacked Fields in Breezewood.

"Anyone know what's out here?" Fields asked.

I slowed, swerving carefully out of their path. "Small towns, pastureland."

"Government land?"

"Possibly."

About a mile later, we passed another vehicle. This one was also abandoned. Nothing else showed up ahead. I began breathing again.

"Why'd you really get out of the military?" Fields asked.

"When we began dealing with China, our policies changed drastically. Nothing made any sense to me. Our food deal with China sent me over the edge."

"Yes," she said. "Chinese farmers were sent over here in droves, and American farmers went bankrupt. That boner infuriated a lot of people."

"That was around the time of my discharge. I wasn't even twenty-two years old and no longer wanted to be a part of an organization that kept making decisions that made no sense."

Fields lowered her window and tossed out what was left of her ice pack. "Nothing was more brainless than that stupid…"

"Uh-oh." The scene straight ahead made me cringe.

A group of vehicles blocked our path. Nearly a dozen unmarked cars, arranged in an overlapping chain, spanned the highway. Not one body lay on the pavement. The bodies stood in front of the vehicles. They were all armed with shotguns. They wore camouflage fatigues and stood at ready alert, their weapons aimed straight out. At least two dozen of them formed a chain, each standing just two yards from one another.

It was a very efficient roadblock, with the Jersey barrier preventing me from switching to the oncoming lane.

"What ... is this?" Reed whispered hoarsely.

My pulse was thumping. "A roadblock..." My voice sounded far away.

"Wh ...What ... do you think ... they want?"
Stupid, Reed.

155

But he couldn't help it. He was frightened, as was Fields, who sat forward, gripping the automatic in her lap.

"They obviously want us to stop," I said.

As I slowed down, Reed groaned.

"Now what?" I asked.

"You won't ... want to hear this."

"Probably not, but tell us anyway."

"My friend says they all have little black dots on their foreheads."

***

His face dark and ominous beneath his cap, the soldier marched up to my door and stopped about three feet away, his shotgun held straight out.

My insides heated up. Once again I found myself staring at a gun barrel. It had become a daily occurrence in the last few days and had turned my nerves into tingling needles scratching my flesh.

A second soldier circled the front of the van and marched over to the passenger door. He stopped about the same distance away and stood in the same manner as his partner, his shotgun pointed directly at Fields. She turned around very slowly to gape at me. Her face was as white as a sheet. Her eyes lowered to the .380 in her lap.

She wants me to take the gun and use it.

"Can't," I whispered, barely moving my lips. "Too many of them."

"We're toast," Reed whispered anxiously from the back seat.

"What ... do they want?" Fields whispered.

"Us," I whispered back.

"Why?"

156

"It doesn't matter. We don't have much of a choice."

The soldier on my side tapped my window with the tip of his barrel.

"Get out," he said flatly.

Grab the .380 and take them out.

That wouldn't be a bright move. The two shotguns aimed in our direction did not waver. I had no doubt that they'd shoot us at the slightest provocation. If they actually were the new batch of soldiers the military had perfected over the years, they'd be unstoppable. Their young faces revealed no expression at all. In my experience, no expression meant these were real cold, calculating killers.

"Get out," he repeated.

Once again, I considered grabbing the .380. My right hand was only inches away from it, my lower body concealed in the darkness of the cab. They couldn't possibly see my hands. I could grab the gun and stick it in my pocket. When I needed it, I could whip it out and pick off one or two before they nailed me.

The soldier at my door obviously thought I was taking too long. He suddenly reached out with his left hand. Grabbing the side mirror by its metal base, he ripped it free. It was done with minimal effort—as if he'd merely pulled back his arm to swat a fly. He held up the mirror.

Fields gasped. Reed groaned softly.

The mirror was then dropped to the pavement with a clatter.

"Out!"

157

He'd done it quickly and easily, his eyes on me all the while. The shotgun in his right hand hadn't moved. I realized then that going for the .380 would be the stupidest move I could make.

"It's been nice, guys."

One last attempt at bravado might give Fields and Reed a shred of hope.

I grabbed the handle and pushed open the door. I wanted to slam it in the soldier's face, but he'd immediately stepped back. This alone helped ease my guilt for not testing him. Even if my silly plan had worked, the other soldier would have shot Fields and Reed. And since he was using a shotgun, the spread would be at least six inches in diameter. I would have been in the line of fire and killed as well.

We had to do as they said, but I realized that if they'd wanted to kill us, they could have easily done it. Anyone capable of calmly pulling a mirror loose from the side of a van, running down a moving car, or picking up an adult with one arm, could kill with ridiculous ease.

A heavy wave of guilt quickly swept over me.

This is my fault. I brought them as well as myself into this. If only I'd listened to my gut and left Reed in St. Cloud ... If only I'd let Fields jump out of the van when she'd wanted to.

It was much too late for ifs or regrets. I had to bite the bullet and let them take us. I had no desire to sacrifice any of us for the sake of idiotic, ill-fated heroics.

I climbed down, slamming the door behind me. The soldier motioned with his shotgun.

"Where to?" I asked.

He pointed to one of the cars.

"What about my...?"

The tip of the barrel poked my lower back.

I walked toward the designated car. I considered running, maybe even ducking between cars and making for the woods, but I knew it would be just as futile as anything else I'd considered. These men could run down a moving car. I had to keep remembering that.

He circled me, reached out, and pulled open the rear door.

I risked a quick peek before I slid in.

No one.

So far, so good. That meant once I got in I could wait until he slammed the door. Then I could slide across the seat, kick open the other door, and try to make it to the bushes just beyond the shoulder.

Then that gun barrel once again pressed against the small of my back.

I risked a glance toward the van to see if Reed and Fields were also being escorted to other vehicles. But as soon as I started to turn my head, the soldier behind me lowered his shotgun and shifted his feet.

Duck... Get out of the way quick and roll...

My brain started working a little too late. Something hard and heavy cracked me on the back of my head.

The night instantly grew pitch-black.

159

PART TWO: THE WAR MACHINE

CHAPTER ELEVEN

Something slapped my shoe, wrenching me awake.

I opened my eyes. Yellow haziness penetrated the darkness, making everything soft and blurry. A whiff of some kind of disinfectant assaulted my nostrils.

I rubbed my eyes. When I opened them again, my vision gradually cleared. A table lamp about fifteen feet away had provided the haziness.

I lay on a couch. Two soldiers stood off to the side, watching me. Their faces were identical and showed no emotion. Their eyes were Asian, and I immediately thought of what Fields had told us about what she'd seen in Breezewood. They wore combat fatigues and baseball-style caps, and shiny black boots. Their uniforms had no name tags, patches, or ribbons. Their automatics—they looked like Sig Sauers to me—rested in holsters over their right hips.

Cold nausea rushed down my back.

What the hell is happening?

One of the soldiers brought up his arm and jabbed a thumb behind him. He clearly wanted me to get up.

I forced myself into a sitting position, and a heavy pounding began near the crown of my head. My arm weighed a ton, but I managed to bring it up to gingerly feel the lump. The memories swam back immediately: The roadblock. A small army of these jerks all armed with shotguns. I'd been ordered out of the van and escorted to one of their cars. And, when I'd turned around—or rather tried to—the lights had gone out.

Obviously, they'd brought me here while I was unconscious, probably to some secret government facility that they didn't want me to know anything about. They'd probably planned to blindfold me but resorted to the head tap when I tried to resist.

At least, I hoped that's what had happened. I didn't want to consider the possibility that I wasn't supposed to see what they'd done to Reed and Fields, assuming my two friends had been escorted from the van as well and not just shot on the spot.

If the latter was the case, why spare me? Why not them as well? And if they were still alive, where were they?

Too many questions. I strongly suspected I wouldn't get any answers from these two. My anxiety intensified the throbbing pain in my skull.

"Stand."

If you don't, they'll yank you to your feet. You'll throw up on both of them and be shot for messing their uniforms.

Why would two of them be sent here? Either of them could carry me over one shoulder without breaking a sweat.

Even if I wasn't so groggy, none of this made any sense, especially by military standards. The world had gone down the tubes. Very few people were still walking around. So why was any of this necessary? And why would anyone go to the trouble of bringing me in?

I took a deep breath and forced myself to stand. The effort immediately drained me. Dizziness made my head swim, and I nearly fell back down. One of the soldiers quickly shifted toward me. He probably thought I was up to something. I would have been if my head hadn't been throbbing so much.

I knew I would have to get away. Hopefully, Reed and Fields were here as well. If I could gain enough time to investigate, I might be able to find them.

But that thinking was premature. I had no idea how long I'd been unconscious or how far away the van was. If I'd been out for a couple of hours, we could be anywhere within a hundred-mile radius of the roadblock. We might also be less than a mile from it.

"Move." The other soldier extended his left arm toward the doorway.

I took a couple of steps. They were shaky, and I nearly stumbled. I bent, rested my palms on my thighs, and took a few breaths. The pair waited silently and made no move to hurry me along. I found this strange. They didn't seem the considerate type, and they'd been barking orders at me.

As I recovered, I surveyed the room.

It seemed to be a reception or waiting area, with the near end occupied by two chairs flanking a small table, and a coffee table facing the couch where I'd been dumped. The coffee table was empty of magazines or any sort of reading material. Checkerboard tiles covered the floor, each about the same length as my shoes, which made them a foot square. I quickly calculated a twenty-by-twenty area.

A waiting room?

A small black box hung from the ceiling in the corner and faced the door behind me. No tiny red light winked from its center. If it was a video camera, it wasn't working.

On the other side of the room, I saw a desk with a small cubicle behind it and an open doorway feeding into a dimly-lit hall.

Gathering my strength, I slowly straightened again.

My escorts led me to the doorway. I spotted a closed laptop sitting on a green blotter on the desk. A gray office phone with several rows of buttons sat off to the side. No lines were lit.

We went out into the hall. Fluorescent lights spaced at wide intervals lit portions of the tile floor with a cold white glow. An EXIT sign highlighted the far end of the corridor, which appeared to be about sixty feet away. This was a large building. That same aroma of disinfectant clouded the air. An artificial coolness suggested the place was air conditioned.

I felt like shit but still wanted to make a mad dash for it. I knew they could easily outrun me, but somehow I might be able to outmaneuver them. Adrenaline provides certain advantages in impossible situations.

They must have sensed my hesitation, because I felt something solid now pressing into the small of my back.

"Walk."

Reluctantly I began moving toward the EXIT. When we got within about ten feet from the doorway, one of the soldiers said, "Turn right." It was another dimly-lit corridor, and the smell of disinfectant grew stronger.

This facility didn't make sense. Why would it continue to operate while the rest of the world had practically shut down completely? This definitely reeked of a military operation. No other organization could still function under such extreme circumstances.

That's what puzzled me. With the majority of the world gone, the military had become unnecessary. And from what I'd seen during the last few months, there was no need for a government, either.

This hall was much longer—maybe a hundred feet. There were no doors or markings, only the next EXIT sign straight ahead.

A thought hit me.

Decrease your pace; sustain the tempo for about twenty yards then burst into speed.

If I could zip through the EXIT doorway, I might be able to trip them as they followed me through. Maybe I could grab one of their guns, shoot them both, and begin my search for Fields and Reed.

That's when another thought arose in my aching head.

You're too old for this. The men behind you are in their mid-twenties.

I couldn't ignore the obvious; I was way overmatched. If they came from the same group

Fields had encountered in Breezewood, they could easily catch me.

Enter, thought number three.

These two men have been ordered to take me somewhere. Someone has gone to great lengths to bring me here.

This realization gave me an edge. If they hadn't killed me by now, I could press things a bit to try to expose the source of the orders.

I decreased my pace.

Almost immediately, I felt the tip of the gun barrel nudging the small of my back again. Time to exercise my new strategy.

Gain some distance.

I hastened my step. If I could widen the space between us by even a few yards, I might be able to dodge around a corner and shake them up a little.

I quickly realized just how hard a blow I had sustained. My limbs grew warm and thick after the first ten yards, and I began breathing heavily. I struggled on, forcing myself to keep up the increased pace, breathing deeply, my mouth open, my calves and thighs on fire.

About twenty yards later, I glanced behind me.

They were still right behind me. I was nearly out of breath, yet they continued breathing normally. Frustrated, I slowed back down and let my heart rate return to normal.

Would conversation do me any good?

These two hardly spoke. They were professional soldiers. They lived to complete their mission and spoke only when giving or acknowledging orders. I couldn't imagine them engaging in any meaningful discussion.

Still, it might be worth a try.

"Where are we?"

No response.

"What building is this?"

"Shut up."

So much for chatting; best keep walking and wait for my chance.

I'd keep on looking for opportunities to goad them, but the time might also come when they'd lower their guard. Even superbly-trained soldiers have weaknesses. No matter how good they are, nobody's perfect. They could turn at the wrong time, reach for a door awkwardly, or even blink. If an opportune moment arose, I'd knock their heads together and grab a gun.

Just before we reached the EXIT sign, one of them said, "Turn left."

Inside the threshold, another corridor awaited us. Unlike the others, this one was well lit and carpeted. I spotted two black plastic signs mounted on the wall straight ahead. Their white lettering made my heart skip a beat:

←PROJECTS A-M

PROJECTS N-Z→

This was definitely a government installation.

"Turn right," one of my escorts said, as we reached the signs. Ten feet later, we encountered a solid metal door. One of them reached around me and pulled it open. "Inside."

I hesitated.

Yet again, the gun nudged my lower back.

Briefly I considered driving my elbow into his jaw. That would probably have been a seriously bad move. Stupid, too. His jaw was most likely made of steel, and he could shoot me much faster than I could execute the blow.

My body trembled in anger, as I stepped through the doorway.

The door clanged loudly behind us.

Shivers raced down my back. For a moment I imagined I was about to be brought down to hell. When the door clang stopped resonating, a heavy silence followed, intensifying my feeling of isolation.

We were standing on a landing at the top of a staircase with nowhere to go but down.

The gun barrel still in my back, a bolt of heat jabbed me deep in my gut. I spun around and stood my ground. I didn't know if it was anger or fear fueling me; both emotions tend to mesh together in a frightening situation. Sometimes one of them forces you to act, sometimes both. You often don't know which emotion causes it. In this case, it might have been panic or the fear of what awaited me at the bottom of the stairs. Or, maybe I was just tired of being shoved around.

"What happens if I don't want to go downstairs?"

The gun barrels lowered simultaneously, both stopping at my kneecaps.

I didn't move.

The cocking of the hammers, loud and frightening as they bounced off the walls, made the decision for me.

Cursing myself, I turned and descended the stairs.

We went down twelve steps to another landing, turned right and went down another flight of twelve. Then another landing, another turn, and twelve more steps.

We descended a total of five flights, with each step appearing to be around ten inches tall—sixty stairs equaling fifty feet. If our journey had begun on the main floor of the facility, we had gone five stories below ground level.

A bomb shelter?

The panic returned. The bottom landing faced three metal walls and another solid metal door. A six-inch-square black box mounted on the wall beside the door rang of familiarity. The tiny red blinking light within its center brought back an avalanche of memories.

Some kind of scanner. High security clearance.

It was beginning to make sense.

"I didn't bring my card with me," I said flatly.

As if by rote, one of my escorts shoved his automatic into my back. Then, shifting around me, he reached out and applied the back of his left hand to the center of the black square. The door clicked.

A cold blanket of utter dread wrapped around me.

These two are chipped.

Chipped. Superhuman strength. Razor-sharp reflexes. No emotion. No expression.

The memories thundered back.

Following eight rough weeks of Basic Infantry Training, the military sent me to Louisiana for eight brutally intense weeks of Advanced Infantry Training. Once we'd all been tested and chosen for our individual MOS, our military occupational specialties, we were paraded into a hot, stuffy classroom. There, for two hours every afternoon for the next two weeks, we watched training film after training film showing different phases of the military's plans for future technology in the battlefield.

High-tech weapons. Ultra-specialized aircraft. Remote explosives. Super soldiers.

I remember our instructor, his khakis immaculately ironed, his brush-cut shaved to the skull on the sides and buzzed flat on top, standing off to the side of the big picture screen, speaking loudly and impersonally, his gaze cold and vicious, like a shark during an attack.

The wave of the future, recruits. You are gradually becoming obsolete. In five years, this country will no longer need soldiers like you. America will require a stronger, smarter, more efficient fighter. Ordinary flesh-and-blood soldiers are outdated. You are vulnerable. You tire, grow weak, hungry. You require rest and nourishment, and cannot function properly when wounded or captured. You have become the weakest link in our global defense program.

The two behind me were such super soldiers. Anyone could figure that out. But what did all this have to do with me, especially now, since I'd been out for nearly twenty years?

That damned gun nudged me once again. I forced my thoughts back to the present and pushed open the door.

In contrast to the dimly lit corridor and staircase, this area exploded with light. A solid glass wall faced us. Behind it, a sea of processors and other supercomputer hardware filled a large open area beneath a veritable blaze of fluorescents. Long tables covered with laptops and other electronic equipment also filled the room. Giant but blank video screens covered the far wall.

One of the soldiers again waved his hand over the scanner beside the glass door. At the sound of the click, he pushed it open.

We went down a long aisle of processors, stepping carefully over knots of exposed fiber-optic wires, clusters of extension cords, and tangles of power strips. The floor was made of two-foot-square, vented metal tiles, the kind that had been used in the old-fashioned data processing centers during the latter years of the 20th century.

Another metal door stood at the far end of the room. Once again, one of my escorts reached around me and waved his hand over the black box next to it. Another click, another door pushed open.

Three long rows of tables filled the small space, with a dozen laptops set up on each table faced by an adjustable office chair.

A large conference table touched the far wall. A complex phone system sat in its center. Six Styrofoam cups had been left on the table surface.

Signs of a brain at work here—or at least a human being?

"Sit."

"Where?"

They both pointed to the chairs.

I sat.

"Now what?"

Without another word, they stood at parade rest behind me.

I glanced at the laptop keyboard.

"Mind if I play Solitaire?"

No reply.

"What are we waiting for?"

Ditto.

At least the chair was comfortable. I sat back, closed my eyes, and tried to relax while thinking of a possible escape plan.

CHAPTER TWELVE

About ten minutes later, I heard the scanner at the other end of the room click. The door opened. A tall, broad-shouldered man around fifty appeared in the doorway. He wore a starched-collar white shirt with the sleeves neatly pressed and a red tie whose knot showed no hint of a crease or wrinkle. He had the unmistakable look of retired military.

I figured him for a full-bird colonel, maybe even a brigadier. His blond hair was cut close to the skull. His small, deep-set blue eyes hardly blinked. His gaunt cheeks had been shaved so closely they gleamed in the fluorescents. His strong chin and muscular neck displayed discipline, leadership, and determination.

He stared at me for about thirty seconds, his gaze steady as he took in everything from my hair to my dirty, sweat-stained shirt. Once he'd finished his inspection, he closed the door and marched briskly down the aisle to my table.

"Alan Moss," he announced in a clear voice.

"We know one another?"

"You do not know me, Moss. I know you."

I strongly suspected I was about to be interrogated. I'd been in these situations before and knew how these people operated.

"For a moment I was afraid my memory had jumped ship."

"Your memory is fine."

"How would you know?"

"I know."

His statement made me suspicious. "Who are you?"

"That is not important—at least, not right now."

I wasn't in the mood for deception or fancy sparring. They'd brought me here against my will. They could at least tell me what this was all about.

"Why am I here?"

"That will become evident."

"Let me guess. I forgot to pay my taxes."

He said nothing.

"I just remembered; there's no more IRS. I guess I lucked out for once."

His blank expression didn't change. "Your file said you challenge authority but nothing about you being a smartass."

"File?"

"We have a current, up-to-date file on you, Moss."

I'd been out of the military nearly twenty years. They had no reason to continue maintaining my file. He must have been talking about something else.

"What sort of file?"

He didn't reply.

"I deserve to know."

Still no reply. A splash of heat flared up, nearly choking me.

"You stopped me at gunpoint, knocked me out then hauled my unconscious ass here just so we could play stupid guessing games? Frankly, I'm disappointed."

"Everything was done for your own protection."

"Knocking me out was done for my own protection?"

"You resisted."

"I turned around."

"Your orders were to get in the car."

"I turned my head so I could see what these clowns were doing with..."

"You disobeyed a direct order."

"I'm no longer in the military. How can I disobey a direct order? Besides, only an officer can issue a direct order. I didn't see any brass on the nutcase that slugged me over the..."

"You were instructed..."

"By a psycho with a shotgun?"

"The people to whom you are referring are a platoon of specially assigned military personnel."

"They apparently didn't feel the need to identify themselves. They were much too busy pointing guns at us, shoving us around, and hitting me over the head. One of them even damaged my van."

"You were given a direct order to comply with their instructions. You are lucky you were not shot."

The more he spoke, the more he sounded like a high-ranking officer.

"I took my last direct order just before I got out of the Army. I haven't taken any since."

"As I said, subduing you was necessary for your own protection."

"How the hell did you know where I was?"

His steady gaze did not waver. "You cannot possibly be serious."

His response revealed the obvious. Triangulation, GPS coordinates, cell-phone tracking, satellite monitoring and, of course, their on-going experimentation with microchipping the last five decades. I hadn't forgotten how devious the government was. The chip program they experimented with during my military days had been strictly voluntary for personnel desiring three-day passes. We were all given a full week to sign up.

Sensing a scam in progress, I didn't add my name. As a result, I was scheduled for immediate riot-control duty at Pakistani Brighton. Before being deployed, I was given a battery of inoculations. One of the shots was injected into my forearm. At first I'd thought it was for tuberculosis, but I could never find out for sure. After my discharge, I tried several times to get a doctor to scan my forearm but wasn't able to find anyone to cooperate with me.

"I was chipped, wasn't I?"

His silence told me the frightening truth. Despite the heat rippling up my back, I fought to stay calm.

"We were told all chips would be removed or deactivated upon discharge. Care to expound on that?"

"You happen to be government property, Moss."

Government property.

That statement should have triggered another flare-up, but I suddenly realized I no longer cared. Everything that had happened had obviously changed my outlook.

He turned to the laptop behind him and punched some keys. The screen flared to life. My old military photo covered the right half. A page of vital stats covered the left.

"Your service photo."

"I never did go for that cue ball look."

"You were nineteen. A good soldier: disciplined, tough, intelligent, and resourceful. What happened?"

"What the hell do you think? I got out and began living like a normal human being."

"You turned arrogant, self-indulgent, undisciplined."

Their stats hadn't stopped with my honorable discharge. They also included the year I was married, the year my wife and I divorced, the three different addresses we'd shared during our marriage, and my latest Orlando address, as well as stats about my detailing business and employees.

"Something interesting?" he asked.

"Why don't you people ever get your facts right? I'm six feet tall, not five-ten, and I'm no longer in the one-seventy category. Last I checked I weighed one eighty-seven."

He continued staring at me, his expression the same weird blankness you'd expect from a department store dummy. It was eerie, as if he'd just switched himself off. Then he blinked, and some color returned to his cheeks. "Any pertinent questions other than height and weight issues? Are you not concerned why we have your records after all these years?"

"I already asked why I'm here, but you didn't give me a straight answer. I figure you're military, and the two apes behind me are also military. You've said I'm government property, so I've got a pretty fair idea why I'm here. But right now, I'm more interested in where I am."

"I am sure you are."

"And what this place is."

"It would be much easier to show you."

He punched a few more keys. The screen turned blank. He marched over to the door then turned back to me. "Coming?"

I'd rather be leaving.

"Do I have a choice?"

"You wanted to know what is going on."

I jabbed a thumb at my escorts. "What about Tough and Tougher?"

"They do only what they are told."

"What have they been told?"

"They will follow us until I say otherwise."

"Nothing in their present instructions about killing me?"

"Not in their present instructions."

I knew better than wrestle with that statement. This bozo wanted to show me something; he couldn't very well show me anything if I was dead.

I got up rather stiffly, my thoughts looping as I followed him through the doorway.

***

I could tell the white walls of the well-lit corridor had been recently washed, the drab green rug vacuumed. The residue of an ammonia-based cleaner permeated the air.

177

The disinfectant.

There were three brown metal doors spaced at equal distances along both walls, each with a standard doorknob but no markings.

"You never did say what this facility is," I said. "Or where this is."

"No," he said, not missing a step. "I did not."

I struggled to control myself. I would not get the answers I needed by losing my cool. "You wouldn't by any chance want to tell me where my friends are, would you?"

He stopped walking and turned. "Friends?"

"I had two people with me when your roadblock crew got us. One of them is a nurse. She's slender and attractive, with brown hair and green eyes. The other's a former teacher. He's around my age, maybe an inch taller than me, and at least thirty pounds lighter. He has light-brown hair and blue eyes. You wouldn't by any chance know what happened to them, would you?"

His blank expression revealed nothing. "I gave strict orders to have you brought here. My instructions did not include anyone else."

"What about my friends?"

"I was told you were alone when you were brought in." Then he turned and resumed marching down the corridor.

The bastard was lying or had received the wrong information. The folks communicating with him could be winding down. I couldn't let myself think of the other alternative.

"I wasn't alone," I said, catching up.

"You are now."

It was getting much more difficult to control myself. I wanted to slap a chokehold on him, or slam his face into the wall.

"I've dealt with people like you before. Why do you think I got out of the service when I had the chance?"

He still didn't lose a step. "What sort of people are you referring to, Moss?"

"People in authority—officers, politicians, bank managers, department heads, CEOs—you're all cut from the same mold. You play games with people's lives and treat them like they don't exist, and when they try communicating with you, you baffle them with bullshit. Truth and honesty aren't exactly in your vocabulary, are they?"

"You sound like an outsider, Moss. I find it hard to believe that only twenty years ago you were one of our finest fighting men."

"I just want to know where my friends are— and of course why you're operating a top-secret facility while the rest of the country has gone down the tubes."

When we were about ten feet from the end of the corridor, he turned and gazed at me as if I'd just grown another ear. "What makes you think this country is at its end?"

He was good, all right. And no different from the other bureaucratic morons I'd dealt with in my military days: cold, calculated, and tough as granite. Tell no tales. Give away no secrets. Don't let the enemy know what you plan to do. Distract then plunge, hard and quick.

"Are you trying to tell me it's business as usual out there? That nothing's happened to turn this planet into a giant graveyard?"

"I have no idea where you are getting your information, Moss."

"I've obviously been hallucinating. It's been a doozy, too. It goes something like this: There's no power, no water, no cell-phone service, no Internet—no communications of any sort. And to top it off, everyone I've stumbled across during the past few days is dead, dying, psychopathic, or wandering around like a zombie."

"Interesting." He motioned to the door. "May we proceed?" He waved his hand over the scanner. It clicked immediately.

Damn. He's chipped as well.

It only stood to reason; if they'd chipped enlisted men they'd certainly chip NCOs and officers.

He pushed open the door and we entered a tiny alcove. The area, about the same size as an elevator, made me feel trapped and helpless. My limbs turned to ice as the door closed behind us. With the three men surrounding me, I felt even more claustrophobic.

My guide clicked the scanner beside the door facing us. "You were not hallucinating, Moss. Everything you have seen during the last few months has actually happened. However, what you are about to see will explain everything."

"You're going to show me something that'll explain why everything I've seen doesn't necessarily mean the world has ended?"

"As soon as we step through this door." He eased it open, and we entered yet another long hall. Walls of glass displayed the large open areas on either side of us. They were well-lit and carpeted, with a desk, some filing cabinets, and a couple of chairs.

A platoon of troops took up the rest of the two areas. On one side, soldiers of both genders stood at attention in three long rows, all dressed in full camouflage. I counted twenty in the front row. The back rows were about the same length. None of them moved. All displayed the same face and body structure. In the center of one room, a similarly dressed female stood on a podium. She quickly fell forward and landed on her outstretched palms. Without pausing, she removed her left palm from the floor, rotating the arm perpendicular to her body. She then performed a set of rapid, one-arm pushups. The action was effortless and perfect. From full extension she touched the floor with her nose then rose back up, her right arm remaining straightened.

The woman completed twenty repetitions, switched arms, and did twenty more, finally leaping to a standing position.

She nodded once, and the entire class repeated what she'd just done. No one spoke or counted. Everyone moved in unison until the exercise was finished. Then they all leaped simultaneously into the attention position and remained perfectly still.

In the room on the other side of the corridor, men and women in police uniforms stood at full attention in four long ranks. They also had the same face and body structure. The demonstrators for this group, two men, faced each other on a large rubber mat. Both were stripped to the waist, revealing lean, well-muscled physiques. The one facing us gripped a large hunting knife.

The one with his back to us nodded.

His opponent attacked, his blade glistening in the fluorescents as it lurched forward with blinding speed. The victim grabbed his assailant's wrist so incredibly fast I saw only a brief flash. It was done with deadly accuracy, twisting and snapping the opponent's wrist in one fluid, well-coordinated motion while elbowing his attacker sharply in the jaw, pulling with his other arm and slamming the other man to the mat. Still holding the attacker's broken wrist, the victim calmly grabbed the knife and sliced the tendons. The attacker didn't flinch or resist. There was no blood. The glistening blade remained clean.

The attacker leaped up from the mat and examined his mangled wrist. He took it in his other hand, made a few adjustments, and closed the gaping wound by pulling the skin together.

Damn. Strong, fast, resilient, intelligent ... and indestructible?

The realization slapped me cold. The military had finally completed their project. The day of the super soldier had arrived.

I considered it a mixed blessing that our enemies were all dead.

At least, I *hoped* they were.

CHAPTER THIRTEEN

"What *is* all this?" I asked.

"Welcome to the New Order," my escort said, turning to face me.

Totally unbelievable. Nothing I'd stumbled across during the last few days could compete with what I was witnessing here. "You're trying to tell me these ... creatures ... have taken over?"

"Moss, you are indeed hallucinating if you think everyone is gone. Yes, there are millions dying every single day, but do not for one moment think there will be no survivors." He waved an arm at the window. "This is living proof."

At that moment I knew he was out of his mind.

"But they're robots—or some form of perverted human clones."

"We call them Technologically Advanced Beings—TABs, for short."

"They're robots."

"They are just as real—just as flesh and blood—as you are."

"I bleed. They don't."

"TABs are superior, humanized clones made up of genetically-processed material that is tougher, more durable and more flexible than any known metal alloy. They do not feel pain, are incapable of injury, and are three times stronger than the average human. They can reach running speeds of forty miles an hour—as fast as the average full-grown horse."

"That sure will come in handy if they see a horse wandering around and decide to arrest it."

He ignored my comment. "As I said, they are stronger and faster. They are also ten times more intelligent. Their brains are New Age computers."

"And you're crazy."

He cracked a slight smile. "Yes, there has always been a fine line between genius and insanity."

"Yeah, I've seen evidence of that a few times before. I saw it in the Army, mostly. I also saw it when I invested a great deal of my money in the stock market then lost most of it in three months, when we were told our economy had taken a slight dip. I know all about crazy people and intelligent people, and you know what? I've always had trouble telling which is which. But that doesn't seem to matter now. Nothing means much anymore."

He gestured toward the door where we had entered the hall. I turned and walked toward it. He and his guards followed. One of them opened the door, and once again I found myself in the tiny alcove surrounded by my three escorts.

Once inside, he resumed talking. "You are wrong, Moss, dead wrong."

"So are you. No matter what you or your cronies think, you can't repopulate the country with robots."

"As I have stated, they are highly-sophisticated, superbly generated clones. They are superior to humans in every way. They will soon turn this planet into what it was meant to be."

That clinched it.

"What the hell are you talking about? 'Meant to be?' By whom? And just what would that Utopia be? A giant video game operated by a handful of power-mad fools?"

"Why are you skeptical? You have seen what they can do."

"Yeah, I've seen. Apparently, they can also run down a moving car, pull the people out of it, and snap their necks like a twig. That's just what this dying country needs—an army of robots running around, killing what's left of humanity."

"I do not know what you are referring to."

"Oh, you haven't dispatched some of these ... what do you call them ... TABs? You don't have them out among the rest of us?"

"We have several units policing certain key areas."

"'Policing?' You mean like picking up cigarette butts and candy wrappers?"

"They are gathering data. We need to know the numbers of victims, damage spots, cleanup estimates, and power analyses. They observe what they see and photograph it with cameras built into their visual program. The data are transmitted to our servers, where everything is copied, stored, and transferred to our command center. We need these vitals to help us decide where and when to restore power. But none of the TAB programs authorize killing."

I wasn't surprised. Like most high-level officials, this jerk had no idea what was actually going on. "Well, guess what?"

I saw a brief startled look in his eyes. The guards remained impassive.

"I assume you are referring to some sort of isolated software error that can be adjusted. We can comb the data recordings and see if any of our TABs has malfunctioned. If so, we can transmit a reboot order and then upload corrected programming. It would not take long. So far, we have dispatched only two TAB platoons. One is monitoring the Washington, D.C., area, and the other is overseeing the Breezewood section. They represent our first wave. Of course, there will be glitches in everything new." "Glitches?" My gut tightened. "That should be reassuring to the people who are dead because their necks were snapped by mistake."

"Unfortunate, but necessary."

"Killing innocent people is never necessary."

"Collateral damage has always been a hazard of war. You were active military. You have heard the phrase before."

"It always seems to come up whenever computers or other expensive high-tech devices malfunction and civilians end up dead."

"Computers can and will malfunction, Moss. They are built by humans, and they process what is programmed into them. If the programming is faulty…"

"Sure, it all comes back to human beings and their shortcomings—except it always seems to be other human beings that have to pay."

"As I said, unfortunate but necessary to achieve our ultimate goal."

"And what would that be?"

He stared at me, as though he was carefully weighing his response. "What is the ultimate purpose of a computer?"

"To serve humanity; to perform tasks that are too mundane, time-consuming or dangerous for people."

"No, Moss. The ultimate purpose is to replace humans. Anyone who thinks otherwise is foolish."

"And what happens to humans once they're replaced?"

"Moss, you should know more than most what humans are capable of."

"In other words, these creatures have been designed to make the world a safer, warmer place?"

"People have been struggling to extinguish one another since the beginning. This country has been slitting its own throat for a long time, ever since we became multicultural, pitting one group against another, classifying everyone according to which group he belonged to. Sooner or later, ethnic warfare had to start—and it did.

"You saw it happen, Moss. You were stationed in Brighton, I know. If it were not for the national emergency, the Latinos there would have killed off all the Pakistanis, or vice versa. Then the winner would have attacked the blacks, the Arabs, the Iranians, and so forth. All would have died eventually."

"So it's better to kill everyone off all at once and be done with it."

"We had nothing to do with that."

"Really? This damned plague was just a coincidence?

"As difficult as it might be to believe, yes. Though it was not entirely a natural occurrence."

"What does that mean?"

He hesitated, his gaze momentarily lowering. "Things got out of hand."

I just stared at him.

"We did not know what it was … at first. We thought it might have been an accidental release of an experimental biological agent, such as one of those they had been working on at Fort Detrick. But our investigations failed to track down the source.

"Then the National Security Agency picked up a peculiar conversation between a Chinese diplomat and his home base. It took a while, but we finally determined what was happening."

He paused again.

Am I crazy? Is he stopping to receive some kind of radio message?

"The Chinese had secretly been imbedding a biological agent into all of their paper and cardboard products. It was so subtle our best instruments could not detect it. The substance stays inactive until it comes in contact with human flesh. Then the microbe jumps into the pores of the skin. Once it enters the human body, there is no stopping it. It was brilliant."

He sounded downright admiring.

"Brilliant? They're on the verge of killing nearly half a billion people, and you think it's brilliant? That's not brilliant. That's genocide."

"No, not really," he said quietly.

"How could it not be?"

"Moss, China could not have accomplished this if the American people had not met them halfway."

"Now what are you talking about?"

"People have been sleepwalking through life for decades. The computer age has been a godsend in many ways. It relieved a lot of uncomfortable responsibility. People were no longer required to make decisions, analyze, remember, or learn. Computers began doing it all. People wasted no time letting machines take over their lives."

"What does that have to do with anything?"

"For quite a while, this country has been declining on the global intelligence scale. By the turn of the last century, our average IQ had dropped below 100. That means half of the national intelligence quotient was 90 or lower, with many close to retardation. In the years since, the national average score has dropped another ten points."

He was taking too long to make his point.

"So we've become a nation of dunces. So what? Does that give China the right to wipe us out?"

A quizzical stare from my captor. "How many Americans would you guess have taken pharmaceutical drugs?"

"I'd say just about everyone."

"And what percentage has taken antibiotics?"

"Fifty?"

"Eighty-seven point five, at last calculation."

It came to me in a flash. Antibiotics. Flu epidemics. What Fields told us. What I'd feared all along.

"Do you understand now?"

189

"The doping? That nationwide vaccine drive last year?"

"Where did the vaccines come from?"

"I don't believe it. I can't. I won't."

"When people began exhibiting strange symptoms, our Centers for Disease Control went to work studying possible causes. They could not find anything immediately, so they sent out bulletins asking other countries for data on similar cases. It was China that sent us the most useful information—including the formula for a so-called effective vaccine."

This was becoming more and more difficult for me to accept.

"It became a simple matter of telling the nation to visit neighborhood pharmacies and free clinics for a vaccination. Moss, when you have spent the last hundred years instructing a population to take medications for everything, the process eventually becomes an essential part of their lives. They assume that taking a particular drug for depression will make them feel fine. If they have trouble sleeping, they take another. For an ear infection, another. For the flu, yet another. So when the epidemic started, they assumed they needed to be inoculated. Everyone did it—an overwhelming majority. That vaccination drive was more successful than even the Chinese had expected. The vaccine actually boosted the microbe's effectiveness. People died within days instead of weeks or months."

This was incredible—totally mind-boggling.

"So ... you're saying the Chinese committed biological warfare against us, but they couldn't have done it without our help?"

"They provided the biological agent, and we complied by using it."

I could barely grasp what he was telling me. "Un-fucking-believable," I said, barely above a whisper. Then, as I forced myself to recover from this horrific news, I uttered the most important question: "Why?"

"Because China owns us."

***

I didn't want to believe him. I'd heard all sorts of things over the years. I'd learned most were false, and the particularly depressing ones were always fueled by fear. But right now I wasn't as sure. Too many frightening things had happened in so little time. Even so, I refused to believe our country belonged to China.

"How can anyone buy America?"

"I did not say China bought America—I said China owns America."

"What's the difference?"

"This is what happened. It was done gradually, in steps, so no one noticed outside of those directly involved. China started growing into an economic powerhouse because of cheap labor and a government that decided they could keep iron-fisted control over their people and society while still doing business with the rest of the world. They used both to great effectiveness—at least at first. American companies found out they could have their products manufactured in China for much less than it cost here, even with the large transportation distance involved. Pretty soon, China was awash in cash—American cash—and they started investing that cash in the best place on earth to do business: the United States.

"At the same time, our government went on a spending binge, to the point where it could not meet its obligations just from tax revenues. About forty years ago, during the bailouts, when so many insurance companies and banks and the auto industry were either bought or went bankrupt, in many of those cases, China provided the financial relief. And by the second term of Barack Obama, the country was borrowing 40 cents of every dollar spent—much of that from China as well." Another pause. "Eventually, the government ran up so much debt that it could not even cover the interest payments. We tried to negotiate more favorable terms with the Chinese, but they refused—and the United States defaulted. You know what happened next."

We stood there for a moment, staring at each other.

"Okay," I said in resignation. "The Chinese decided to wipe us out so they could claim what is now rightfully theirs. Meanwhile, you're preparing this TAB army to … what, take the country back?"

Silence.

"Fine. Whatever. But if you've built the Brave New World, what do you want with me?"

He actually smiled. "You really do not know?"

I got it right away. "Ah. It turns out your little clone army isn't immune to the Chinese bug—but I seem to be."

"Yes, Moss. It turned out that the concoction the Chinese sent over was not a vaccine at all. It was an antibiotic that became particularly toxic when mixed with certain antibiotics already present in the bloodstream."

"What kind of antibiotics?"

"Strange as it seems, the ones in most common use—including those found in antibacterial soaps. The human body has a tendency to accumulate them in the fatty tissues. When people received the Chinese chemical cocktail, it traveled to those same tissues, combined with the residual antibiotics, and disabled many of the body's vital functions."

"So the doping campaign was the final nail in the coffin."

"Yes—except that it seemed to work only with people whose immune systems had already been weakened or damaged by years of antibiotic misuse."

"In other words, people who hadn't taken antibiotics on a regular basis wouldn't suffer the more severe effects of the doping?"

"Even so, the mixture would retard other bodily functions. After several weeks of intense study, our research department was about to discover the nature of the discrepancy—as well as the exact mixture of chemicals—when three of five of the panel members slowed down and died. After that, we discontinued the study."

Discrepancy. Research. This was beginning to make deadly sense.

"So this is why I'm here."

"Yes, Moss. As I said, you are government property."

"I became my own property when I was discharged twenty years ago."

"You would like to think that," he said, almost sneering.

"That's what my discharge papers say."

"There was a disclaimer on your DD-214, stating that in the event of a national emergency all previous arrangements made regarding your discharge would be deemed null and void."

"Bullshit. I've been out for too many years."

"That does not matter."

"It matters to me."

"Moss, you do not have the option of leaving."

"What do you intend to do?"

"We are going to study you to find out why you remain unaffected."

"I'll tell you why. I never took antibiotics, and I didn't get the shot. Now can I go?"

"You never took antibiotics? I find that difficult to believe."

"The last time I took anything like that was when I was in high school. I don't know what the Army gave me, but I haven't taken anything since I got out, just vitamins and mineral supplements. I hate meds, period."

"You were given a heavy regimen of vaccinations and boosters during your three-year stint."

"As well as that chip you stuck in my arm?"

"The chip was part of the program at the time, yes."

The urge came on automatically. I knew it was hopeless to resist, but the panic—as well as the anger and the frustration—took over. I raised my right arm, but as soon as I did, one of the clones grabbed my wrist and elbow, imprisoning them in an excruciating, viselike grip. My arm instantly grew cold then numb. My shoulder felt as if a blowtorch had been placed directly beneath it. I gasped, cringing under the pressure.

A moment later, the pressure vanished, and my arm, now a useless piece of flesh, dropped limply to my side. The guard then grabbed me around the waist, lifted me up, took two steps back, and set me back down. A moment later, the barrel of an automatic pressed snugly into my lower spine.

"Was that really necessary?" My captor regarded me curiously.

I massaged my tingling shoulder. The flickering fire in it gradually ebbed. "I needed to vent."

"What did you think would happen?"

"Watching you drop to the floor with a broken jaw or bloody nose would have been highly entertaining."

"You actually thought you could outmaneuver the TABs?"

"Like I just said, it was just an urge. You pissed me off. I wasn't thinking straight."

"Those demonstrations you saw in the hall, they did not register?"

"It doesn't matter. I'm not going to submit to your tests."

"Then this conversation is over." He nodded to the TABs, one of whom nudged me with the gun barrel.

I led the way out of the alcove and down the corridor. I didn't think they'd shoot me, but I had no illusions of resisting further. Being picked up and handled as if I'd been a small child was humiliating. But at least now I fully understood my predicament: If I couldn't escape this nightmare, I'd die in this building.

***

A doorway awaited us at the end of the corridor.

Beyond it, that same staircase we had descended before descended farther into a black abyss. A small-watt bulb leaking slim strands of yellow light above a doorway sliced the darkness, and I gripped the metal banister on the way down.

The foot of the stairs, pitch-black as the inside of a cave, gave no evidence of light beyond it.

The next corridor, damp and murky and smelling of mildew and vomit, made my insides churn. Tiny overhead bulbs positioned at wide intervals barely lit our path. At the end, a narrow metal door opened to yet another dark corridor. The strong, sour smell grew in intensity, adding to my nausea.

Despite the gun poking my back, I proceeded slowly, barely lifting my feet. While the TABs were obviously equipped with infrared vision, I was forced to feel my way. The passageway was clear, but the unevenness of the black concrete floor made my journey difficult.

Tiny bulbs flickering from the areas we passed reflected vertical bars on both sides of the corridor. Some sort of prison, obviously. I'd no doubt remain here until they came and took me away for their tests.

A cell awaited me at the end of the corridor, on the left. The bulb in the center of the far wall splashed a flimsy illumination over the dirty cot beneath it. The shadow of a toilet and small sink jutted from the western wall. The floor was bare.

The gun poked me one last time.

By now, I had become much too tired and sore to resist, but for some stupid reason I decided to take a whack at it anyway.

Just spin around and kick one of them in the crotch. Or let both of them have it in the jaw. It doesn't matter that you haven't done any serious physical training in years, or that they can break your neck like a twig, or pull a mirror off the side of a van without breaking a sweat. Just spin around and hope for the best.

I realized that any effort I made would be laughable. They'd just pick me up and set me back down again.

Bad boy. Naughty, naughty.

But somehow I needed to communicate to them that I was a fighter. Anyway, I was sick and tired of letting them lead me around.

Just as I started to turn, one of them shoved me inside the tiny cell, nearly knocking me over. Before I could regain my balance, they slammed the

197

heavy door loudly behind me, echoing in heavy waves down the corridor.

The two of them contemplated me for a few seconds then turned and marched away briskly, their boots echoing sharply on the concrete.

"How about breakfast?" I called after them, figuring it was worth a try.

No reply.

"I like eggs, bacon, and toast. Coffee would be nice, too. And if it's not too much trouble, bring me a toothbrush and some mouthwash."

I heard only the slamming of the door at the end of the corridor.

Silence followed.

Loneliness, isolation, claustrophobia, and panic stabbed at me all at once, though my strongest sensation was relief. The gun poking my back had grown tiresome. The TABs had grown tiresome as well. Their silence, lack of emotion, and bored manner terrified me. I didn't want to accept the awful fact that the world I'd known and loved all my life had been taken from me ... to become theirs. But as bleak as everything seemed, I couldn't give up, or submit to defeat.

I checked my cell door. It held fast. The sink spigot produced a trickle of cold water. The strong sulphurous smell irritated my sinuses, but at least it was wet. I cupped my hands beneath the slender stream and splashed my face. Despite my aching joints and the nausea filling my gut, its tingling chill invigorated me. I took a little drink.

The toilet worked. A small roll of toilet paper sat on the dirty floor beside it.

I kicked the bottom of the cot. Hopefully, anything living inside it would be scared away. I yanked the frayed blanket from the slender mattress and shook it vigorously. Nothing but dust and dirt. It was the same with the filthy pillow. After picking up the mattress and shaking it as well, I flipped it over and replaced it on the metal frame. Weary from my efforts, I sat, rested my elbows on my thighs and my head in my hands, and tried to make sense of what I'd learned.

If I believed what I'd been told, America had been destroyed by the Chinese. But had the Chinese survived? Had the rest of the world?

One thought kept coursing through my brain. Nothing would ever matter again.

My only concern at the moment was that these people—whoever they were—decided they had some use for me. It was my only hope. My only way out of this. If someone needs you, it gives you an edge. A bargaining chip. The trick was to make sure I remained useful while I planned my escape.

I had to find Reed and Fields, get us out of here, and drive home see my mother before it was too late.

Reed and Fields were still alive. They had to be. I couldn't let myself think they'd been killed. If I suspected it even for a moment, I knew I'd give up. But I couldn't give up. I couldn't let these psychos beat me.

Despite the fears weighing on my mind, I had to view my predicament more objectively. They'd brought me here because I'd been in the military. They believed they still owned me and had a use for me. Reed wasn't in the military. Neither was Fields.

But since Reed and Fields were still functioning, these people might want to study them as well. If they needed lab specimens to monitor the effects of the doping, three cases would be much more reliable than just one.

Fields was a nurse. She would be considered valuable. Reed was involved in software and was also a high school teacher. They might consider his expertise in education useful for their research.

If they had plans for me, they had plans for Fields and Reed. They might be keeping them in a wing not far from here. Judging by the intense silence, I suspected I was the only one in this dark, foul-smelling tomb. I couldn't see anything moving in the darkness. But with only the single bulb barely lighting my own bed, I was lucky I could see anything.

I decided to try a long shot.

"Anybody else in here?"

Nothing.

"Reed? Fields?"

Silence.

I had to find some way to escape—I had to.

Get up and check the cell bars again.

I sat up, but my lower body remained molded to the cot. I could feel myself growing more exhausted by the second.

Get up and pace, dammit.

Ideas came easier and clearer when I was up and about, burning energy. I could also do a few pushups to get the blood flowing, and pump more adrenaline into my system.

Then the urge to lie down took over. Exhaustion set in, and sleep nudged me. The lump on the back of my head began throbbing again. I obviously needed rest. It had been a very long, stressful day.

I closed my eyes and let the darkness take me to quieter places.

CHAPTER FOURTEEN

A strange sound wrenched me awake.

I sat up sharply and squinted at the darkness. Sleep clouded my eyes, and I rubbed them.

Except for the tiny bulb flickering from the wall two feet above my bunk, everything was as dark as a tomb. I couldn't tell if it was night or day, or how long I'd been sleeping. An hour? Four hours?

My surroundings revealed nothing. The minuscule aisle bulbs emitted a faint orange hue, highlighting the cell bars. I listened but heard only the heavy silence pressing against the bars of my cage.

A dream, no doubt.

I lay back down and tried forming an escape plan. Given my present predicament, all such thoughts seemed impossible. The cell door wouldn't budge, and I was much too big to squeeze through the bars. Since I couldn't flush myself down the toilet, I'd have to wait until someone released me.

The officer I'd talked with said they wanted to study me. They couldn't accomplish that from this cell, so they'd have to take me somewhere else— possibly a nearby lab. That might provide access to all sorts of equipment and give me an opportunity to cause enough confusion to effect an escape. I'd probably have only one chance, and if it didn't turn out, I'd be killed.

The idea of dying didn't concern me at the moment; I cared only about finding Reed and Fields. I'd have to figure out some way of disabling a TAB or two in the process, but I couldn't see any way around that. I had no idea how to do it—or if it was even possible. But I had to try. In the meantime, my best bet was to work on some sort of...

A toilet flushed, jarring me from my thoughts. The sound resonated up and down the corridor, but I suspected it had come from the adjoining cell.

I sat stock-still and listened closely. It took about a minute for the tank to fill back up, after which the heavy silence resumed. I got up and cautiously approached the bars. The hazy darkness from the other cell revealed nothing. But then I noticed a break in the flickering bulb above the cot. Someone had moved in front of it, blocking its light. The quiet shuffling of footsteps made me shiver.

"Someone there?"

Silence. A shadow approached the bars. The owner's face moved closer and became visible.

It was the man I had talked to upstairs.

***

I told myself I was dreaming or hallucinating. Life and logic had literally jumped ship, wandering off together into the sunset. My mind had obviously followed.

I refused to believe what my eyes were seeing. Yet something about this man's face—his eyes, perhaps, or his blank expression—made me suspicious. A strong sensation of wrong swept through me. It was the same feeling you get when you walk to your car in a crowded parking lot and realize the moment you glimpse the unfamiliar brown sweater in the back seat that the car isn't yours.

In this case, there was no familiarity when our eyes met. The picture was off. The man I'd talked to earlier was alert. He dressed and walked smartly, oozing authority. Proud yet economical in his movements, calm yet fired up about his plans, he remained devoid of emotion when I tried to slam my fist into his face.

Although I hadn't heard this man speak, somehow I knew he wasn't the same person. The face was similar, but there the similarity ended. The semidarkness of the corridor clouded the overall picture, but I could still distinguish certain details. His eyes were lackluster, his features gaunt and pale, his cheeks unshaven. His clothes were dirty and a size too large. The shirt tail hung loose, the pants baggy.

The hopelessness in this individual's demeanor registered most of all. His body trembled. The hands gripping the bars also trembled. He seemed to be using them to hold himself up.

"Didn't I just talk to you upstairs?"

"You weren't ... talking to me." His voice was weak and raspy, and he sounded like a much older man.

"It sure looked like you."

"That was ... my clone."

Of course . . . A clone. Should I be surprised?

Still, some things didn't add up. The officer had spoken like a human being—delusional but human. The TABs hardly spoke, so I hadn't even considered putting him in the same category.

"I didn't realize," I said.

"They've been at it ... a while," he said, clearing his throat.

"How long for ... the TABs and you?"

He coughed and cleared his throat. "It started a couple of years ago for the TABs ... a couple of months for me."

I realized he hadn't spoken with anyone for a while. He was gathering his thoughts. "When they realized the Chinese meant to do us in, their best minds got together ... to develop a way of surviving the plague and fighting back with a smaller but superior force. To do both, they needed to convert the data in the human brain into programmable material ... and storing it in a chip."

"They can store the contents of a person's brain in a chip?"

"The pertinent data was all they really needed. Isolating and eliminating the disposable material ... that was the most difficult part. The disposable stuff comprises nearly ninety percent of the brain. They basically separated out the unnecessary files. When they finished, they uploaded what was left in the chips. But the first generation of TABs rejected the implants. Then they discovered that Asians were somehow more receptive to cloning and that they could take the chips without too many side effects. They also figured they could make the Asian TABs more difficult for the Chinese to detect, so they could infiltrate certain installations—but by then it was too late."

"How so?"

"The vaccination program—the doping—it killed off most of the best minds working on the project. It derailed the effort."

"But I've seen dozens of functioning TABs, and they were amazing."

"We were able to create a small group of them ... to help us get at least part of the country back. But we also recognized it would take a massive effort to repel the Chinese, one well beyond our present capabilities."

He coughed again, but I could see he was feeling a little stronger. "Something of this magnitude would require a minimum of ten thousand TABs deployed in each state. It would take more resources and more personnel than we could possibly marshal. So we decided to start small and see what we could do locally. Our main objective was to search for the unaffected.

"Then I began having trouble with my equilibrium, and I occasionally dozed off in the lab, sleeping hours at a time. Two of my colleagues also began succumbing to blackouts. One day they stopped showing up. A week or so later they returned, but I noticed something was very different about them."

"Cloned?"

"It was an intelligent decision, actually. Cloning is the most efficient way of getting things done. A clone's DNA is made up of pre-existing data, so to speak, but you can reprogram it, make it do exactly what you want. When we started the project, everyone was in agreement about what should be done. Then a couple of the members decided to induce certain changes the rest of us found objectionable."

"What sort of changes?"

"Experiments."

The realization hit me. "You mean human experiments?"

He nodded. "You have to understand we were researchers, scientists, people who ... who suddenly found an enormous supply of human subjects they could study—subjects that were powerless to resist. Most of them were dying, anyway, so there would be no repercussions ... and we needed not feel guilty or regret."

"But what are you talking about? What kind of experiments?"

"First, we needed to separate the subjects into groups in various stages of the disease: untreated, partially doped, severely doped, and unaffected—immune. Next, we subjected each group to various tests."

"What tests?"

"Heart rate, respiration, sensitivity to heat and cold, galvanic skin response—all the normal, usual physiological evaluations. Then we began mental and psychological evaluations. Basically, we were studying ways to counter the disease effectively while looking for physical advantages to help us against the enemy."

"That all sounds kosher to me."

"Yes, but the problem was we found nothing useful—nothing to help fight the disease, and nothing to help fight the Chinese. That's when some of my colleagues began suggesting more ... dramatic experiments."

"Like what?"

"All sorts of horrors: water-boarding, submerging in sub-freezing water, electroshock, asphyxiation—you name it."

"Jesus. Why?"

He looked at the floor. "The short answer is ... because we could."

"Good God."

"If we were going to build a superhuman race, we needed to test the normal limits of human endurance."

This was unbelievable. Even in a dying world, these people were making things worse.

"The damned thing is, we learned a lot. We were able to use much of the data to program out almost all human weaknesses in the TABs."

"'Almost all?'"

"Yes."

I almost hated to ask the next question. "What didn't you fix?"

"It had to do with one or two of the short-term memory subprograms we installed in a trial batch."

"'We?' Meaning you?"

"No, not by me; a couple of the more ambitious researchers inserted them into the main program. I wasn't privy to those particular programs, so I don't know for sure what they contained. I only know the data were taken from some of the more aggressive subjects in the studies. They added the programming to a new chip and installed it immediately."

Aggressive subjects. Frightening.

I took it all in for a minute. "So you were part of all this."

He looked at me squarely. "When the disease began affecting me, I lost track of what was going on. Up until then, though, yes, I was part of it. I was doing my best as a scientist to overcome the disease and help to save my country."

"Including torturing helpless victims?"

"If we couldn't save them, we had to save ourselves."

Now I looked at him squarely. "You think you've saved anybody?"

He ignored the question. "Things changed completely when some of us came down with the disease. It changed the direction of the research." He sighed. "The others took what we had learned about cloning and reprogramming, and they cloned and reprogrammed … us. Before we knew what was happening, our jobs were being done by our replicants, and they placed us in these cells … just in case our clones malfunctioned."

"You mean…?"

"They've kept us alive in case they need to replicate us … again." He shook his head and turned away from me.

"Wait a minute. This doesn't make sense. Your clone isn't a scientist; he's in command of this place."

He turned back to me, looking puzzled. "Don't you understand?"

"I guess not."

"I *was* in charge."

My mind strained to grasp what I had just heard. This feeble man once commanded the obviously secret complex that now held me. He and his cronies had somehow developed the ability to replace infected humans with functioning doubles, and apparently they didn't have to wait forty or fifty years for Nature to run its course.

"Then who are you?" I asked.

"My name is Nathan Forbes, and I was a colonel in an Army special command."

"You were a colonel and a scientist?"

"Yes."

"And you ran this facility?"

"Four of them, actually; one in California, one in Florida, one in Minnesota, and this one."

"But now your clone has taken over?"

"Yes, except that we lost contact with the other three installations. As far as we know, we're the only one left."

"And the TABs ... they're on the loose only from here?"

"That I don't know. Before I succumbed, we were all communicating and sharing data. But we haven't heard from our sister facilities for some time."

"So this place could be all that's left?"

"It would seem so."

Unbelievable.

"I've got a question, Colonel."

"Yes, Mister...?"

"Moss."

"What's your question?"

"Why don't the TABs talk? Your clone speaks very well, but the TABs just bark orders."

"It wasn't our original plan. We had been trying to create a superior grade of soldier, one that could think independently and take the initiative. Apparently, my replacement Forbes decided that only the administrative clones should be able to think rationally and communicate well. He must have regarded the TABs as strictly military instruments, capable only of following orders."

This was incredible. The problem I faced was suddenly much bigger than my escaping and finding Fields and Reed. I had to do something about it—I had to find some way of destroying the TABs.

"Do the TABs have a kill switch? A power-down button?"

He rubbed the back of his neck. "As I recall, their chips are all connected wirelessly to the main server. If you can find it, you might be able to switch them off—unless, of course, my clone has installed a defense program to switch the programming to an alternate source in the event of sabotage."

"Is it possible they've done that?"

He coughed wetly. "I honestly don't know if they've had enough time."

"Then I've got to find that server."

"We've got more than a hundred and fifty processing units up there."

"What should I be looking for?"

He shook his head. "I used to know."

"Please, try to remember." I hated pressuring him. He was obviously winding down, having a difficult time trying to concentrate. But I had to find out. Otherwise, we didn't stand a chance.

He lowered his head and pressed his skull against the bars. "I seem to recall the term 'XL' … 'XL7000' or something like that. We took delivery of a batch of processors less than six months ago. I think one of them is loaded with the program."

"How many of the new ones are there?"

"Twenty or so."

"Are they all up and running?"

"As far as I know."

"What's the program called?"

He went silent again, searching his fading memory. "Look for 'TAB,' or 'TB,' or 'T1'—anything starting with a T is worth checking."

"They couldn't come up with anything more complicated or misleading in the event of a hostile takeover?"

He sighed deeply. "No one was expected to gain access to the lab. Even now, you'll have to get through the TABs to do it. If you can hack into the program, you can shut them down."

"What if I can't?"

"I'm afraid it's your only chance."

By now, fear had taken over his pale features. He appeared older than he did even minutes earlier. I could tell he was going fast.

"My mind … sometimes … after a few minutes of normal thinking, it … doesn't work like it … like it used to."

"I understand." I felt bad for the man and especially bad that I couldn't help him.

"What ... were we talking about?" He looked like he'd just awakened from a nap.

"Powering down the TABs. Is there something I need to know about them? A weakness, perhaps?"

"Remember, a clone is a dupe ... of the original. These TABs ... they're duped from us."

"Meaning?"

"Their brains have absorbed our knowledge—and our weaknesses. They chose one of us. He was the prototypes."

"And he was Asian."

"Yes. All the latest TABs are his clones."

"Why?"

"Because they thought his characteristics would work the best."

"Like what?"

"He was extremely logical—rigidly so. No room for creative thinking. So they used that ability and programmed his chip to favor the left side of the brain. Once given orders they would follow them to the letter."

I sighed. "Sounds hopeless."

"No."

"Why not?"

He managed a weak smile. "They overlooked the man's weaknesses."

"Such as?"

"For one thing, he's claustrophobic. He's also afraid of heights. And he has quite a fear of the dark."

My thoughts raced. I couldn't waste time wondering about the significance of that statement. I'd try to figure it out later. Meanwhile, I had to get him to tell me as much as possible before he went blank. "Why am I here?"

"Are you ... military?"

"Twenty years ago."

"That's why."

"Why?"

He didn't reply at first. His head had lowered again. He appeared to have fallen asleep.

"Colonel?" I struggled to come up with some way of bringing him back. A touch of the past, perhaps? Something he'd be comfortable with? "Where are you from, Colonel? Where did you grow up?"

He raised his head. For the first time, pride showed among his gaunt features. "I was born right here in Somerset County. My family farm ... isn't more than a few miles from here. I left to go..."

He started to slip away.

"Go on, Colonel. You're on a roll." My pulse raced. I couldn't let him stop, couldn't let him give up.

"What you need to do," he said, struggling with the unconsciousness that was enveloping him. "Play ball with them. Give them ... what they want. Otherwise, they'll bring you back here and you'll stay here ... until you're dead."

"What do they want?"

"You're military ... and ... you're ... not affected. They ... want to study you ... to clone you. They want your tactical experience."

"I came here with two others. They're not affected, either. One's a nurse, the other a former teacher."

214

"They'll definitely want the nurse ... to aid in the experiments."

"And the teacher?"

He shrugged. "Who knows?"

"Any idea where they could be holding my friends?"

He was nearly gone. "Experimentation wing ... directly above us ... two floors ... across the ... hall from ... computer room. The TABs ... they'll bring van ... specimens ... need ... nurse."

"The teacher, Colonel..."

"If ... don't want for cloning ... use ... for ... ex ... peri ... ments."

He went silent. I would learn no more. But I decided to heed his warning and do what he'd suggested. I just had to figure out the best way of doing it without alerting my captors. If he'd told me the truth, I didn't have many options left.

And very little time.

***

Just then, the door at the far end of the corridor banged open. The sound of heavy footsteps bounced off the concrete walls. My pulse started racing. I wondered if Death Row inmates experienced similar sensations of panic, isolation, and fear. I wasn't going to be taken to the gallows or the injection table, but I was certain the lab held similar horrors. Also, being cloned then brought back here to die later on would be just as terrifying.

The shadow in the hall became broader and more distinct as the footsteps grew louder. My heart thundered and my limbs grew cold. I felt as if I'd just been lowered into a vat of chilled mud. One of the TABs had come for me. His expression would be stone-faced as he opened the cell door. He'd order me to come with him. I'd have no choice.

So many military men had faced this horror while serving their country. They had been captured by the enemy, taken to his camp, and tossed into his prison. Occasionally, they were given meager scraps of food. They'd been taken from their cell at various times of the day and night. The sessions sometimes lasted a few minutes; other times hours on end. They'd been subjected to torture, excruciating pain, and mind manipulation. When it finally ended, they were taken back to their cells and strung up with hemp, fishing line, or barbed wire. They were bruised, bleeding, and numb with pain and fear. Some bore it silently; others whimpered like idiots. Our enemies knew how to play these games, and thoroughly enjoyed them.

Of course, in this case, the enemy was a product of my own country. I wasn't trespassing on foreign soil, I was home. In America. The Land of the Free. Except that America wasn't America anymore, and those of us not yet dead were no longer free.

The TAB stopped in front of my cell. Since they all looked the same, I couldn't tell if this was one of the two that had brought me here. It didn't matter. I cared only about the gun in his hand. It was the same automatic my ribs and gut had grown to know so well during my recent tour of the facility.

The TAB reached out and applied his palm to the scanner. A loud click echoed through my cell.

He pulled the door open with his free hand and gestured with the gun.

Play ball with them.

The colonel's warning registered strongly, but the soldier in me wanted to test them to see how valuable I was to them. If they really needed me, they wouldn't kill me. Otherwise, I could die right here and save myself a lot of unnecessary physical and emotional torment.

I remained on the cot.

The gun gestured.

"I'm not going anywhere."

Without a word, the TAB marched briskly into the cell and stopped about a foot from my bed. Bending slightly at the waist, he grabbed my left arm just above the elbow. It felt like my arm was trapped in a vise, but I didn't have the time to grit my teeth or grimace. In one smooth motion, I was yanked completely off the cot.

The pressure on my arm increased dramatically. It was what you'd expect if a horse suddenly bolted with your arm trapped in the stirrup. The force was horrendous. Although I weighed nearly two hundred pounds, I was easily tossed three feet in the air, before gravity slammed me to the concrete floor. I landed on my side, the breath knocked out of me. I lay there, dazed, a cluster of bright stars swimming past my vision. Unconsciousness beckoned, but I wasn't allowed the luxury of closing my eyes and surrendering to the darkness. I was grabbed by the belt and lifted as if I were a light suitcase.

My right side tingled from my shoulder down to my toes. My neck hummed. My hip buzzed hotly.

The hard surface of the floor slapped the bottoms of my shoes when the TAB set me back down, pressing the gun barrel into the small of my back, urging me forward.

So much for testing them.

I now had a much clearer picture of what lay ahead. This country had fallen into the hands of these vicious, superhuman freaks. It wouldn't be long before their growing army ventured out in their vans and calmly did away with what was left of the population.

I had to find some way of defeating them.

My gut churned hotly as I staggered out of the cell.

CHAPTER FIFTEEN

Wincing at the hot pain engulfing my right side, I trudged up two flights of stairs as instructed then down the first corridor we encountered.

Halfway down the hall, we stopped in front of CONFERENCE ROOM 1-A. Like the other doors, this one had a scanner. The TAB waved his hand over the blinking red dot, opened the door, and pushed me forward.

The room was small, smelling of coffee and a strange and unpleasant mix of perfumes and colognes. Eight people sat at a long table, one at each end and three on each side. Four males and four females, with everyone dressed in business attire and seeming to be between forty and fifty years old. Colonel Forbes's clone was not in the room. He was probably in the lab, supervising experiments or watching his toy soldiers capture victims on the streets.

Eight Styrofoam cups sat on the shiny table surface. Those not staring at me were studying file folders. They occasionally sipped coffee. All of the males and three of the females appeared normal, their eyes clear. The fourth woman sat perfectly still, her eyelids half-closed and heavy. She was either falling asleep or in the process of zoning out.

The TAB nudged me closer to them. Ignoring the stinging pain, I forced myself to stand as smartly as possible. I didn't want them to know I was hurting or what had happened in my cell. If the TAB's internal program was hooked up to their databanks, they'd find out anyway. They might be tempted to clone me immediately, rather than waste time studying me.

The man sitting at the head of the table was unmistakably career military. His close-cropped silver hair ended at the base of his neck, in line with his earlobes. His sideburns stopped at the tops of his ears. His clean-shaven cheeks revealed smooth, pink flesh. His piercing blue eyes exuded authority.

He sat at attention, his palms down flat on the table, equidistant from the opened folder in front of him. He was dressed impeccably in a light-blue pinstripe suit. The Windsor knot of his maroon tie was perfect, as was his starched collar. The white handkerchief poking out of his breast pocket formed a sharp peak. I imagined his black dress shoes gleaming beneath the table.

Observations from my old Army days kicked in. In boot camp, I'd learned how important it was for the right people to know your strengths. My perfect scores on the rifle range had earned the respect of my DI's. They had treated me like royalty when I won a special shooting award for my unit. I garnered the respect of my peers, as well as the Cadre commanding my survival training unit, on my safe return one week after being dropped off in the middle of the Mojave Desert, armed only with a hunting knife and one day's ration of water in my canteen. Likewise, I'd earned the respect of my company, as well as the entire Brooklyn Police Force, during the Brighton Beach riots, when I'd saved the lives of undercover narcotics officers and several hundred civilians by finding pipe bombs and disarming clusters of C-4 explosives.

This would be no different from my military days. I was older, but the situation had not changed. Once again, lives depended on me.

The silver-haired man sized me up. Those icy-blue eyes probed me, starting at the tips of my shoes and stopping at my face.

The colonel's halting words filled my head.

Play ball with them.

Playing ball, to me, translated into something else, something I was much more comfortable with, something I could do in my sleep.

Tell them what they want to hear.

"Sergeant Alan P. Moss?"

His voice was forceful, sharp.

"Yes, sir?" Ignoring the pain in my side, I straightened to my full height. Everyone glanced up from their folders. The man at the opposite end of the table raised his head sharply. The silver-haired man blinked. He hadn't expected cooperation. He'd certainly read my file and seen that in spite of my fine record, I'd received two formal reprimands, one of them issued by a field grade officer. I'd also received dozens of oral reprimands, several formal warnings, and I was put on report half a dozen times. I knew better than to act too cooperative. It would cause suspicion. But showing them reasonable respect was the intelligent way to go. Second-level officers relished discipline. It made them feel superior. They despised troublemakers but admired a turnaround, and they always took credit whenever a hard case chose the right path.

"I am Brigadier General James Eldon," the silver-haired man announced, straightening even more in his seat and increasing his height by at least two inches. He gave me another quick once-over and nodded. The rest of the table watched passively.

"You look fairly fit, Moss."

"I like to stay active, sir."

"Most let themselves go very quickly. I am glad to see you are not one of them."

"Thank you, sir."

He went back to my file. "This says you were a troublemaker, Moss. Discipline problems?"

"I was young, sir. Immature. Stupid sometimes. I also drank a lot."

He nodded. In his language, I'd just apologized for past sins. Officers loved that, particularly generals. It made them feel more godlike. "This also says you were an excellent soldier. You did well at Brighton and equally well in Arizona, during our border patrol campaign."

"I did my best, sir."

"You saved lives. Located and disarmed bombs. Risked your life every day."

"It was my job, sir."

"In my experience, Bomb Squad personnel are required to have nerves as thick and as tough as steel cables. You look like you still have good nerves, Moss. Am I correct?"

"Yes, sir."

Just then, the heavy-lidded female knocked over her Styrofoam cup with her elbow. Coffee spilled down the side of the table, splashing her slacks. She didn't notice as she slumped forward, her face slamming onto the tabletop.

No one else reacted except to glance for a moment then returning to watch me.

The general reached for a communications unit in front of him and pressed a button. A crackle came through the box immediately. "Sir?"

"Johnson just dropped. Bring someone up here at once to collect her."

"Yes, sir."

"Be prepared for a cleanup. She spilled coffee."

"Yes, sir."

I recognized the voice's flatness. It was a TAB.

The general returned to my file. "You were a top-notch sniper, as well."

"Yes, sir," I said, as flatly as I could.

"You know how to kill people as well as save lives."

"Just another job, sir."

"You were our best sniper, this says."

Now seemed the perfect time to see if I could ruffle anyone's feathers. "I killed men, women, and children. I did it well and didn't hesitate. I obeyed orders. I would've kept doing it if the Army hadn't changed my MOS for the final six months of my tour."

Silence. Nothing.

Are these people alive?

The general glanced at my folder again. "You served only three years, Moss. It has been nearly two decades since you were discharged, yet you still sound proud."

"I am proud, sir."

223

"Even now?"

"I'm proud that I served my country."

"And if you are ordered to kill again?"

The door clicked open. A TAB entered, carrying a towel. He walked over to the conference table, bent over and wiped up the spill then picked up the woman easily, slipped her over his left shoulder, and left the room. Again, no one reacted. The whole incident took only a few moments. I was impressed—and appalled.

"Moss?"

"Sir?"

"I asked you a question."

"I was granted an honorable discharge nearly twenty years ago, sir."

"Are you aware that your discharge papers require you to automatically revert back to government property in the event of a national emergency?"

"Yes, sir."

"We are definitely in the grips of a national emergency."

"I'm aware of that as well, sir."

"What else are you aware of, Moss?"

"I assume, sir, you're telling me I've just been recalled."

"You assume correctly, Moss."

A pause. The icy blues probed me. The man's features tightened.

"Anything you wish to say that might cause a problem for us?"

This was no time to offer resistance. I'd learned long ago that you choose your own battlefield. You never fight the enemy on his own turf—especially when he expects it.

"Nothing, sir."

"Good, Moss. Something in your file is missing, however. I want it filled in immediately."

"What is it, sir?"

"Why did you decline to reenlist when you were given the chance?"

"I didn't like what was happening, sir."

"Explain."

"Things were going on that didn't make sense. It seemed like we no longer cared about anyone sneaking across the border. Then the Army took my rifle and transferred me to a Quonset hut to keep tallies on spent ammo. No explanations."

"None were necessary. You were an E-5. A noncom; still an enlisted man. You were given orders to obey, not question."

"I understand, sir."

"Then what was your problem?"

"I was a field man, sir. A grunt. I liked action. I had problems when they stuck me in that Quonset hut."

"What sort of problems?"

"I get bored easily. When I'm bored, I get drunk and look for trouble. Like I said, I was young and full of myself."

His eyes stayed on me. I could sense him sniffing for signs of dishonesty or betrayal. I kept cool and stared straight ahead. Then he suddenly pushed back his chair and stood smartly. He was about two inches taller than me and obviously very

225

fit. He was at least fifty years old, but I could tell there wasn't an ounce of fat on him.

He approached me and stopped about a foot away, as officers do when they want to intimidate you. I was overwhelmed by his aftershave as well as the rancid coffee stench coming from his parted lips.

"How is your eyesight, Moss?"

"Pretty good, sir."

"Not good enough, Moss. We want great. Are you up to the challenge?"

"Yes, sir."

"Without even asking what the challenge is?"

"I'm willing to accept it, sir, whatever it is."

"Good." He spun around, returned to the table and sat back down. "My colleagues will be conducting a series of experiments." He gestured toward those empty stares. "We are going through the worst catastrophe in our nation's history, and those of us still able to function need to band together to get things running again. This is still America, and we are ready to bounce right back and show the rest of the world—whatever is left of it— just what we are made of. Understand?"

"Fully, sir."

"My colleague, Senator Cameron, will fill you in on the details. Senator, tell this man what we want."

Senator?

The man at the other end of the table stood. He was about my height, broad at the waist, thinning on top, and around the general's age. His features were heavy and bloated, clear evidence of heavy drinking. He spoke in a voice that was uncharacteristically flat for a politician. "We will be conducting an intensive study to see if a man your age—a former soldier—can still function in the field. Since you have obviously not been affected by the disease, we will study that as well. You will be required to spend some time in our lab to undergo a series of tests."

"Any objections, Moss?" the general interjected.

"No, sir." I knew better.

"Once these tests are conducted, we will do a lengthy examination to determine if you can return to active duty. If you pass our requirements, you will be dispatched with a small platoon on a necessary mission. As you must know, many of the affected are still wandering around out there, causing havoc. They are looting, pillaging, and murdering anyone who gets in their path. Our soldiers are programmed to round up these troublemakers and truck them back here for immediate dispersal to their various destinations."

"Destinations?"

"We are setting up several studies at the moment, Moss," General Eldon said. "The more we progress, the more studies we will conduct. We need to get this country back on its feet as soon as possible. We cannot tolerate delays."

"We have a full battalion at the ready," Senator Cameron said. "They are stationed in various police barracks around the National Capital area."

"How many?" I asked.

"That number is not important for you to know," the general said.

Probably because they've only got a few dozen TABs in working order.

"There will be more as our operation gets under way," the senator added. "We are evading the Chinese. We know they are operating in our area but at a limited capacity. Our present concern is to marshal as many of our present resources as possible…"

"That means you, Moss," the general interjected.

"Those still functioning are of use to us and need to be brought in," said the senator. "Former military, such as you, are of great value to us for obvious reasons. We cannot have the affected killing off our remaining resources."

"The troublemakers need to be spotted immediately and eliminated," General Eldon said. "Your field experience will help us immeasurably. Our soldiers have been programmed in many different methods of combat and tactical maneuvers, but they have not accumulated enough experience to act correctly in every given situation. They tend to … overreact when faced with confusion or resistance."

Overreact? Like running down innocent people, pulling them out of their vehicles and breaking their necks? These idiots are as crazy as bedbugs.

"A seasoned soldier with your experience will be invaluable to all of us," he said.

"Do you want these troublemakers shot on sight?" I asked.

"Only if they resist. We would like to study them first, but with some it will not be possible and prove a waste of time. Understand?"

"Yes, sir." I now understood it very well.

"Your escort will take you to the lab for two days of testing," the senator said. "If you meet our requirements, you will be taken immediately to the armory, where they will outfit you with full gear and any weapon you consider necessary for your tour."

They wanted me to kill for them again. They actually wanted me to lead their TAB army. If I didn't pass their tests, or showed weakness or hesitation, they'd clone me, put my replicants into the field, and stick me back in my cell to die, as Colonel Forbes had said.

The lab was across the hall from the computer room. I had to somehow find some way into it, where I could disable the TAB program. Then I could move about freely and look for Reed and Fields. It sounded impossible and probably was, but it was my only shot.

"Any other questions, Moss?" the general said.

"None, sir."

"Good." He turned to the TAB guarding the door. "Take Sergeant Moss to the lab."

***

The lab was located halfway down the hall, directly across from the large, red metal door marked COMPUTER ROOM.

Things from this point on would be tough. The scanner made the door inaccessible. If I wanted to gain access, I'd have to use some ingenuity—and I couldn't make any mistakes.

After we'd reached the green door marked LAB, my escort waved his palm at the scanner. The door clicked. He pushed it open and nudged me with his automatic. My heart thrashed as I went in.

Fifteen large cages had been shoved against the wall, each containing a naked male subject. Three males sat cross-legged on the cage floor, their heads lowered. Three others lay on their backs, not moving. Five older males lay on the floor, not moving. The sixth sat in the corner, sucking his thumb. The remaining three cages contained elderly males, all dead.

Naked females sat imprisoned in similar cages against the opposite wall. The first six contained teen girls. The remaining subjects were in the forty-to-sixty range. The teens pulled at the bars while the others repeatedly pounded their heads against them. One girl shouted something incoherent. The others whined and whimpered. The rest were deeply affected, and lay on the floor of their cage. Two were obviously dead.

The smell of urine and feces, not totally absorbed by the air-filtering unit, made my eyes water.

In the center of the room, a naked man lay strapped to a table angled at around sixty degrees. The bottom edge of the table was submerged in a galvanized tub of ice water. His bound feet shivered with cold just inches from the frigid water. He cried out, struggling frantically, but the heavy black straps pinning his chest, waist, and thighs to the table held him fast.

Beside the table, a female technician faced a monitor, busily typing away at a keyboard. Slender and fairly tall, she was dressed in a long white lab coat. Her thick black hair was tied in a knot at the base of her neck.

The table, attached at its center with hydraulics, lowered slowly, until the man's naked flesh entered the water, submerging him up to his genitals. His screams shook the walls, growing weak as he struggled violently, his efforts pulling him toward unconsciousness. Knots stood out all over his bluish flesh.

The man remained submerged for about one minute. When he stopped struggling, the technician raised the table, until only his feet remained in the water. She felt for a pulse then busily scribbled into her pad.

Another female in a white lab coat emerged from behind a partition and walked over. She was about the same height and build, with thick brown hair hanging loose. The first technician said something to her, and the second female turned in my direction to pick up a flash drive from the table behind her.

It was Fields.

CHAPTER SIXTEEN

I watched numbly, unable to move or even breathe.

If I could believe my eyes, Fields was assisting this bunch in the involuntary cloning of human beings. Had she become a member of this psychotic crew?

Colonel Forbes's three words thundered in my head.

Specimens ... need ... nurse.

At the time, the actual image hadn't registered. I'd been too busy gleaning him for information—too busy thinking of some way of pulling the plug on this government-manufactured nightmare. I never would have thought of Fields helping them—actually joining them.

She was a nurse, for God's sake. She'd been trained to help people. To relieve suffering. To aid them in their time of need.

How could she be a party to this?

Had I been wrong about her?

Had she lied to Reed and me?

Was she a spy planted by Colonel Forbes's clone, or was she working for General Eldon?

I had to confront this possibility. Her behavior might have been staged for my benefit. At the roadblock, maybe she'd feigned fear and confusion. Maybe she hadn't really wanted me to go for her gun. Maybe it was just an act to persuade Reed and me that she was just as scared as we were.

I imagined her being escorted from the van while another TAB grabbed Reed, knocked him unconscious, and hauled him away. I imagined her relaxing comfortably in the back seat of their lead car, confident she'd done her job of luring us into their trap. I imagined them bringing Reed here and tossing him in one of the cells. I imagined them coming for him, escorting him here, stripping him, and fastening him to a table, while Fields slipped into her lab coat and started the cloning process.

How could I have been so wrong about her?

If she was one of them, as attractive and desirable as she was, they'd have no trouble luring me into their trap. Using their equipment to monitor my chip, they'd taken her to Breezewood and waited for me to show. They'd even roughed her up a little to gain my sympathy. They probably even gave her a bonus for it. She hadn't stumbled upon the trio of TABs, as it appeared. She'd gone with them to find me and make sure I drove to the roadblock.

I should have been suspicious when she didn't shoot me at the gas station. If she'd been as terrified and as enraged as she let on, she would've just blown me away.

Part of me started to believe all this, while the other part told me I was being stupid, that Fields had been brought here just as I had, that she'd been ordered to the lab. She had no choice. If she didn't comply, she'd have been executed.

How could anyone fight them? How could anyone stand up to these superhuman clones?

That was the part of my reasoning that didn't make sense; that told me I wasn't being stupid. Even if she'd wanted to resist, she couldn't have found a way. Sure, this was a lab arrayed with deadly instruments lying within easy grasp. Possibly she could have picked up a scalpel, sliced the brunette's jugular, and released the lone survivor from the examination table. She could've unplugged things, disabled the lab...

My thoughts spun, and my imagination ran wild.

No, I concluded. She was one of them. That fact alone made me want to grind my teeth. But if I was right, it meant I wasn't the only one in danger. Every functioning veteran imbedded with a chip would be snared in a similar way and brought here. They'd want as many of us as they could find to help them.

I wanted to kick myself for playing into their hands. I also wanted to wrap my hands around her slender neck and...

Another nudge of the automatic in my back snapped me out of my rage. The TAB gestured toward that empty exam table awaiting me.

A shiver ran down my spine. I'd seen a couple of these bad boys before. The military employed them on terrorists and illegals suspected of subversive dealings. We'd used them with great success on Muslim terrorists to locate sleeper cells.

At each end, sturdy straps were bolted into the metal frame—in case the patient/subject was uncooperative. For intensive sessions, the interrogators would add a leather harness with snaps for electrode placement. I didn't see that apparatus, but based on what the colonel had told me, I knew it was nearby. I did notice the straps bolted to the table's sides and dangling loose to the floor. They secured the victim's chest, waist, and thighs. I saw a black hood made of heavy material lying on a table against the wall. Beside it, an array of wires extended from power outlets on the wall. And underneath the table, there was a foot pedal, which I knew controlled the application of electrical current.

Torture or involuntary cloning—some choice.

The TAB gestured for me to lie down on the table.

My nerves quivered, and I trembled. These people were going to copy my body to create a new line of TABs, and they would empty my brain to program them.

The gun pressed into my back again.

My time for action had run out.

Panic hovered frighteningly close, like the hot, salivating jaws of a predatory beast. I forced myself to ignore it by trying to remember what the colonel had told me, but too many things prevented me from thinking clearly. I wanted blood, not answers. I needed to take action. Drastic action. Extreme, violent action.

I had to disable the TAB then kill Fields and the brunette. Fields was busy working and wouldn't notice anything else going on in the lab until it was too late. My adrenaline was pumping at a frantic rate. I could probably snatch a scalpel and slash her throat before my guard could get at me. At this point, I had lost any illusions of surviving—I wanted only revenge. For Reed, for the poor slobs on the table, for the others dying elsewhere in their cells, and for all the other military men and women who would be brought here for this evil plan. Last, I wanted revenge for myself, for letting these savages bring me here.

I was right for not believing anything the colonel's clone, the general, or the senator told me. They wanted only to create their own personal empire, enforced with battalions of superhuman clones.

I had to stop them. I'd faced overwhelming odds before. I'd seen what this New Order held for all of us. I didn't have much to lose.

The hood.

Something about it nagged at me.

Why would they need a hood? Light deprivation? Isolation? A fear tactic? Was waterboarding part of their repertoire?

The colonel had said something about the clones. Something very important, yet I still couldn't focus.

The gun poked me again, this time harder.

The sudden contact pumped even more adrenaline into my system and forced my brain into deeper focus.

The TAB, essentially a walking computer, operated very much like a human. Without the use of its eyes, it would be forced to rely on auxiliary information, and I might be able to subdue it during the transition. If I could just grab that hood from the table, maybe I could subdue the guard long enough to disable it completely.

Movement to my right made me start. Fields had left her station and was walking toward me.

My first instinct was to lunge at her, but something about her made my scalp buzz, and I didn't move.

Her eyes were totally blank. Her expression told me nothing. I saw no familiarity, no kindness. No hint of emotion whatsoever.

How could she do this? How could she...?

No hint of emotion. *My God.* The realization slapped me in the face.

Was this a clone, too?

She approached the table and reached for the straps. The TAB kept his distance, staring at me as I climbed on the table.

At that point, his gun was about two feet away, too far to try knocking him off balance. A kick to the groin? I had no idea what was down there. A TAB wouldn't need testicles, so I had to pass on that. Besides, I'd seen clear evidence they weren't programmed to feel pain.

How else could I get him to drop the gun?

Then Fields did something unexpected. She reached for the hood on the wall table and handed it to me. Her face still showed no emotion. Given my predicament, I had no choice but take it from her. I was about to say something nasty, when her left eye suddenly twitched.

Twitched? Or blinked?

Did clones blink? Or was this my imagination?

No. It wasn't a twitch or a blink.

Fields just winked at me.

Was this actually Fields herself?

Her eyes shifted from my face to the hood in my hand, then furtively to the TAB at the foot of the

237

table. She brought up her left hand to pull back her hair, and subtly pointed to her head at the same time. When she brought her hand down, she pointed to the hood.

That's when I remembered: Colonel Forbes had told me the Asian clone model had suffered from claustrophobia. Fields had somehow figured this out and was trying to tell me what to do next.

She gestured for the TAB to help her strap me in. He holstered the gun and reached down for the chest strap on his side of the table. As he did, he lowered his head toward me momentarily. I quickly brought up the hood, pulled it open, and covered his face. He immediately lunged out with both arms, but his movements were imprecise, as if he had no concept of space without the aid of his eyes.

Capitalizing on his confusion, I pushed myself off the table and leaped onto his shoulders, forcing him to the floor and using his muscular bulk to cushion my landing.

The TAB flopped around helplessly beneath me, rolling from side to side while groping clumsily for the hood. He wasn't going for his gun or trying to push me off. He had obviously switched to full panic mode. The Asian's claustrophobia must have penetrated deeply into the TABs' behavioral programming.

"Keep his head covered." Fields rushed the technician, who'd grabbed a scalpel and charged at her.

I kept my weight on the TAB's shoulders, using all my strength to hold the hood tightly around his head. Fields grabbed a loose hospital gown and, like

238

a toreador, whipped it in the air and around the technician's head and neck. She immediately dropped the scalpel and, like the TAB, grabbed at the air, as if she had completely lost her spatial sense.

Fields pulled a Phillips screwdriver from her pocket. With her left hand, she held the gown wrapped tightly around the woman's head; with her right, she took the screwdriver and plunged it into the technician's left ear. She gave it a counterclockwise twist, and the woman collapsed to the floor.

The move astonished me so much that I almost lost my grip on the hood.

Fields sprinted in my direction.

"When I say now," she whispered, dropping to her knees beside me, "yank it up. Grab the backs of his ears and hold on tight. We have to do this fast. Once he can see again, he'll recover immediately. Got it?"

I nodded.

Fields positioned the screwdriver just a few inches from the TAB's left ear. She took a deep breath and gawked at me. I could tell she was scared. She took another deep breath and focused on her task. "Now!"

I ripped off the hood, grabbed the TAB's ears, and put all my weight on them. Fields quickly stuck the screwdriver into his exposed ear and twisted sharply. The TAB stopped struggling and went limp. His eyes immediately dimmed.

Winded and shaking from my exertions, I sat back on my haunches. I wanted to kick myself for thinking what I had been thinking.

"Good job," I said, my voice shaky. "But how did you…?"

She put her hand to my mouth then pointed to the tiny black camera positioned above the door. Another one tilted down from the ceiling at the opposite end of the room.

"Any idea how many of them are still in charge?" I whispered.

"They've kept me pretty isolated since they brought me here."

"Well, now they've got two less."

"They can be turned back on, you know."

"I was afraid you'd say something like that."

"A turn of the screwdriver only powers them down. Their main chip is inside the center of the forehead, and the power-down is temporary and used only for maintenance, or a quick reboot in the field. If I don't power it back up, it automatically brings itself back up after three minutes."

"Then I guess the only way of putting them out of commission permanently is to kill the program."

She jumped up. "We've got to move. We might only have seconds to get out of here."

"I have to get to the computer room."

"It's got a double scanner," she said.

"Are you authorized?"

"Just Forbes, Eldon, Cameron, and the TABs. Quick, follow me."

Grabbing the hood from the floor, she moved to the technician. She picked up the scalpel, grabbed

240

the female's wrist, and sliced off her hand. There was no blood. Fields then stuffed the severed hand, the screwdriver, and the hood into her lab coat pockets, jumped up, and headed for the corridor.

I yanked the pistol from the TAB's waist holster and checked the clip. Then I joined her just as she pulled open the door.

Across the corridor, she waved the detached hand across the scanner. We heard the click as the computer room door unlocked.

Red lights flashed brightly from the ceiling panels. Sirens wailed loudly from speakers, turning the corridor into a chaotic nightmare.

"The TABs must be hooked directly to the security program," I yelled over the sirens.

"No doubt. When you turn one off, the program automatically does a search on the broken link and assumes there's been a security breach."

"Any idea how long it'll take them to get here?"

"Judging by the size of the corridors, I'd say no more than a couple of minutes."

We rushed into the computer room.

"Do you think you can find their operating system?" she asked.

"Don't know, but it's our only chance."

The walls of the computer room were obviously sound insulated, because the wailing of the sirens went silent as soon as we shut the door.

The room was about half the size of the lab. Rows of processors spanned the area, and data readouts flooded the array of monitors on the walls.

Eight people sat facing the far wall. Three of them had already collapsed onto their keyboards. One sprawled face-down in the aisle. The others continued punching keys, oblivious of us or their fallen comrades.

As I stepped over the fallen geek, Fields whispered, "What are we looking for?"

I approached one of the vacant work stations. It displayed Chinese characters, a multi-digit serial number, and several tiny, strange-looking icons. Apparently, computer people were just as impossible to understand in China as they were in America.

Then it came to me. XL7000. Colonel Forbes had told me China had sent over a batch of twenty.

"Look for XL7000," I told Fields, and she immediately rushed down the aisle, examining each screen and computer unit.

I went down another aisle, stepping over another dead programmer while checking for logos, model numbers, and brand names. I suddenly felt someone behind me and spun around.

One of the programmers had abandoned his monitor to come over and see what I was doing. He was about three inches taller than me, forty pounds lighter, and at least fifteen years younger. His hair was blonde and unruly, his cheeks sunken and pink. Judging by the stray blotches of peach fuzz on his chin and above his nose, I guessed he hadn't started shaving yet. His expression was typical of other geeks I'd known—a mixture of contempt, confusion, and dismay. He gawked at me as if trying to determine what species I was.

"Haven't seen ya before," he said. "Got top clearance?"

Since I hadn't the time to work up a convincing lie, I tried the truth. Sometimes the truth actually helped things along. "Where's our latest batch of XL7000's?"

He blinked. "Huh?"

"The last batch we just got from China."

"We get everything from China."

"I'm looking for XL7000."

"Who are you?"

Now was the time to inject a helpful lie or two. "I'm an inspector."

He tilted his head. "What kind of inspector? Where's your badge? And I just heard sirens out in the hall. They looking for you and the brown-haired babe?"

I didn't have time for this. At any moment, an army would burst into the room and blow us all away. I lifted my shirt tail and whipped out the automatic. "I've forgotten my badge. Will this do?"

He gasped, backing up and raising his arms.

"Now that we understand one another, maybe you can take me back to your station."

"Sure ... uh ... sure." He blinked furiously and grinned awkwardly. "Yeah. My station."

Relief washed through me. He was affected. Unless the TABs broke in right this instant, we might just be able to pull this off.

"You okay?" I asked him.

He nodded. "I'm good. Good." He ran a shaky hand through his golden mop.

I recognized the signs. It wouldn't be long before this boy froze or slipped quietly to the floor. The shock of someone pulling a gun on him had probably sped up the process.

"Well? Where are they?"

He snapped to, blinking furiously, as if he'd just woken up. "Uh-huh. Now, what were you looking for?"

"The TAB program."

He scowled. "What's the ... whaddya need...?"

"Just open it."

His eyes narrowed. "You want it ... opened up?"

"Good deal. You remembered. I'll even say please." I gestured with the gun.

He turned to his station, bent over the keyboard, and typed in a few keys. I stood close behind him, watching, as the cascade of bright images poured out, overlapping one another. Then, a blue screen with white letters:

TECHNOLOGICALLY-ADVANCED BEINGS
   TB-1000
   A TUTORIAL

Without turning, he said, "What would you like to do next?"

"Turn it off."

He jerked around. His eyes had already gone glossy. He blinked, trying to focus. "Off?"

"Do it—now."

"But you have to..."

"Now, dammit!" I tapped his shoulder with the gun barrel.

He flinched. "But we're not supposed to…"

"Power it down."

His fingers danced frantically across the keyboard, as he brought up the program. Icons populated the screen.

Then Fields rushed over, her face flushed. "We're out of time."

Behind us, on the other side of the processors, the door burst open. The wailing of the sirens invaded the room. Loud clicks echoed throughout the confined space. At least a dozen gun hammers were being pulled back simultaneously.

Quick footsteps approached us.

Another click, this one only a few feet away.

"Now, dammit!"

TABs or no TABs, I was about to reach around the geek. But just then he clicked his mouse. The ARE YOU SURE? delete box popped up. He clicked YES. The screen darkened, then went blue.

The sirens stopped immediately, followed by the TABs first dropping their weapons and then collapsing to the floor

The wonderful silence caressed my ears.

"Is that program on disk?" I asked the geek.

"Flashhh … d-dri…"

His voice trailed off.

"Get it and give it to me."

His eyes had grown darker, his movements slower. He went to reach around to the back of his computer for the memory stick, but his arm dropped, his knuckles thumping the table. I reached past him and yanked it out. He turned to me and collapsed, slamming his head on the keyboard on his way to the floor. The keyboard slid over to the edge of the table, then over the side, swaying and bumping into the table legs when its cord went taut. Key covers broke off and fell quietly onto the carpet. One of them landed on the geek's nose before sliding off.

Another flash drive jutted out from the workstation next to his. I pulled it out and stuck it in my other pocket.

Then I noticed that the room had been filled with TABs—at least three dozen of them. The one that had been behind me lay just three feet away, its gun still pointed in my general direction, the hammer cocked.

The remaining geeks had already left their posts, making a mad dash to the other end of the room and ducking behind the racks of processors.

"What did you do?" Fields asked, her eyes as huge as silver dollars.

"I killed the program."

"They don't have a secondary program? Backups?"

"Good point." I gestured at the fallen TAB's gun then at the geeks. "Escort them out of here."

She picked up the gun, moved toward the huddled group, and motioned them out into the hall.

As soon as they had closed the door, I removed two more automatics from the TABs, walked to the room's entrance, turned, and fired. Holding both guns, I shot out every computer unit, monitor, processor, and any other device that looked the least bit functional. I emptied both clips, found two more weapons, and started the process again.

By the time I had finished, every piece of equipment in the room was a smoking ruin. None of the TABs had budged.

My task done, I joined Fields in the corridor. She smiled at me. "Wow. I sure am glad we didn't have to pull the screwdriver bit on them all."

"We'd both be dead."

"But I think we should get out of here right now, while we're still able to. It's gonna be tough to find a way out of this building."

"We've got to find Reed first."

247

CHAPTER SEVENTEEN

Fields and I had to squeeze a good bit of the way down the corridor past the rows of deactivated TABs.

Dozens of them had flocked toward the computer room, after the alarm sirens began blaring. As we made our way through the complex, I expected a batch hooked up to a separate program to suddenly come charging at us. Or, maybe there was a backup master program located somewhere else that could be engaged, so that all the fallen TABs could rise again and haul us back to the lab for cloning, or the dungeon to await punishment.

None moved as we stepped over them. But just in case, I grabbed an automatic from an exposed holster and handed it to Fields.

Using the female clone's severed hand, Fields clicked open the doors guarding the end of each corridor. We climbed two flights of stairs to a separate wing labeled OFFICE & ADMINISTRATIVE PERSONNEL. Inside that door, a TAB had been standing guard, its gun in hand. It now leaned against the door, and its dimmed eyes told us we had nothing to fear. Fields swiped the hand again, and I pushed the TAB over, as we entered.

Down the long carpeted hall, glass walls displayed the partitioned cubicles behind them. Filing cabinets stood everywhere. Desks with laptops cluttered each cubicle. A section with potted plants, a couch, two chairs, and a coffee table littered with magazines embellished each reception area. A water cooler and coffee station sat quietly toward the back.

Dead or dying workers slumped over their desks, beneath the tables, and in front of the filing cabinets. A woman lay spread-eagle in the hall, papers and binders scattered around her.

The stench was so heavy that Fields and I pulled up our shirts to cover our noses.

"You have any idea where Reed might be?" I asked, gasping through my makeshift mask.

"I heard one of the lab workers say Forbes and the others have to use whoever's available to keep the workflow going, since everyone's been dropping like flies. If Reed's still alive, he'll be on this floor."

"I haven't seen any TABs in the offices. They're obviously equipped with the latest computer software. It seems to me they could do office work ten times faster and more efficiently than the average human."

"They don't have enough of them. I got the idea they want to use them strictly for defense and clean-up. But I did hear someone in the lab say their jobs are about to become obsolete in a few weeks, and that they'll be replaced by a special line of clones more suitable for lab work, like the female we disabled."

"In other words, the clones will eventually take over every conceivable position."

"Eventually."

I nearly laughed. Even with the world destroyed, these stupid bureaucrats were still replacing people with computers.

Fields opened a door marked STATISTICS. The woman at the front desk was blonde, heavyset and about forty, and stared blankly at us. Her name plate said DALE HAWKINS. She smelled strongly of lilacs and something sour. Her lipstick was badly smudged, and her left eyebrow was missing. Her left hand covered the switchboard on her desk. Her right hand rested on a green blotter.

"Hello, Dale," I said. "Still with us?"

Her eyelids lowered. She slumped forward, her face smacking the keyboard.

"I guess not."

Fields hurried around the corner, stopping behind a stack of filing cabinets. "Over here."

I followed her to a door marked RECORDS. This one didn't have a scanner. Fields pushed it open, and we entered a maze of floor-to-ceiling shelves crammed with folders, files, pamphlets, and thick manuals. Rows spanned the length of the room, which appeared to be at least eighty feet long. This labyrinth separated in the center with a narrow aisle cutting across its middle.

We crept down the center aisle, stepping over folders and two dead records clerks, until we reached the other end of the room. To our left, a desk, chair, and a long row of filing cabinets lined the wall. A lone figure sat at the desk, busily working at his keyboard. The shock of light-brown hair made my spirits rise.

"Reed!"

Startled, he shifted in his chair. A grin lit up his face. "He said you'd be coming shortly. What kept you?"

I laughed. "Traffic was heavy."

He squinted. "Traffic?"

"A little light humor. What are you doing here?"

"When they found out I was a software manager, they decided I could be of some use to them. Since they brought me here, I've been sorting files, putting things in order."

"Sounds interesting. And boring as hell."

"This isn't a bad job, Moss. Not really. It's a lot better than worrying about being killed. When they first brought me here, they stuck me in a little room and left me for hours. I was terrified. My friend told me I shouldn't be afraid, that they'd need me for something, but I couldn't help it. Then some lady came in and asked me all sorts of questions about my background, and they brought me right here and told me what they wanted me to do. I was relieved, of course, but every time I saw one of those soldiers, I thought…" He suddenly stopped talking and peered behind us. "Where are they? How'd you get away from them?"

"He switched them off," Fields said.

His eyes grew wide. "I didn't think that would be possible. Is that all you had to do? Pull their plug?"

"The hard part was finding it."

Reed sighed. "That's a shame, in a way."

"Why the hell would you say that?"

251

"They're really efficient, you know. When they have a job to do, they get it done faster than…"

"Reed?"

"Yes?"

"They kill and torture people. Don't get all messy and nostalgic about this."

"I know how dangerous they are, believe me. Even the people in charge of this place are in awe of them. That's why I was installed here."

"To do what?"

"I manage their numbers and make sure everyone knows where they are at all times. They're all equipped with chips and GPS trackers and other software, but the execs don't want to have to monitor everything themselves. Still, they want them constantly watched."

"I guess since the TABs are also the security force, Forbes can't really trust them to monitor themselves."

"Exactly. They want a steady flow of stats from the TAB GPS coordinates going into the system. As soon as I get an updated readout, I enter their serial numbers into separate files and send an alert to whoever Colonel Forbes has assigned…"

"That's enough, Reed," I interrupted.

"Enough of what?"

"Enough of this shit about how efficiently the place is run. Shut it down. Delete it. All of it. Every damned thing you've done since you've been here. And take out any flash drives you've got and destroy them."

Reed's blue eyes widened. "That's a lot of lost work, Moss."

I couldn't bear any more of this crap. I yanked the flash drive from his laptop, dropped it on the floor, and mashed it with my shoe. Then I grabbed the laptop, slammed it to the floor, and jumped on it, until it shattered beneath my feet.

Reed stood up, paralyzed in shock. But a huge swell of relief washed through me, as I stared at the jagged pieces on the carpeted floor. I'd escaped being cloned, closed down the TAB program, and destroyed their monitoring system. Unless they had offsite backups, I'd hurt them beyond repair.

Still, I knew we shouldn't celebrate just yet. A few more loose ends lingered.

***

Dale Hawkins had slipped out of her chair and dropped to the floor while we were with Reed. She lay on her back, her pudgy arms outstretched, and her dead, glazed eyes gazing at the fluorescents.

"Poor Dale." Reed squatted and stroked the dead woman's shiny blond hair. "She was such a sweet lady. When they first brought me here, she came back to my workstation and brought me coffee and doughnuts."

I remembered how cold and callous Reed had sounded in Cocoa, when we'd first arrived at the dead family's house. Now, as I watched my friend sharing a final moment with someone he'd known only briefly, I realized he didn't lack for compassion.

"She had a son somewhere overseas," he said. "He was serving in the Navy."

I tapped him gently on the shoulder. "You can tell us about her later. Let's get out of here."

253

We hurried back out into the hall.

"I think we've got to go up one more floor," Fields whispered. "It's just a hunch. They didn't let me see too much when they brought me here."

"Your hunch is right," Reed said.

I said nothing as we kept moving. I could feel my legs weakening, but I knew we couldn't stop or dally, no matter how exhausted or hungry I was.

When we reached the windowless door, I suddenly froze. A heavy feeling of dread gripped me, sending ice slivers sliding down my back.

None of us moved.

"They could be waiting for us on the other side," Fields said.

I turned to Reed.

"He doesn't know."

"Any suggestions?" I asked Fields.

Still staring at the door, she produced the gun I'd given her. "They're not taking us again. Not easily." She drew closer to the door, crouched down, and listened, her ear pressed to the metal surface. Reed and I waited behind her. I pulled my gun from my waistband and took it off safety. It was a Sig Sauer. I'd handled them before and never had a problem. They fired accurately and rarely jammed.

"Uh-oh," Reed whispered.

"What's wrong?"

"He says the camera in the stairwell is working."

"Stairwell?"

"That's what's on the other side of this door."

Fields turned toward us. "Does he know if anyone's monitoring it?"

"He says we should assume the worst."

I knew then what had to be done. "Open the door."

"Then what?" she asked.

"We've got to reach the main level. It's the only way out of here. I don't even know if they have elevators in this building. But if they do, they're probably not working."

Fields blinked. "They'll see us. They'll know where we are."

"They already do. I'm chipped. They always know where I am."

Reed's eyes widened. "When did they…?"

"Twenty years ago, and they've never deactivated it. But that doesn't matter. Like I said, we've got no choice."

Fields took a deep breath, applied the clone's hand to the scanner, waited for the click, and pushed it open.

I rushed through and they followed me. The small, square black camera, mounted on the wall one flight up, faced our landing—just as Reed's friend had warned. I was too far away to tell if its tiny red light was on, but I assumed it was.

"Cover your ears," I told them. Then I aimed and put a slug directly into it. Shards of metal and plastic caromed off the walls, dropping and bouncing when it hit the stairs. The noise was deafening in the confined area, resonating over and over in pulsating waves.

The sudden silence seemed nearly as loudly as the gun blast.

My eardrums hummed in protest as I lowered the Sig.

Fields kept her hands over her ears. "Finished?"

"For now."

I turned to Reed, who also kept his ears covered. "Where to?"

He lowered his hands. "He says up."

"How many flights?"

"One."

"Let's do it, then."

***

The door at the top of the stairs opened into a long carpeted aisle at the center of another endless maze of cubicles. At the opposite end, an EXIT sign smiled brightly. I couldn't see any sign of life and guessed by the now-familiar odor that bodies lay in many of the cubes.

"I think the coast is clear," Fields whispered, and we hurried down the aisle.

"Wait," Reed said, his face turning turned pale.

Behind him, two TABs appeared in the aisle, blocking the door we'd just come through. Both had their guns drawn.

"My God," Fields said, backing up.

Forty feet beyond us, two more dashed through the door beneath the EXIT sign and marched toward us. They also had their guns drawn.

My heart skipped a beat. Four TABs. A backup program we obviously hadn't known about had automatically kicked in. We were screwed.

Fields sidestepped, nearly bumping into me. When I saw her hand reaching for the gun in her belt, I grabbed her arm. She cringed then pulled

256

away. I held on. "Pull that gun out and we're all dead." She relaxed her arm.

"Are you possibly thinking of some way out of this?" Reed whispered.

"I'm working on it."

"Work faster, because my friend just told me we've run out of..."

"I knew we would meet again," a familiar voice said behind us.

Alert and just as bright-eyed as he was during our first encounter, the clone of Colonel Forbes stepped into the aisle. He wore the same shirt, tie, and slacks he'd worn when he first showed me around the facility—everything as pressed and impeccable as if he had pulled it all from a display window. His highly-glossed low quarters glittered in the reflection of the overhead fluorescents. A shiny, well-polished gun barrel extended from his right fist. It was aimed at me.

Now there were five guns trained on us and seemingly no escape. I should have been frightened. I wasn't. Rage engulfed me. I had to forcibly keep my arms at my sides to avoid going for my gun and getting us all killed in the process. I could barely see through my fury. I forced my eyes shut and took a deep breath.

You can't let them win. Not now.

I was in no mood for bullshit, especially from someone who'd selected me as an immediate candidate for cloning.

"I thought I gave all your toy soldiers a well-deserved nap," I said.

257

"There is such a thing as a backup program," Forbes said. "You could not possibly think that we would undertake this operation without one."

"Now what fun would that be?"

"Perhaps I should explain a few things to you, Moss, while I have you here."

"We've got some time. Just don't make it too long. I bore easily. Besides, we've got places to go."

Forbes stared at me impassively. Like most top-ranking officers, colonels expressed emotion only on specific occasions. Aspiring to be in the public eye and in the political arena trained them to control their visible displays. "Very noble of you, Sergeant Moss. Feigning bravery. You would have indeed made terrific soldiers if you had given us time. We would have definitely adjusted that attitude."

"Not enough perks, Colonel. And my attitude has always suited only me."

"It will not help you now."

"I'm still confident we're getting out of this dump."

"Little hope of that. You and your friends have not evaluated your situation properly. The TAB program was a major investment and so essential that we developed three independent backup programs to ensure nothing threatened or delayed their mission. You managed to deactivate one of them when you destroyed the computer room. Two more remain safely out of your reach."

Two more programs. Terrific. My gut throbbed heavily.

Still, there was something about his cadence, the way he spoke, that made me think we actually had a chance. In any case, at this point I had nothing to lose.

"In other words, Colonel, you're continuing to develop the very individuals who will annihilate the rest of our species—including you."

"You see the TABs as something negative, obviously."

"I've seen how they operate and heard about what they can do when they're on the loose. They're no better than street gangs, only you can't kill them or stop them. I have no doubt they'll eventually wipe out everyone."

"As you were told before, the program has not yet been perfected. There is bound to be a glitch or two in any new effort such as this."

"Glitch? Tell that to the people who are now dead because of your clone army."

"The future never comes without sacrifice."

"Yeah, and where you guys are concerned, it's always somebody else making the sacrifice."

"That would be true in your case, Mr. Moss."

"What a surprise."

"But it need not be unpleasant—if you cooperate."

"Now why should I do that?"

"Hand over the flash drives you took from the computer room."

"What makes you think I've got them?"

"We watched you remove them in the computer room. You have them in your pocket. Now hand them over."

"If you tell me something first."

"Make your request brief. You are running out of time."

"How many of these robots are controlled by the backup programs?"

"At present, there are one dozen TABs in Auxiliary Program Number One, which we implemented when you breached our primary operations program. These four here, as well as eight others guarding the front and back gates. They are programmed to shoot anyone coming in or going out."

"Bummer. I was all set to get back on the turnpike and look for my van. All our stuff's in it."

"Three dozen more are controlled by Auxiliary Two and five dozen in Number Three. The program you powered down is our main application. It controls two hundred clones out in the field, as well as the four dozen protecting this facility. We need the flash drives in your pocket to restart them." He gestured with his gun.

"And if I decide not to give them up?"

"Then I will shoot your girlfriend. Then your skinny friend. Then I will shoot you and take the drives myself. I will count to three."

"Why not just kill us and take the flash anyway?"

"You are still of value to us, Moss. So are your friends. I will not kill you unless you force me to."

"Thanks all the same, but I won't give them up without a fight." My mind raced to find some way to get us out of this mess. I spied several laptops on the desks behind the wall near the colonel's left side. I had no idea if there were any flash drives in them.

If I could get to one of them, I might be able to cause a diversion and avoid getting shot. Forbes was hell-bent on retrieving that flash. It was the only way he could keep his legion from becoming a huge pile of robotic trash.

"Moss, I will give you one more chance. Hand over the flash drives."

My brain continued to whirl. I needed to get to those laptops. Create a diversion. Somehow disarm the colonel.

Reed winked at me.

I stiffened. Was it possible Reed had picked up on my thoughts? Could he have figured out what I was up to? No one was that perceptive, least of all Reed, who hadn't taken his eyes from the colonel's automatic. But the faint grin on his slender features told me he might have some idea of what was going on.

Then it hit me: It wasn't Reed at all. It was his friend.

I didn't know why I hadn't thought of it before. His friend had no trouble reading or evaluating things. Or slipping around to see what was going on elsewhere. He knew I'd been in the military. He knew I'd been wounded. He even knew I was wounded more than once. He could analyze emotions and moods. He lived in Reed's mind and knew everything Reed thought and felt. He'd no doubt slipped into my mind a few times as well. Even if he hadn't, evaluating my expression would not be much of a stretch for him.

If I was correct, distracting Forbes was possible. Getting through this without being shot would be tricky, but not out of the question.

"In other words," I said, "if I do as you say, we'll be all right?"

"Hand over the flash drives and the three of you will be escorted safely back to the lab."

I'm about to grab the second one from my pocket, I told Reed's friend. *I don't know if it's the real one or a different program.*

"Sounds like a deal." I started to reach into my pocket.

Forbes inched the gun forward. "Slowly, Moss."

I wasn't about to go for my gun. I'd eat five bullets before it cleared my body.

"I'll do it," Reed said. "I don't mind. I wouldn't dare try anything that would get us all killed. All right, colonel, sir?"

"Shut up. Moss, give the drives to your friend." He turned to one of the TABs. "Stay with him and make sure he does nothing stupid."

Reed took the drives from me and slipped past Forbes. A TAB immediately followed. While the others stood guard over Fields and me, Reed went into the cubicle, bent over the laptop, and removed the flash drive.

Now's the perfect time for distraction, I told Reed's friend.

"You're not doing it right, dammit." I went into the cube and grabbed the drive from Reed. I wasn't sure if he'd switched them yet. I had to assume he had. "I know what to do here."

"No, Moss, it's all right. I can…"

"Stop this." Forbes made an effort to get between us.

"You two are acting like stupid little kids," Fields said, edging past him.

I slipped the other flash into her left hand as she passed then gently pushed her away. "He's the one being the asshole."

"You're the asshole, Moss."

"You are."

"I think the Army did something to your head."

"There are plenty of assholes who were never in the Army, dammit. You're definitely one of them." I pushed Reed's shoulder.

"You are." He grabbed the TAB's left arm for balance. The TAB pushed him away, nearly knocking him down.

"I can't believe I let you two drive me all the way from Breezewood." Fields inched toward another laptop and slapped me sharply on the shoulder. "I should've been looking for two axe murderers instead."

Forbes fired a shot into the ceiling. Bits of popcorn sprayed everywhere, dropping silently to the floor and onto his shoulders and shoes. Everyone froze.

"You." He gestured to Reed with his gun. "Put that flash drive into that laptop. Now!"

Reed did as he was told.

Forbes again gestured with the automatic. "Move away."

Reed obeyed, and the colonel logged on. The TAB/CL Program populated the blue screen. He went into the tutorial and entered another command. The screen changed to a series of icons.

Forbes suddenly and awkwardly tilted his head. "What?" He spun around and gawked at me then stared at the TABs behind me. Then he spun around and gazed at Reed. He opened his mouth, stiffened, and stopped moving completely. His eyes went dark. The TABs' eyes also went dark, and one by one they collapsed.

Reed appeared totally confused. "I didn't ... have time to ... to do anything. My friend told me ... he said he'd do something."

Behind Reed, Fields gestured to the laptop. The light-blue screen clearly displayed the TB2/CL Program icon—but it also displayed the prompt: PROGRAM ENDED. RESTART?

"I guess the administrative clones were hooked up to the same program as the TABs," Fields said.

"That wasn't very bright, was it?" Reed said.

"It saved us a lot of aggravation. By the way, good work." I wanted to kiss both of them—especially Fields.

"I did it while he was distracted," she said. "It was easy. He even opened it up for us." She switched off the laptop then removed the flash drive and handed it to me. "Who distracted him?"

"Reed's friend, I suspect." I put the flash back in my pocket. "That was perfect timing."

Reed blinked. "He didn't say what he was going to do."

"What did he do?"

"He said he made some sort of noise close to the colonel's ear."

I turned back to Forbes, pulled the gun from his fist and tapped his head with the metal grip. It made a dull sound--as if I'd whacked the top of a table. "How about that? He really was a clone."

"You had doubts?" Fields asked.

"I've had doubts about everything ever since I woke up in this place. But now I'm wondering how many flash drives these programs are on."

Fields shook her head. "It doesn't matter, does it? Everyone in this place is dying. You think anyone left will bother powering everything back up? Besides, we just switched off the main guy. Or clone. Or whatever you want to call him. He was calling all the shots."

That made sense. In fact, it should have made me feel great about the whole thing. But I couldn't help being suspicious.

"You're still doubtful?" Fields asked.

"I can't help it. Whenever the government gets its hands on something, it really fucks it up."

"We can't think of that right now," she said. "We've turned it all off. Just the three of us. And it doesn't matter how many other backup programs they've got. We found the main one and switched it off. To tell you the truth, I never thought we'd get this far. And I truly never thought we'd get out of here alive."

"I hate to burst your bubble, but we ain't out of here yet."

CHAPTER EIGHTEEN

When we finally reached the main wing of the complex, we found no one in the administrative offices. I'd expected to run into more TABs, or even someone still functioning as a human. Just in case, I kept my gun out and cocked. But I was soon distracted.

At the end of the hall, something around the corner blazed with light. Bright golden bars streaked the beige carpeting with hazy parallel strips, as the light peeked through the open blinds.

We stopped moving and stared for a long moment, squinting from its glare, its power. Relief flowed down my body like warm honey. I was seeing—noticing—my first sunrise in a long while, and it had never seemed so beautiful, so magnificent. Suddenly, momentarily, I felt like a kid again. No worries. No problems. Another day of fun and frolic lay ahead. I truly believed a beautiful summer day awaited us. Everything felt new again. The morning meant birth and a fresh start—and hope.

But first, we needed to regain our freedom.

As my mind returned to reality, anxiety ripped through me, and I reluctantly turned away from the beautiful specter, back into the grotesquely dark face of cold, terrifying reality.

The front entrance. Outside. Escape. Leave this place forever. Run away from the death.

"Let's get out of here," I told Reed and Fields.

We broke into a fast gait and sprinted down the hall, leaping over the bodies lying on the floor and jutting from doorways. The recirculating air-conditioning system had done much to neutralize the smell; otherwise, the atmosphere would have been unbearable. This, more than anything else, compelled me to get away. In just a few days, the generators would eventually run down, and the ventilating system wouldn't be able to handle the growing stench of death.

The mere thought of it forced me to maintain my speed. As I bolted along, I couldn't help thinking how much I'd changed. Even with my military background and our experiences during the last few days, I now found myself in a constant state of nausea. The passing of the years had filed down the sharp, competitive edge that once had made me a tough, driven soldier, one who considered death nothing more than a means to an end or a growing number on my locker door.

When my father died five years earlier, I had viewed the event as a quiet passing, followed by a permanent absence. We hadn't been close for years. I'd only seen him a dozen times or so since my military days, and though it hurts to say it, his death meant very little to me. His funeral remained etched in my memory, not because of how much it had affected me, but how badly it had affected my mother.

But now, after being a reluctant participant in this endless plague of darkness and destruction, I viewed death much differently. Death was darkness, a state in which all signs of life, hope, and happiness had vanished. Death was permanent. Unable to undo. Impossible to ignore. Witnessing so much of it did little to numb the senses. In this battlefield of immeasurable loss, it had achieved the opposite. The only thing keeping me from giving up was the knowledge that relief awaited us straight ahead, just beyond the front entrance.

I lacked food and rest, and I found myself growing weaker with each step, but I fought it with every fiber of my being.

Don't give in. Don't even think about it.

I couldn't even allow myself to think about Reed and Fields. I could hear them gasping for breath just a few feet behind me, which told me they were keeping up. Hopefully, they could continue. They had to, for all our sakes.

We had to fight our way out, even if it meant crawling through the entrance doors with our last breath and dying outside, in the sunlight.

There, our struggle would continue. We'd need a vehicle that worked and also a way of getting through the locked gates. Otherwise, we'd die in this massive, sour-smelling tomb of concrete.

I fought the dizziness and the ever-increasing weight of my legs, which had grown as heavy and as cumbersome as concrete pillars.

Keep moving. Do not under any circumstances stop. Never look back.

Reverting again to my military training, I focused on my objectives—freedom and safety—and ignored the knot of heat growing in my chest, as I forced my aching, worn-out body forward.

What seemed like ages later, we reached the lobby. The sun pressed its powerful radiance against its wall of glass doors, forming silver spears pointing at the slumped figure in the wheelchair in front of the entrance.

It was General Eldon—the real General Eldon.

***

Dressed in a crumpled white shirt, baggy black pants, and brown slippers, he gripped a gun in his right hand and rested his forearm on the arm of the chair to keep the gun steady. Its barrel pointed in our direction.

Reed and Fields bunched in close behind me. Fields pressed her left hip against my right and shifted her weight, keeping her right side out of sight. I heard her gun sliding out of her waistband.

I gently tapped her thigh while leaning into her. Even though we were exhausted, scared, and sweaty from running, I could smell the residual lilac scent in her hair.

Stay focused.

"You're not gonna do anything stupid, are you?" I whispered to her.

"Like what?"

"Like shooting a dying old man in a wheelchair?"

"He's pointing a gun at us."

Defeat and agony registered prominently in the general's sunken cheeks and bloodshot eyes. Even at a distance of twenty feet, I could see that he'd had enough and probably couldn't take much more.

"He doesn't look like he's strong enough to pull the trigger," I said.

"Are you willing to gamble our lives on that?"

She was right. I was stupid to assume anything at this stage. But I didn't want to shoot the man if

269

we didn't have to. We'd seen too much death, and I'd done entirely too much killing in the last few days. The prospect of shooting this man in particular made my insides ache.

Fields moved her face closer, and I found it hard to focus again.

"I've got your back," she said. "Try not to get shot."

"I'll do my best." My limbs stiff and as cold as ice, I took several cautious steps toward the crippled husk. I kept my eyes on the gun and hoped I hadn't been wrong in my evaluation.

Just as I reached him, he slowly raised his head. His blotchy cheeks and the bruises on his forehead made him appear twenty years older than his clone. His eyes were glossy and out of focus. The lids kept lowering as if he was fighting off sleep. His bruised, withered forearm resting on the arm of the wheelchair did not drop. And the gun remained in his trembling fist.

"You don't really want to use that, do you, General?"

He squinted at me, as if trying to determine who I was. He then took a deep breath and whispered, "I thought ... you were ... the clones ... can't let them ... escape." He coughed wetly.

"It's over, sir." I pulled the pistol out of his hand. He didn't resist. He coughed again, and took another deep breath.

"It ... got out ... out of hand." The words came out brokenly and ended in another coughing fit.

"The clones were designed to kill off everyone else?"

"They were supposed to ... rescue the unaffected ... bring them here ... for study." He took a breath. "The others ... supposed to be ... taken to ... Walter Reed ... for ... treatment."

"It's all right now, General."

"You need to ... to go back ... kill the program."

"It's done, sir."

He sighed wearily.

My rage evaporated. The tears staining the general's cheeks told me he was a decent man who'd genuinely wanted to serve his country with an ultimate dream. He could not possibly know this dream would shatter and become a nightmare.

Rage would be wasted on this man. Pity was the only thing left. I had none, but at least I wouldn't have to kill yet another human being. I wanted only to walk away. But I also couldn't leave him like this. He was, after all, an officer and entitled to some respect. My intense anger for what he and his peers had done would stay with me to my dying day, but I couldn't hold it against him now.

"Are the gates locked, sir?"

He jabbed a shaky thumb at the guard's station on the other side of the double doors then doubled up in pain. "Controls ... at ... guard's ... desk," he stammered, coughing.

I could tell he had only minutes left. Making him more comfortable might give him a semblance of dignity. "Would you like to lie down, sir?"

He nodded, so I pushed his wheelchair over to the leather couch in the waiting area, pulled him up, and set him back down. He'd probably weighed two hundred solid pounds in his prime, but now he felt

271

as if he weighed no more than eighty. Even so, I had difficulty. My own weakened condition plagued me, and I nearly let him slip from my grasp. I knew I should've asked if he wanted to go out the conventional way—a bullet in the line of duty—but I couldn't bring myself to do it. In any event, he was very close to death.

Now lying on his back with his head propped up, he stared at me, and his eyelids lowered once again. This time, they stayed closed. I felt for a pulse. It was very weak.

"Who … are … you?" he asked in a soft, raspy voice.

"Sergeant Alan Moss, sir."

"Sergeant … Moss … yes … Moss?"

"Sir?"

"It wasn't … supposed … to…" He began coughing again. The coughs grew softer, weaker. His eyes closed, and he lay still.

I stood over him for a moment. I felt for a pulse. There was none. The man's worries were over. Snapping myself back to the immediate reality, I turned to face my friends. They had already moved to the guard's station and were studying the controls.

The security system consisted of four monitors, all of which were working and showing views of the building's exterior—including the front gate. The console beneath the table was clearly marked. The gate would open with one press of the appropriate button. I pressed it, and the chain-link gate slid open.

***

The exhilaration I felt when we pushed through the glass doors compared to being splashed in the face with a bucket of ice-water. I stopped cold and stood on the concrete landing outside, my eyes closed. I greedily sucked in the fresh country air as if it was some rare healing elixir from a mystical land. It had a fresh sweetness I'd never noticed before, and I knew it would never again intoxicate me as much.

I took in the special scents of fresh grass, pine from the trees, the sharp bouquet of the flowers growing along the steps down to the parking lot, and I noticed that the sourness of death was missing. It made me realize at once how powerful it had been, how it had consumed us. The sweet air and the morning sunshine rejuvenated me, and the exhaustion, soreness, and stiffness plaguing me only moments before began to recede.

Then the fresh air turned normal again, and I opened my eyes. Standing beside me, Fields squirmed out of her lab coat and dropped it on the ground while gazing up at the bright, clear-blue sky. On the other side, Reed leaned against the steel rail at the top of the steps, scanning the parking lot.

Without another word we descended the concrete steps. My knees wobbled a little, but I managed. Now was not the time to submit to the exhaustion, nor the throbbing I still felt in my hip from being tossed to the concrete floor. I could submit to that when we were a safe distance away.

The enclosed lot was about half the size of a football field, yet less than two dozen vehicles and a row of eight unmarked vans sat quietly in their designated spots. The researchers valuing their lives had probably fled and would never return. I couldn't blame them.

273

Three TABs lay off to the side, peering up at the sky with dead eyes. Their guns were drawn, but they didn't move. Another TAB lay at the far end of the lot, his gun drawn as well. Like his comrades, he remained motionless. We glanced at them but said nothing. They'd ceased being a threat.

"How picky are we?" Fields said, as she scanned vehicles in the lot.

"I really don't care," I said. "Just so it has a key in the ignition and runs."

"I'm fond of that model, too." Hair bouncing, she strode toward the row of vans.

About a minute later, the roar of an engine shattered the silence, and one of the vans jerked out of its spot, zooming toward us with Fields behind the wheel. Reed and I scrambled into the back, and she floored the gas pedal as I pulled the door shut. When we had roared through the open gate, I took my first—and last—look at the building that had nearly become our tomb.

The facility looked nothing like I'd imagined. With its sandblasted block walls, metal roof and tinted windows it was roughly twice the size as the average bank. But with so many underground levels, its mass rivaled that of a thirty-story skyscraper.

Surrounded by ten-foot, chain-link fencing and concealed by a large pine forest cresting the hill and sweeping down the rise, the complex nestled comfortably in the hillside. Its mile-long driveway, a modest, two-lane dirt path cut into the heart of the forest, could barely be seen from the main road.

Like many secret governmental facilities, the building was unmarked. It had no visible sign or even a mailbox. Its security system was most likely motion-monitored, its sensors fitted into the branches of the pine trees surrounding the property.

Passersby or airline passengers probably would have considered it just another research facility. The locals would pass the driveway daily without paying it much notice. No one would imagine it directly responsible for a legion of robotic clones recently dispatched to annihilate what was left of humanity.

Now, with most of humanity dead, none of the remaining few would know that the legion, like the power stations that had once served as the life-blood of society, had been permanently switched off.

***

We reached the Turnpike just fifteen minutes later. I'd been right—the facility hadn't been far away at all.

Our van remained where we'd left it, in the slow lane, sitting beside an abandoned SUV parked near the guard rails. Straight ahead, most of the roadblock remained. Six TABs lay motionless in front of their black sedans, their shotguns dropped to the ground.

"They're still here?" Reed asked.

"They were probably waiting for more military victims when I switched them off," I said. "I wasn't the only one the general's clone wanted for his collection."

The van hadn't been touched. The food we'd taken from the Cocoa Beach family had gone bad, but our canned reserves would suffice, as well as the whiskey we'd lifted from Carla and her friends. Our gun collection hadn't been disturbed, and

275

neither had the ammo canisters we'd taken from Carla's van.

"No one's been near it," Reed said, climbing in.

"Anyone coming this way would spot those bastards right off and immediately turn around," I said.

"But they're not moving," Reed said. "Anyone can see that."

"They've only been down for an hour or so," I said.

"Let's get out of here," Fields said. "This place is creeping me out, big-time."

I grabbed the door handle and was about to jump behind the wheel when a heavy cloud of dizziness slapped me square in the face.

No time for this, dammit.

I shut my eyes for a moment and wished the discomfort away. We had to trudge on. We weren't far enough away to feel safe.

Fields got in and squirmed into her seat. "You okay?"

Her voice sounded a mile away.

"I'm fine." I barely heard my own voice over the beating of my heart. But I was okay. I really was. I could make it. All I had to do was climb in and start driving. After twenty miles or so, I could let Fields take over and...

Just then, my legs turned cold and gave out. I went down, and my right knee cracked the bottom of the doorway. A giant bolt of pain shot brightly up my leg, and my side turned hot and tingly. The dizziness returned, and I collapsed to the pavement.

The blackness was surprisingly comforting.

I awoke in the passenger seat of the van. The seat had been reclined as far as it would go, and my seatbelt held me fast. Fields was driving. Reed lounged in the back seat, as always.

The last thing I remembered was the dizziness ripping through me as I'd tried climbing into the van. My right knee throbbed quietly. Then I remembered. My legs had given out, and I stumbled. Everything had gone black.

"I was wondering when you'd come around." Fields munched on a potato chip from the bag in her lap.

"What the hell happened?"

"You blacked out."

"I don't remember a damned thing."

"That's why it's called blacking out, silly."

Reed handed me something wrapped in a paper towel.

"What's this?"

"Tuna fish on rye. I made some for us earlier."

I took it eagerly, unwrapped it, and stared at it. *Food. Actual food.* I began slobbering even before I bit into it. My taste buds exploded with the exciting assortment of flavors. It tasted so wonderful, I ate more.

"Did they feed you at all after they brought you to the facility?" Fields asked.

I finished the sandwich and wiped my mouth with the napkin. "Those morons weren't exactly interested in my well-being."

My hunger no doubt had prompted that blackout. I wanted more but didn't want to overindulge—at least, not yet. I sat back and noticed the darkness pressing heavily against the windshield. "What time is it?"

Fields glanced at the clock on the dash. "Seven-thirty."

"How long have I been out?"

"About four hours."

"Damn. I must've been dead."

"We checked your pulse every once in a while to see if you were still alive."

It was a dark and starry evening, with more stars twinkling in the darkness than I'd seen in a long time.

"I could use a strong drink."

Fields shook her head. "I wouldn't advise it. You ate that sandwich entirely too fast. Whiskey on top of that will play havoc with your blood pressure."

"Fields, you're much too young to be my mother. Reed, hand me something."

"What do you want?"

"I really don't care."

While Reed used my flashlight, Fields said, "By the way, where the hell are we going? Reed said something about driving to your mother's place in some rural area north of here. Elk River. Deer Run. Something like that."

Reed handed me a wet, semi-cold can of Sprite. I glared at him.

"You said you didn't care."

"You're dehydrated," Fields said. "Shut up and drink it."

"We'll all have stronger drinks later," Reed said. "Once we reach your place and can relax for a while."

They were right. If I drank whiskey right now, I'd be shitfaced in minutes. I didn't want my mother to see me in that condition. I popped open the can.

Fields said, "How long did you live in Elk…"

"Deer Creek." I downed a good portion of the liquid. It was still cool from the melted ice, and it perked me up just as much as the tuna sandwich. "I grew up there. Where are we, by the way?"

"We just passed I-70 at New Stanton."

"It took you four hours to get here? Breezewood's only…"

"We found a place to pull off and rest after about half an hour. You weren't the only one who was half-dead."

I wanted to curse myself for my thoughtlessness. After all, they'd been through the same trauma. Being forced to assist in those disgusting experiments, as Fields had been, was probably even more distressing.

"Thanks for taking over," I said, penitently. "Did you have any problems at the rest stop?"

"We didn't see a soul. There were a couple of SUVs, but no activity. How far away is this place?"

We had half an hour or so more before getting off the Turnpike at Allegheny Valley, then at least ten minutes before finding Bakerstown Road, which would take us to my grandparents' farm. "Maybe forty minutes."

A warm lump filled my throat. I found myself growing more uneasy by the second. I didn't know if it was because of what we'd been through or the uncertainty of what awaited us.

Was I afraid my mother was already dead? Or, worse, was she just a few days from dying? Could I find the inner strength to take care of her, knowing she had only days left on this earth? Could I look into the beautiful chestnut eyes of the lovely woman who'd borne and raised me, knowing she would soon become an empty shell? Could I face the horror of knowing that this woman would no longer know who I was?

Hopefully my Uncle Joe was still around and hadn't been affected. Last I'd heard, he was still living in my grandparents' house next door and was always available whenever Mom needed something. He and Mom had been fairly close as kids and had grown much closer after Dad died. They were the only two members left of my family. I hadn't even wondered about him when I received Mom's email, possibly because I'd been concerned only about her.

My childhood had always been my happy place. I'd spent my early years exploring the fields and woods on the farm, tending to the chickens and cows, mending fences, and learning to operate the tractor so I could help bush-hog the pastures. Those years were my happiest. I don't believe I'd ever been as happy since.

Until the world had fallen victim to the mass scourge of death, I'd felt sorry for all the members of my family who'd died. I'd pitied them for dying. I'd even pitied myself for being forced to live the rest of my life without them.

The plague had changed everything, and I found my sympathy turning to envy. I finally realized that the dead were the fortunate ones. They'd lived their lives without being forced to view the horror facing those of us still living.

"Were you close to your parents?" Fields asked.

"Until I was around fifteen or so."

"What happened?"

"As I grew older, my father couldn't relate to me as a grown man. He treated me as a child all my life. Like most people, I resented it."

"He lost control. It's common that fathers don't know how to handle things like that."

"He always did like calling the shots."

"How about your mom?"

"She always treated me with respect. Besides, it was always easier for me to talk to her. How about your parents?"

"They both died when I was little. A car accident. My aunt and uncle raised me."

"Are they still alive?"

"They both went a couple of weeks before ... well, before I left Walter Reed. I don't blame you for wanting to see your mom again. I'd want the same thing."

"I have to see her before ... well, before it's too late."

"Do you have any idea if she's all right?"

"No," I said, hoping with all my heart we hadn't run out of time.

CHAPTER NINETEEN

The old farmhouse was gone.

The cozy four-room, two-story dwelling that had once been a major part of my childhood had vanished.

"Sure this is the right place?" Fields asked.

Behind us, the van's headlights cast a golden haze at the small grove of trees straight ahead. For the last hundred years, the house had sat proudly in front of the grove. A black emptiness had taken its place.

"I grew up on this piece of land." I couldn't take my eyes off the bare patch of black earth. I felt as if someone had just reached into my chest and ripped out a large piece of my heart. "Of course, I'm sure."

"What do you suppose happened?" Reed asked softly.

On impulse, I switched on my flashlight and directed the hazy beam at the hilly terrain just beyond the trees. Everything looked the same. Even the square black silhouette of Uncle Joe's garage sitting at the top of the hill remained unchanged.

I switched off the light and the darkness rushed back. A genuine sadness filled me—for my grandparents and my parents, and the wonderful life we'd shared in this very spot, where bare earth now claimed our past.

It had become a grave. A grave of memories.

Once again I was glad my grandparents were both gone. It was bad enough that the world we knew and loved had vanished. Knowing my childhood home had also vanished would have surely destroyed them.

"My friend says it was burned to the ground," Reed said.

"How does he know?"

"He can smell the ashes in the soil."

My gut churned heavily. "Can he tell when this happened?"

"Not very long ago."

Was it arson? An accident? Why hadn't Mom called to tell me about this? Why hadn't she mentioned it in her email?

I took a few stiff, awkward steps forward, until I stood on the spot where the kitchen had once been. I expected to close my eyes and see images of Mom cooking dinner. Putting groceries in the cupboard. Gathering up dog hair from the linoleum floor with her broom. Dad coming home. Mom greeting him at the door. Christmas morning, with the tree sitting in front of the living room window, the presents stacked beneath it.

Other than the vast, throbbing emptiness, I felt nothing. Only the cool night air whispering through the trees around us gave me any notice.

"What now?" Fields asked.

"Next door." My voice sounded hoarse.

"What about next door?"

I forced myself through the shock of all this and turned toward the hill leading to my grandparents' house. Slivers of light poked through the pines separating the properties. It was a sure sign that someone was there, and my heart lifted at the realization.

Not long after my father's death, Mom told me she'd been thinking about moving in with Uncle Joe. Too many memories had made it too painful to be by herself in the little farmhouse. Uncle Joe had lost Aunt Patsy just before Dad died and had been living alone in my grandparents' house ever since. Hopefully, Mom was there now.

"It's where ... if she's still ... she should be there."

Suddenly I heard the unmistakable sound of a pump-action shotgun, and a tall, broad-shouldered figure moved toward us.

"What's your business here?" The figure had stopped about twenty feet away, his features shrouded by the darkness. I could tell who it was by the way he rested the gun in the crook of his arm. A huge lump formed in my throat. "U-Uncle Joe?"

The gun barrel lowered abruptly. The figure moved closer, the headlights revealing his features. A heavy wash of warm relief rippled through me. The man had been an important part of my childhood. He'd taught me to milk cows and mend fences. He'd also taught me to operate a tractor when I was ten years old.

"Good to see ya, boy." He moved closer. In spite of more than sixty years of back-breaking farm work and more than seventy years of life, he stood tall and proud. His white hair had thinned on top but remained thick and wavy on the sides. His cheekbones were heavy, his nose straight and broad, his lips deeply etched with fanlike cracks.

His large hand reached out for mine. I wanted to hug him, but he'd never been the hugging type, and I didn't press the issue. His grip was still amazingly strong. A lifetime of farm work kept a man tough.

"How long's it been?" he asked.

"I saw you at Dad's funeral. Five years ago."

"Seems longer. The years play tricks."

"Definitely, although the days for tricks are probably now close to the end."

"A damn shame what's happened." He glanced past me. "Who'd ya bring with ya?"

"Fields and Reed. They're my friends."

"Where ya comin' from?"

"Reed and I have come from Orlando," I said. "Fields…"

"Washington," she interjected.

"D.C.?"

"That's the one."

"Orlando…" He scratched his neck. "Florida?"

"Yes." I swallowed uneasily. Hopefully he was just rusty with geography, and his age had slowed down his recall.

"You three old friends?"

"We met on the road," I said.

"We're very close," Fields said. Her remark surprised me but made perfect sense. You don't go through hell with someone without bonding with them.

My uncle cupped his hand over the stubble on his cheeks. "You made it all the way here?"

"It took a while," Fields said.

"Trouble along the way?"

"You could say that." I saw no reason to go into detail. We were all tired and hungry, but one important item on my mind had overshadowed everything else. My pulse sputtered when I opened my mouth. "How's Mom?"

Uncle Joe didn't speak. Chills ran down my spine. My heart raced.

"Is she ... did she...?" I just couldn't get it out without my throat closing up.

He sighed deeply. "Let's go inside. We'd better talk."

***

The overhead light fixture gave the kitchen an eerie golden hue. The large room hadn't changed much over the years. The white plaster walls, the cabinets my grandfather had built from scratch, and the large Coca-Cola clock Uncle Joe had picked up at a flea market many years ago and nailed on the wall above the refrigerator, all remained the same.

But the smell was different. The sweet aroma of my grandmother's fresh-baked bread had been replaced by stale coffee and mustiness.

As Reed, Fields, and I collapsed into chairs at the kitchen table, Uncle Joe made coffee from the old blue spatterware coffeepot. His hand shook as he set the pot on the burner of the ancient gas stove. I couldn't tell if the shaking was the result of his age or from the sadness inside him. I wanted to spare him from telling me what happened, but I'd come a long way to see her again, and I had to know.

"When?" The word came out hotly, and sounded raspy. Neither Reed nor Fields moved. The silence became thick and intense, like a heavy black tarp tossed over the room, covering us.

Uncle Joe leaned against the stove and stared at the coffeepot. "Two days ago," he whispered hoarsely.

Two days.

The last few weeks had become tangled and unruly. An endless series of nightmares strung together by fear, anguish, and sleepless nights. How long ago did we escape the government facility? How long ago was it since I'd sat in that dark, filthy cell, plotting my escape? Since we were stopped at the roadblock? Since I'd met Fields? Reed?

How long ago did I receive my mother's email?

I wanted to go back in time and undo a few things that might have changed this sad homecoming. If I hadn't stopped to help Reed. If I hadn't stopped in Cocoa. Or outside Jacksonville. If I hadn't stopped in Breezewood for gas. Or picked up Fields.

I'd missed seeing her by two days. Judging from what I'd encountered in all the others, she probably started winding down long before that. The fact that she'd been affected before I left Orlando should have told me something. I'd been in denial. I'd wanted to see her, hug her, hold her.

I wanted to tell her I loved her one last time.

But even if I'd gotten here three days ago, she wouldn't have remembered me. She would've looked into my eyes and seen a stranger.

Could I have endured that? Would I have wanted to see her in that state?

"Was it ... I mean, did she...?"

"She went pretty fast. It was for the best." Uncle Joe turned away from the stove and from us and stared at the blackness rubbing the window facing the back yard. It must have been horrible for him to watch his baby sister deteriorate before his eyes and not be able to help.

"She talked about your dad. How it was when they met. She was moving around a little slower, and you could tell something was wrong. Then she started talking like we were kids again, when all of us helped work the farm after school, before Lou, Ray, and Nick grew up and left home, married and started their own families. For two days that was all she talked about. Then one morning she came downstairs. I was fixing breakfast, and she stared at me and asked who I was."

He turned to face us. His eyes glistened. "She didn't remember me, and when I told her who I was, she didn't believe me. Got real scared…"

"Where is she?" I'd heard enough.

"Out back. On top of the hill. There's that buckeye tree across from the garage. She liked climbing it when we were kids, so…"

"I want to see her."

"Boy, it's late. Ya need to rest."

"I have to see her." A warm cloud encircled me like a shroud. I found it difficult to breathe. Fields stood up, but I waved her down. "Alone. Please."

No one said anything as I grabbed my flashlight from the counter and went back out into the darkness.

***

The mound was fresh but packed well. I sat down on the cool grass just a few feet from the buckeye tree and turned off my flashlight. The moonlight provided enough illumination to let me see the grave, the trees, and the woods beyond the clearing.

It was a quiet night. The breeze whispering through the trees sounded no different from the old days. Other than the hooting of an owl and the distant barking of dogs, I heard nothing else.

I gazed up at the sky. There were even more stars up there than an hour before, when I had awoke in the van. Perhaps the night air was clearer. Or maybe the stars had gotten word of the devastation on this planet and shined brighter to celebrate.

The reasoning was ridiculous. Stars had no feelings. They were oblivious of us. Oblivious and uncaring. Man was but a passing shadow in the fathomless universe. A mere flicker, like the final heartbeat of a dying bird.

I sensed my mother sleeping peacefully. I didn't know where her spirit was, but I didn't think it was far. She wouldn't stray from this place if she could help it. It was her home, and she was always truly happy here. It was the same with Dad. Hopefully they were together again, this time for eternity.

Tomorrow I'd find some daffodils to put on her grave. As a child, I used to pick them for her at the foot of the hill, when the school bus dropped me off. The flowers grew wild just off the curb. Mom would put them in a glass vase, fill them with water, and place the vase on the kitchen windowsill. When the flowers died, I brought her more. It never failed to light up her face when I gave them to her.

A brush of warm breeze caressed my face, and I closed my eyes, knowing it was Mom welcoming me back. Tears filled my eyes, and my inner spirit grew warm as well. It was her spirit touching mine, and I tried to hold on to the sensation as long as I could. But the warmth vanished only a moment later, and I was alone again.

"I love you, Mom. I'm sorry I couldn't be here sooner, but I'm here now, and I'll never leave home again."

***

Fields and Reed sat at the kitchen table, devouring a large plate of cold cuts Uncle Joe had taken from the fridge. Six bottles of chilled Rolling Rock and a large bottle of Jim Beam stood in the center of the table. The coffee brewing from the pot on the stove gave the room a warm, tangy aroma. I actually felt that if I closed my eyes, I could easily imagine my grandmother at the stove, preparing dinner.

"You okay?" Uncle Joe sat down at the head of the table, reached for the Jim Beam, and poured himself a glassful.

"Reasonably." We exchanged looks. Neither of us said anything else about my mother. There was no need to. I could clearly see the grief on his face. I knew he could see it on mine as well.

When the moment had passed, he gestured to the empty chair beside Fields. "Have a seat. You must be starvin'."

Fields placed a bottle of Rolling Rock beside my plate. I preferred the Jim Beam, but my thirst won out, and I took a healthy slug of beer. The sensation of the cold brew sliding down my hot throat made my eyes water. I put down the bottle, sighed, and busied myself with chipped ham, cheese, and what looked and smelled like fresh-baked bread.

Reality hit me. The quiet hum of the fridge, the cold beer, and the fresh cold cuts—it got me thinking. When I'd first seen the overhead lighting, I'd figured this area still had a functioning grid. But this setup had a much more permanent feel.

"I wouldn't think you'd still have full power."

"Found a home generator last year," Uncle Joe said. "Got it real cheap. It's got about half a tank left, and its auxiliary is full. That's about two months' worth. After that, we'll need to drive down to the local feed store in Bakerstown and find some butane. They won't mind. No one's there anymore."

I bit into my sandwich, chewing slowly. As with Reed's sandwich, the inside of my mouth lit up like fireworks. I had another slug of cold beer and felt better than I had in days.

Uncle Joe lit a cigarette. I didn't remember him smoking, and he must have seen my look of surprise. "Took it up a little while ago," he said, coughing. "Went to the little grocery just up the road for some beer, and there was old Rollo, lying on the floor behind the counter." He blew some smoke toward the light fixture. "Knew Rollo the last fifty years. I guess the ol' boy was five, maybe eight years older than me. Said he opened the register, got kinda dizzy, and dropped. Just lay there on his side, mumblin'."

"Mumbling?" Reed asked.

"Rollo was a mumbler from way back. He'd stand at the counter, his glasses on, lookin' at receipts and mumblin' to himself, and when you asked about it, he'd look at you like you just sprouted another head."

I remembered Rollo very well. He was a nice old guy, and always gave me candy and gum when Dad and I walked up the hill to see what railroad magazines Rollo had in stock. My dad collected railroad memorabilia.

"What else did he say?" I asked.

"Said, 'Take what ya want, Joseph, don't matter none no more.'" He frowned and pushed more smoke toward the ceiling. "I took a couple cartons of Luckies then closed his register, picked him up, and took him into the back room, where he'd been livin' by himself since Grace died. Set him down in his chair and asked if he wanted me to do anything else, but he was gone, so I figured it best if I just left. Ol' boy's problems are all over." He grimaced. "I smoked these as a kid but gave 'em up when I got this cough. No sense prolongin' things now. If ya can't do what you want at a time like this, your head just ain't on straight."

No one replied.

But that wasn't what was foremost on my mind.

"What happened to the house?" I asked uneasily.

Uncle Joe's eyes turned dark. His face tightened. "I burned it to the ground."

Reed and Fields both gasped. My uncle's fierce expression told me something awful had happened. Why else would he do such a thing? I tried

292

desperately to read through the dark mask that had slipped over his face. As I stared, I could feel a similar mask slipping over my own.

I'd seen death and destruction everywhere, and faced my own death many times during the last few days. I'd killed people and robbed their homes. I was kidnapped, manhandled, injured, imprisoned, and nearly strapped to a table to be cloned. In spite of all that, I'd made it home—but not in time to return to the house where I'd grown up.

"Why?" The word tore out of my throat with the force of a fireball.

"Had no choice. Once your mom moved back here with me, we both decided to sell the place." He took a sip of Jim Beam. "Figured it'd be best, since she couldn't bear to go back to it, and a house needs people livin' in it to keep it up."

He shook his head and his features darkened again. "Things just didn't work out that way. About a year after your dad died, she decided to sell it. Bunch of jerks from the wrong end of town bought it and did their best to turn it into their own personal dump. They brought over their hick buds, had all kinds of drunken parties, worked on their ATVs and motorcycles in the front yard—made a damn nuisance of themselves. For a while, the neighborhood was after me to do somethin' to get rid of 'em. I wanted to shoot 'em and be done with it, but your mom wouldn't let me. I tried tellin' her I could dump the bodies somewhere in the back forty, for the coyotes, but she always left the room whenever I brought it up."

"So what did you do?"

"Not too long ago, we decided we'd go into hock, buy the place back, and bring out the Fire Department to burn it for training." He took another swig from his glass. "Then this damn plague started and one by one those hicks dropped dead. The last one keeled over riding his ATV. I dragged him into the house with the others, poured gasoline on the kitchen floor, and lit a match."

"How did Mom take it when ... when she saw the fire?"

"She never saw it, just stayed in the house. Stayed indoors for weeks. Stayed in her room most of the afternoons and kept the windows and doors closed so she couldn't smell the smoke. I don't recall her ever looking that way again."

He reached for the Jim Beam again and refilled his drink. "The epidemic didn't kill her, boy. Those idiots that bought your house and turned it into a dump were the ones that pulled the heart right out of her."

My gut burned with rage. I didn't know if I was angrier at the people who'd bought the house, at Uncle Joe for being forced to burn it down, or at how it affected Mom. "I was hoping ... that is, I thought about maybe moving back into it once we got here."

"Boy, you're old enough to know how things change when ya least expect 'em to. You also know the changes almost always make things worse."

"It doesn't make this easier."

"Anyone ever promise you things would be easy?"

294

I felt like a naïve kid when he said that. But he was right. If anyone surviving any of this didn't see that by now, they had their eyes closed.

"So tell me about your trip here." Uncle Joe glanced at Fields. "Ya mentioned D.C. How bad did those government leeches fuck things up, if you'll excuse my French?"

"They did a remarkable job." Fields opened a second bottle of beer. "Before they all started dying, they were working on an army of robots to clean up."

"Robots? You kiddin' me?"

"They were programmed to go out and clean up the streets."

"What the hell for? Nobody's left to give a crap."

"It's a long story. Maybe tomorrow, after we've all had some sleep."

Uncle Joe nodded. A few minutes later, he led Fields and Reed upstairs and showed them the three spare bedrooms. Reed went right off to bed while Fields enjoyed a long, hot shower in the upstairs bathroom.

While we were alone in the kitchen, Uncle Joe grew silent. I could tell something was on his mind. When he finally spoke, I could hear the sadness in his voice. "I'm glad ya came back home, boy."

"You don't sound glad."

"I am and I'm not, 'cause of what it all means."

"What's it mean?"

His eyes bore into mine. "This place is yours, now."

"What?"

He sighed and his eyes crinkled up. "I don't have much time. I know it and so do you. Before you got here, I was wonderin' what I'd do. Couldn't have just anyone come in and take over. There ain't many folks with workable noggins still wanderin' about, but a lot of 'em are country trash like the batch that ruined your old place. I sure as hell don't want 'em showin' up here."

I nodded.

"You're still young," he said. "Ya haven't been stung by the bug yet, and maybe you never will. You can live here until it's your time and get a few things done while ya still can. Or just take it easy and bide your time, like I've been doin'."

This was hard to take. I'd just lost my mother. Now I had to come to the realization that my uncle would soon be gone as well.

"But you seem all right. You might have ten more good years left."

His eyes glistened as he lit another cigarette. "A few weeks, maybe less."

He was still alert and still functioning. He was a big, strong man. He'd lived this long. He could easily live another couple of years.

"But you look just fine."

He shook his head. "It may seem that way, but it's happenin'. Yesterday, I tried to remember my daddy's first name. I remembered it this mornin', but then I tried rememberin' Patsy's middle name. Couldn't do that, neither."

"That could be just your age."

"Wish it was. But we've got to expect the worse. Just do me a favor, all right?"

"Name it."

"When my time comes, lay me out up the hill, beside your mom. It's a good spot, gets lots of sunlight in the mornin' and shade later on, when it's cool."

I just nodded. It's difficult to speak when your heart is bursting.

CHAPTER TWENTY

Five days later, while Uncle Joe burned trash out back, Fields, Reed, and I fixed lunch. We discussed Reed's idea of taking riding lessons from Fields, who'd learned to ride horses as a child in Maryland. My mother was an equestrienne and had kept horses since she was able to walk. At one time she owned a dozen but sold off most of them when arthritis started up in her knees and hips, preventing her from working with the animals and mounting a saddle.

Her three remaining quarter horses stayed out in the pasture behind the barn. Uncle Joe had said they were getting too fat, just soaking up all that grass and not being exercised regularly. Reed, excited about the prospect of learning to ride, began chattering away when he suddenly went silent.

"Something's happened," he said softly. "Something ... bad."

We found my uncle lying on the ground, about twenty feet from the burning trash cans. He'd apparently just keeled over and died.

Despite my initial shock, I was grateful it had happened so quickly. He'd been slurring his words the last two mornings, spilling his oatmeal and coffee during breakfast, and forgetting to close the refrigerator door on several occasions.

He was a large, solid man, and much too heavy for us to carry to my mother's gravesite. Reed and I found a ladder in the four-car garage Uncle Joe had built years ago for the vehicles, as well as for the tractor and its many implements. We set the ladder on the ground beside him, rolled him onto it, and carried him over to the designated spot beside the buckeye tree. Being so close to my mother's grave again was difficult, but the birds singing from the trees nearby consoled me. For an instant I thought I could feel my mother's presence again.

We'd found shovels in the garage as well. With Fields's help, it didn't take us long to dig a suitable grave. We laid my uncle gently in it and covered him with an afghan Aunt Patsy had made for him years ago. We refilled it in and carefully patted the dirt. Reed and Fields took the shovels and ladder back to the garage, while I sat on the grass facing the two mounds.

The death of the last living link to my family shattered me. During the last few days, Uncle Joe and I had spent several enjoyable afternoons together, trudging down the same winding trails I'd explored as a child after school and during the summers. I actually felt like a boy again. Life had reverted back to being as pleasurable as it was before the process of growing up had dulled most of its mysteries, recycling them into silly childish fantasies.

Uncle Joe told me stories about my grandparents I'd never heard before. He'd also told me things about my great grandparents my parents had never told me.

We'd shared a closeness unlike anything I'd ever experienced. Uncle Joe had known me longer than anyone else, and now he was dead.

As I stared at the two graves, the emptiness inside me grew, causing a dull ache in my gut. I felt more isolated than ever before –alone in a strange, dark world.

My feeling of isolation was only natural. I'd spent the last few days talking to the man, sharing his deepest thoughts and reflections. We discussed treasured family memories and laughed about things I'd done as a child. He told me things he'd probably never told anyone else. I was the last person he'd communicated with. In just a few days, his spirit had bonded with my own, and his memory wrapped itself permanently around my heart.

The tears drifted down my cheeks as I said goodbye to him.

***

Three weeks later, Reed snuck out to the barn right after breakfast. Usually, he'd wait for Fields to help him handle the horse and place the saddle and bridle on her. But this time, he decided to go alone. He grabbed the halter and lead rope from the tack room and slipped into the horse's stall for his morning ride. When he reached up to slip the halter strap over the horse's head, the twelve-hundred-pound animal instantly reared and spun around, slamming Reed into the wall.

As I finished washing the breakfast dishes, Fields went out to check on Reed when she spotted the horse in the pasture, nervously snatching up mouthfuls of grass.

Reed lay on his back on the straw-covered floor, his head cocked at a terrible angle. Fields immediately dropped to her knees and checked for concussion. His glazed eyes and lack of response told us the worst. She looked up at me. Her eyes had already filled.

"What happened, Reed?" I struggled to keep my voice steady.

"She ... s-spooked," he whispered weakly. "A r-raccoon ... squirrel ... scurried across the rafters ... just before."

"Your friend. Why didn't he...?"

"Happened ... too ... fast."

"Let's take you into the house." My heart raced, and I found it difficult to keep calm. "We'll put you on the couch in the library. It's cool in there and..."

Reed coughed. Blood trickled out of his mouth. "I'm glad you ... brought us here," he whispered. "I've enjoyed myself."

I fought back the tears. I knew he wouldn't want to see me cry. "I'll get a blanket. We can put you in it and carry you back to the house."

He smiled. "No, my friend."

I grasped his cold, weak hand.

"It's ... been an adventure," he said, his voice weakening. He was slipping away.

Now I couldn't help it. The tears began streaming down my cheeks. "It truly has been."

"I told you, Moss. I didn't want ... be ... last one ... left."

I nodded.

"Hope ... you ... and Fields ... won't ... be ... either."

I patted his hand. "So do I, Reed."

His eyes registered surprise. "My friend ... he's ... he's ... gone."

"He helped get us here, Reed. We don't need him anymore."

"But ... maybe..."

"It's all right. Just relax, okay?"

"Maybe ... I'll ... see ... him ... now."

"I know." The knot in my chest tightened.

"Moss?"

"Yes, Reed."

"Take ... care ... of her. You and she ... good ... together." He smiled, closed his eyes, and went silent.

* * *

Fields and I brought the ladder from the garage, rolled Reed onto it, and carried him over to the buckeye tree. We dug a grave beside my uncle's. I said a few words, then Fields. After staring at the fresh mound for a little while, we walked down the long gravel drive leading to the barn.

The horse that had accidentally killed Reed grazed peacefully in the pasture. As we drew nearer, she raised her head and watched us curiously while chewing a clump of fresh grass. I wondered if she realized what she'd done. Since I'd grown up around my mother's horses, I knew I was being silly. Something had spooked the mare, and she'd reacted the only way she knew. She probably hadn't even noticed anyone else was in her stall when she bolted.

* * *

We spent the rest of the day quietly. Fields wandered up the hill that led to the woods, where Uncle Joe and I had enjoyed our daily walks. I sat on the front porch, sipping Jim Beam and thinking about Reed.

In a short period of time, Reed had become more of a friend to me than anyone I'd ever known. I'd hoped we could spend more time on the farm together. It would have been nice, the three of us driving around the neighborhood, looking for other people, or finding businesses still operating. Even if no one else was left, we would have stayed busy and happy.

I couldn't help feeling bitter about what happened. I'd tried my best to keep us all safe, even though I knew I couldn't possibly own every situation. We'd survived all this death and destruction, only to have a freak accident take our good friend from us.

When Fields returned from her walk, she brought out a bottle of beer and sat beside me. We stared at the gentle valley below the farm in silence.

The main road running past the house turned into a hairpin curve around the other side of the barn. As a child, I'd frequently heard the screeching of brakes as passing motorists, underestimating the severity of the curve, slammed into the guard rail.

At the time, the accidents scared me. Now, I found myself longing for such familiar sounds. I wanted to hear traffic. Or someone walking down the road. Or laughter. I wanted to hear anything that would convince me the relentless plague could not conquer us all.

Except for the chirping of the birds, the silence consumed us. We might as well have been sitting inside a tomb.

"This silence is scary." Fields was obviously thinking the same thing.

"Yes."

"Makes you want to be in the middle of a crowd."

"I've always hated crowds."

"Even now?"

"Maybe not quite as much."

"As crazy as it sounds, right now I wouldn't mind being in the ER, waiting for an ambulance to bring in half a dozen criticals."

"Not so long ago, after a particularly hectic week, I'd spend the weekend alone in my apartment with a couple of six-packs, a giant-sized pizza with three toppings, the TV on, and the phone turned off. Those few times I went the entire weekend without talking to another human being are among my fondest memories."

"I know the feeling. But since it'll be this way from now on, it's different."

I had another sip of Jim Beam and thought how it was so much quieter now without Reed. "It wouldn't be so bad if Reed was still here."

Fields drank more beer. "I really liked Reed. He was very bright. I'll bet he was a terrific teacher."

Reed's teaching horror story rushed back to me, bringing along with it a special sadness far worse than what I'd felt when he first told it.

"Knowing him as I did, I'd say he was that special teacher students like us would always remember."

Fields stared at the bottle in her hand. "That's the worst thing about all this. No one's around to remember anything anymore."

That night, as Fields and I sat at the kitchen table, I stared at the hamburger we'd thawed and pan-fried on the stove and found that I had no appetite. I could think only of Reed and his imaginary friend. I couldn't help wondering who the voice belonged to, where it had come from, how it knew so much. It had not only saved Reed's life, it had saved mine and Fields's as well. Without its help, we wouldn't have been able to leave that government facility.

Since it knew things about me and what was going on around us, it could not have been Reed's conscience. I didn't believe in miracles, so I couldn't sum it up as spiritual intervention. If I had been religious, I might have considered it a guardian angel or some other benevolent spirit coming to our aid.

As Fields took a bite of her burger, she noticed my troubled expression. "You okay?"

"Yeah."

"You sure?"

"Uh-huh."

"Anything to worry about?"

"Don't think so."

"Then stop moping."

"I know."

"Remember what Reed said to you just before he died?"

"What was that?"

"He told you to take care of me."

"I remember. I wanted to take care of him, too. You saw how that worked out."

Fields frowned. "It was an accident. I warned him not to handle those horses by himself and not to go into the barn alone. He was inexperienced, didn't know the horses, and when you don't know what you're doing…"

"He still did it."

"He was excited. He liked riding. He would have been a good rider, too. He was a quick study."

Liked. Would have been. Was. Everything about us, about our lives, our dreams and desires and hopes, had become mere memories.

"He also said we'd be good together," she added.

"I remember that, too."

"Well?"

"Well what?"

"What do you think about that?"

I'd thought about it many times. Fields was an attractive woman, but with all that had happened, I'd kept my male impulses under wraps. Our ordeal had never seemed opportune for such activities.

On the other hand, what could be more perfect? The need for accountability had flown out the window long ago.

I still had doubts, however. This was Reed's idea—not hers. I didn't want to have sex with her just because Reed had suggested it.

"You're taking too long."

"Only for the obvious reason."

"Meaning?"

"Reed brought it up. You didn't."

"So?"

"It wasn't your idea."

She drank more beer. "I wouldn't go that far."

"How far would you go?"

"Actually, I've thought about it several times."

I sat up. "Really?"

"There was just too much else going on. It was never the right time or place."

"When did you think of it first?"

She shrugged. "It's not important."

"As far as we know, we're the only two people still functioning in this area."

"So?"

"I suggest we be as truthful as possible with one another. If one of us gets pissed, we can't very well go running off to someone else."

She frowned. "I've never been that kind of girl."

"What kind?"

"The running-off kind. I'd rather just fix the problem early on."

"So when did you think of it the first time?" My curiosity was piqued.

She sighed. "Breezewood. How about you?"

"In their lab."

"Not in Breezewood?"

"I've never been aroused by a female pointing a gun at me."

Neither of us spoke for the longest time. Then I said, "I thought about it a few other times, later on."

"When?"

"When you kicked that female clone's ass. And when you sliced off her hand. And when you kept bumping into me in the hall. And when you leaned against me and told me you wanted to shoot the

307

general. Your hair did a number on me a couple of times. And there was that time you…"

She reached across the table and pressed her fingers gently against my lips. "Moss?"

"Yes?"

"Sometimes you talk too much."

"My ex used to tell me I didn't talk enough."

"I'm not your ex."

"I've noticed."

She pushed back her chair and got up. "I'll meet you upstairs."

Then she hurried out of the room.

EPILOGUE

That evening, I sat by myself on the front porch, watching the star-filled sky. There seemed to be even more activity up there than I had seen the night before, and I wondered once again what could cause such a phenomenon.

Had all this death done something to the night air? Had it caused the darkness to increase in intensity?

Even if I had a clue, it wouldn't change anything. Other than Fields, there was no one else to share my ideas with.

The only thing that really mattered was our immediate future. Most of the population was gone, but not everyone. Based on my experiences on the drive up from Orlando, many of those who were left had no qualms about taking what they wanted. This meant we had to lock the doors and windows each night and keep our guns handy. It also meant being vigilant when we went out in a few weeks to get butane gas for the generator and to find some gasoline for the vehicles. Half a dozen five-gallon cans would probably last us for the rest of our lives. If we found any local stores or markets that hadn't been picked clean, we could take what we needed. And if we encountered anyone else during our trip, I was sure we'd be able to handle them.

I couldn't stop thinking about what was bound to happen. Even though we seemed to be immune, would we eventually succumb to the plague? Would I go first? Would Fields?

Or was something far worse about to happen?

Was there a wing in that government facility we hadn't encountered? A program we hadn't destroyed? Would another army of superhuman clones be dispatched to clean up the streets? Would a platoon use my chip to track us down and take us back to the lab?

I couldn't let myself dwell on such things. In my mind, we'd been through the worst. We'd destroyed as many of their programs as we could find, and since the rest of them were dropping like flies, no one would be left in just a few weeks. It didn't matter if there were other programs. If no one could execute them, they would forever remain in cyber limbo, as non-lethal as an empty gun.

Fields came outside carrying two drinks. She wore one of Aunt Patsy's robes. Aunt Patsy, as I remembered, was several inches shorter than Fields. As a result, the robe showed off much of Fields's shapely thighs—a pleasant sight to behold.

She sat beside me, handed me a glass, and kissed me. "I was afraid you'd gone out looking for another woman."

I sipped the drink. It was rum and Coke, and she'd made it strong.

"Know how long it would take me to actually find another woman around here? One who's still functioning and doesn't drool all over herself?"

"One of the few good things about all this. You can't cheat."

"I've never been the cheating kind."

She rested her cheek against my shoulder. "What kind are you?"

"It's been so long, I can't remember."

She sat up sharply. Her eyes were enormous.

"What's the matter?"

"Please, don't say that again."

"Say what?"

"You can't remember."

She actually looked scared. I couldn't blame her. Reed's fatal accident made us both realize how temporary everything was. Fields and I had to do whatever it took to stay together.

"I won't," I said.

"Promise?"

"Yes."

She took a sip of her drink and looked up at the sky. "A lot of stars are out tonight."

"More than last night."

"Makes you wonder, doesn't it?"

"I've been wondering about that for a while."

She coaxed some hair away from her face. "I have a theory. It's probably stupid, but..."

"Let 'er rip. Who knows? You might actually be right."

"When my parents died in that car accident, I couldn't understand what happened. I was just five or six at the time and pretty clueless about everything. I'd never been told about death before. I knew they'd gone away, I just didn't know where, and I couldn't sleep because I kept wondering if they were hiding and would show up one day, as if nothing happened. This went on for a while, and my uncle and aunt were really worried about me.

"One night, Uncle Ed came into my room and told me that when someone died, his spirit went up into the sky and became a star, and you could talk to them at night if you looked out your window before you went to bed. I asked him how I'd know which stars were which. He said you could always tell which star belonged to you because it would be the brightest, and would twinkle as soon as you started talking to it." She smiled. "Silly, huh?"

"Maybe."

"I believed it at the time, but as I grew older, I realized he'd just told me that so I'd sleep."

"Did it work?"

She looked down and smiled at some memory. "I didn't have trouble sleeping after that."

I drank more rum. "Before all this happened, I would have laughed at such a story."

"And now?"

I sighed. "You can't help wondering. A lot of people have died during the last few weeks. Anyone who believes in an afterlife would wonder where all those spirits have gone."

"It certainly makes you think—no matter what your beliefs are."

I looked up. Many were twinkling, but three of them sparkled like polished diamonds. I didn't know if I believed in the afterlife anymore, but even so, I couldn't help wondering if Reed, Uncle Joe, and my mother were up there, trying to get my attention.

"Yes," I told Fields. "It definitely makes you think."

Fields finished her drink, stood, and reached for my hand. "Time for bed."

I took her hand and got to my feet. Before following her inside, I gave the sky one last glance and felt a sadness much deeper than anything I'd experienced before. It was a sadness for everything bright and cheerful that would never be seen again—at least, not by us.

I knew the sun would rise again the next morning, as it had for billions of years. I knew that for most of that time there was no one to appreciate it. Now, one day soon, it would rise, and again there would be no one alive.

And when the final darkness fell, it would serve as a shroud to cover the dead.

ALSO BY DAVID BERARDELLI